Dear Kayla

Lovely to meet you and
I hope you enjoy the Book!

Emerald

Noose

Gayle Brgwe
(aka Georgie Belmont)

GEORGIE BELMONT

www.georgiebelmont.com

For Matthew

1

The highwayman hung from the charred elm.

Upside-down he was a lethal branch, thrashing in the glare of the moon. But he couldn't stop his nightgown from cascading over his head.

The retired highwayman's bed-sock flew off. My uncle's thugs hallooed. They let the rope bound to his ankle run loose, and he dropped to the gravel.

He scrambled to his feet and burst from the giant white bloom of his gown. 'Lesson learned,' he said.

One of the thugs hurled the frayed rope.

'Whatever it may be,' said the old highwayman, as he dodged the whipping tail.

He tottered a few steps in his withered sock, until the thug snatched the rope and dragged him. Then they strung him up the right way.

When finally he stopped thrashing, they ripped off his nightgown with a hay hook. It wouldn't do for the people of Fairy Cross to think a man murdered fresh from bed, to think it could happen to them as easily. They left him there, my secret highwayman – his secret out – but they never saw me in my dip beside the rutted road.

I cut down the gent from the lightning tree, eventually. I hauled him to the deer den Tom and I were building in the woods, then went back to cover my tracks. I tucked that poor kindly highwayman into his forest bed of birch and moss.

Nighty night, sleep tight the longest sleep. If you get bit by bugs now, who's ever to mind.

2

I wanted to be happy for Tom. I was trying.

'You'll start the week after next?' I said, picking a frond of moss from his blond hair, which these days he wore neatly-parted.

We were huddled together in the deer den. After four years of building and tending, Tom had announced he'd outgrown our hide.

'So soon…' I said.

Tom shuffled on the mossy ground, away from me. He leaned backwards into the corner of the den, and threaded fresh birch twigs into the lattice of the roof.

'Mr Greenwood thinks I'm ready,' he said. 'Even though it's not due for another year.'

I had suspicions about my uncle's motives for promoting Tom earlier than was usual for apprentices. But Tom was proud to have exceeded his elder brother in something, and his father had given him an heirloom tool in recognition.

I said, 'Mr Greenwood?' and laughed. 'What happened to 'Uncle Caesar', or 'Robin Bobbin'?'

'I canna call him those things anymore.'

'They're your nicknames.'

'Lizzie, I have to be serious now, if I want to get along.'

'As you keep telling me.'

Tom sat up and handed me the remaining twigs for the roof repairs. He fussed with the buttons of his new waistcoat.

'I'm not a child, I canna go around calling people daft names. I'm fifteen.'

'So am I. But I've got a whole two weeks on you.' I looked at the thin, pliable sticks in my hands as if they were baby snakes momentarily at rest.

Things had been changing between Tom and me for over a year, but his being made a bobbin turner was different – this was a leap. Within a few weeks his skills would surpass my own, within a few months he'd completely forget what it was like to be an apprentice. These few months were all the time I had left, or I'd have to fight Tom too.

'That's two more weeks,' I said, 'of running the fells, climbing the lightning tree and swimming to swamp island.' Then I added: 'No wonder I'm faster than you.'

'Two weeks makes nay difference,' he said. He pointed at my knee, where I'd ripped my breeches earlier. 'You're unravelling.'

'I know.'

'Any road, I canna do those things with you any longer. I'll be working, like me Da, twelve hours a day, six days a week now, Lizzie.'

'Stop saying my name like that.' I twisted the birch twigs, wringing the necks of those baby snakes before they could turn on me. '*Tom*. You've only been made a bobbin turner, you're not running the stupid mill. You're not better than me.'

For three years, Tom and I had been learning and skivvying alongside one another: stacking coppice wood in the barn while sleeping bats dangled above; delivering swills of wooden blanks for the turners to shape; sorting and packing the finished cotton reels – the bobbins. And whenever we could, watching the skilled craftsmen, like Tom's father, Mr Kirke, turn bobbins on the lathe, perfectly, rapidly, mesmerically…

'Lay off your gawping,' Mr Kirke said, time and again, 'and get scampering with them swills. I'm not stopping work till knocking-off-o'clock, e'en if it's your own fingers I'm gouging in place o' them blanks.'

Big, small or unusual, from every blank emerged a precisely-carved bobbin destined for a cotton-spinning factory in Manchester, and ribbons and ribbons of beautiful creamy birch wood. Each type of cutting tool made a different shaving – wide and long, or frilly and coiled, or so thin as to be translucent as the wings of a fly.

On Saturday evening, when production had finished for the week, the workshop was as a forest after snow. I loved the workshop most like this – when everything was clean and white and still. Fine sawdust coated the leather belts, which connected each machine to the power shaft overhead. These belts crisscrossed the workshop, branches reaching for the sky, and they sprinkled you with their snow when you bumped them. On the workshop floor, the shavings were piled so high you had to wade knee-deep through the springy white coils, releasing the aroma of freshly-cut birch.

When everyone else had gone home for Saturday tea, I snuck in, to feel the mill as mine, and mine alone. But only Tom would ever move up through the ranks.

Tom sighed and threw himself flat on his back in the den. He reached up to the woven branches and tugged at the wilting leaves. His hands and fingers were already marked with the nicks and cuts of a craftsman.

He said, 'But it's alreet for you to be better than me?'

'That's not what I meant. Just that, you know, nothing's changed, we're still friends…even though–'

'Even though what?'

'Nothing.'

'What, Lizzie?'

'You're my uncle's man.'

'I'm not your uncle's man,' Tom snapped. He sat up, and rubbed his eyes like his father did, circling inwards, ruffling his thick eyebrows against their grain. 'I'm me own person. Like me Da's always been, nay matter what you think. It's you who wants everyone to pick sides.'

'But you have to pick sides. If you're not against my uncle, then you're for him.'

'Lizzie–'

I glared at the side of his head.

I'd never told Tom what Uncle Robin had done to the kindly old highwayman. Neither had I told him that I'd buried the fellow, in the hole Tom and I had dug while looking for giants' treasure. Even after four years of keeping the secret, I was too ashamed to tell anyone why the man was lynched.

'There'd be nay need to pick sides if you'd just let everything be,' Tom said, looking beyond the den to the trees, amongst which we'd played so many games over the years. Growing with the saplings, reaching for the sky, intertwining our roots.

'That's not true. What about Billy? It's only me and Gran, and Mabel, who stopped him being sent back. My uncle called him 'defective' because of his bad leg, said he'd be no good.'

'He isn't.'

'It's only been three months.'

'In three months I'd started on the hand-boring lathe.'

'But that was because of your da,' I said. 'Oh, never mind. You want to hate Billy.'

'I don't hate him. Why would I? He's just not pulling his weight.'

'Well, he doesn't weigh much.'

Tom laughed. 'Why're we arguing about Billy?'

'Don't know,' I said, relieved. I discovered a pulled thread on my untucked shirt. I tried to pinch the thread through to the underside where it wouldn't get caught, and create yet another tear for Tom to notice. I said, 'He'll get better at his jobs, you'll see.'

'I won't be in the packing loft to know one way or the other.'

'Which you've already reminded me. You don't have to be so keen to leave me behind.'

'It's not that, Lizzie. If I get me wages docked…'

'My uncle won't really do that, it's just a threat, to get at me.'

'I'm not chancing it.'

'So, you are picking sides.'

'Urgh.' Tom dipped his head under the over-hanging roof of the den and climbed out, brushing crumbled leaves from his breeches. 'Lizzie, I know you're not asking me to choose. Are you? Because you know I canna. I work for your uncle, have done since I was nine–'

'I know that.'

'Me Da works for him, and me brother. Me Mam does the teas–'

'I said, I know. But still…'

'We *live* in a mill cottage. There's no place for us but the mill and Fairy Cross.'

'Me and Gran are just as dependent.'

'Yes, mebby, but in a different way. You're something else.'

I considered this. Something else good? Or something else bad? Before, I would have asked. I edged further back into the den so I couldn't see Tom's freshly-shaven face when I said, 'If the mill were mine, I'd treat everyone better.'

'But the mill's not yours, it was gone before you were born.'

I recoiled against the earthen wall of the den. A tree root jabbed me in the back.

'Sorry.' Tom crouched at the entrance. I kept my eyes fixed on the toes of his polished boots. He said, 'I didn't mean to– Sorry.'

'S'alright.'

'It's not, Lizzie, and I'm sorry. But tis the way it is.'

If Grandpa William hadn't gone off on his adventures, the mill would have been mine without question.

Fairy Cross mill had been an iron forge when he, William Greenwood, inherited the estate. Included with the forge were the coppice woods, manor house, and tumbledown cottages, in one of which Gran and I now lived.

Cannonballs and weaponry were the forge's specialities. But after William visited Paris during the Peace of Amiens – the one year in twenty when Britain and Napoleon's French Republic weren't fighting – he developed a distaste for war and weapons.

During the early years of the Napoleonic wars, William, stuck in the backward hamlet of Fairy Cross, had yearned for his Grand Tour: the educational travels around continental Europe, which all wealthy young Englishmen expected to undertake. To ease his disappointment, he made mischief in Avandale and other lakeland towns until the forge was nearly ruined, and the Greenwood name disgraced.

Arriving in Paris, with enthusiasm and resentment to spare, as Gran's legend would have it, he lost his fortune, and dignity, in a gambling den. Consequently, he never discovered his aptitude for Italian high society or Alpine mountaineering, which he hadn't bothered with at home anyway, though mountains abounded. His Grand Tour extended as far as a down-at-heel boarding house in the Tenth Arrondissement of Paris, where he met Gran.

In those days, she was plain old Hephzibah, though there was nothing plain nor old about her. She listened to, then laughed at, William's woes, then tracked down the scoundrel who'd won his fortune.

The man declared himself to be a count of a little-known Italian principality, but Hephzibah knew a fraud, and a card-sharp, when she saw one. She won back most of the money, though the contest had almost ended in a pistolling duel. She and William fled Paris before the false count could gather his ruffians.

And so, to Fairy Cross, though not directly, where William, and his striking bride, Hephzibah, converted the iron forge into a bobbin mill to take advantage of the burgeoning cotton industry in Manchester, and make a bigger fortune.

My father, Christopher, was born and the bobbin mill grew and grew. And that's when the trouble began. Believing his Grand Tour would take him permanently to pleasanter climes than the soggy northwest of England, William had never intended to return to Fairy Cross. He'd instructed his younger brother, Ambrose, to run the forge on his behalf, with the promise that all the land and property would pass to Ambrose's son, Robert, known as Robin, upon William's death.

When William made a solemn vow he truly and wholeheartedly meant it. But when this mood passed, so did his promise lapse.

3

Grandpa William and I differed greatly on certain matters of honour. Yet I was the one who inherited the consequences of his broken promise, instead of the mill and estate.

Of my own resolutions, there were those I trusted only to Tom, and others that, well, I probably shouldn't have made. I'd assured Billy, the youngest apprentice, who'd come from the workhouse in Manchester three months ago, that he wouldn't be sent back. But he was making things difficult for himself. I was determined, however, to prove Tom wrong. And show everyone exactly how I differed from my uncle.

'Nar then, Billy me lad, let's see how ye've got on with them one ounces,' said Mabel, the packing manager, stomping in her wooden clogs to join us at the sorting table.

Billy's bony shoulders hunched to his ears and he leaned further over the table at which we stood. Though it was summer, he wore a grain sack over his threadbare jacket for warmth; it hung well below his knees.

It was the day after the deer den trouble, and I was checking bobbins for nicks and flaws in the packing loft alongside Billy. He said he was nine years old, though he didn't know his birthday – the workhouse kiddies rarely did. He seemed much younger, but maybe that's because he was always looked so scared.

'Show me five o' the good uns and five o' them bad,' Mabel said.

Billy thrust his hand into the sack of polished bobbins beside him.

'Hold up for a jiffy, lad. Are they goods or bads?'

'Er, good?' said Billy, through a chesty cough.

'Ye should know, laddie, tis your sorting.'

'They're good. Yep, goods, I'm sure o'rr it, ma'am. Sure as chops.'

'Ye need to be,' said Mabel. 'If ye got them all mixed up again, I canna stop Mr Greenwood cutting your meals. Now, which is it?'

'Um…could be bads, ma'am. Could be bads instead, maybe…'cause I were doing the–' He coughed again, and again, to clear his chest, and I tried not to worry that he had consumption.

'Oh, Lordy me,' Mabel said.

She reached behind Billy, who was peering into the sack, and tweaked my arm.

'Ye don't need to stay for this, Lizzie, I know yours are second only to Mr Kirke's himself. Mebby fetch another swill or two from the drying sheds, and haul Tom from stacking to help us or we'll ne'er get this order finished. I'm not getting me wages docked, or how'll I keep meself in white socks.'

'I don't think Tom's with Mr Taylor, Mabel. I think he's, well…because of the promotion and…'

'Ach, aye, course. Forgot he's left us behind for better things,' she said. 'Just tha and me now, Lizzie.'

'And Billy,' I said quickly, before she remembered I wasn't supposed to be here either.

Billy paused with three of the smallest bobbins in his palm. He drew his pinched face close to his hand, as if he'd just discovered three field mice there, wearing little hats and clogs.

'They *all* look perfect to me,' he said. 'How do t'men make 'em so?'

'Alreet, laddie, that's enough o' your dreaming. We're not the museum o' lakeland arts and crafts. Let me just check, Lizzie, which sizes we need most.' She clomped back to her station, where she kept the ledger.

I scooped the handful of perfect bobbins I'd just sorted into Billy's sack. He frowned.

'Try to pick one of these to show,' I whispered.

He tried to smile, but he wasn't very good at that either. He squinted both his red-rimmed eyes and flared his nostrils, which seemed to draw his mouth upwards, but it wasn't a smile; it was the wince of someone who thought you were going to jab them in the stomach.

'Just keep trying,' I said. 'You'll get the hang of it.'

Mabel returned, and said, 'Get me some o' them Gimp Heads, Register Moulds and Convexes. Oh, and some fancy tassels too, your uncle'll be wanting to show them off to this special dignitary o' his, we oughta check plenty in advance. And mind out, Lizzie, he's been round this morning. Don't know how long I can keep pretending I've forgotten ye're not supposed to be up here.'

'Oh, thanks,' I said. 'And sorry.'

'Nay problem, Lizzie. I'm sure he'll find another urgent desperate problem to absorb him soon enough.'

Sometimes I wondered whether Mabel had appointed herself my substitute mother, my own having died in Bath, on the ill-timed occasion of my birth. Some said my mother had been the cause of my father's disgrace, and others that she'd been the cause of his. But either way, my cousins said

– beside themselves with the supposed hilarity – I was the dirty linen.

I picked up the swill I'd made myself, in the usual way with thin strips of boiled oak woven around a hazel frame, and slung it onto my shoulder.

As I climbed down the ladder one-handed, I heard Mabel saying, 'This one. And this one. Hmm, this's alreet. But *this* one, Billy. And *this*.' She slammed each of the defective bobbins on the table. 'Is it a problem with your peepers, lad?'

I squelched across the rain-soaked yard towards the drying sheds.

'Land ahoy, Lizzie!' called old Mr Taylor.

He was outside the woodshed, loading his barrow with coppice poles. The poles knocked upon one another, as if he were playing a dismantled xylophone.

I waved to him. In the sixteen years my uncle had run the mill, he'd not had to pension anyone off. They'd conveniently died instead. No one wanted to ask what would happen to Mr Taylor, who'd been at the battle of Trafalgar, when the time came. And his time was coming soon.

A reassuringly neat solution occurred to me. Could I persuade patient Mr Taylor to teach Billy how to peel bark? Thus ensuring Mr Taylor was indispensable for at least six months, or probably two years in Billy's case.

But peeling bark was done outside in all weathers, and Billy had a permanent, rattly cough. And you had to clamber over unsteady piles of coppice poles with a sharp knife in your hand. Knowing Billy, he'd probably fall on the knife and disembowel himself on the first day. No, he wouldn't be able to peel bark either. Only three months of Billy's trial remained.

I glanced up at the sky, to remind myself there was an expanse above, as well as the muddle below. The clouds were growing tall and grey; it would rain this afternoon. But it was warm, early summer. And the packing loft was dry. Leaks in the roof would ruin the finished bobbins, and my uncle prized the finished bobbins above all else.

These past few months everyone had been put to work on a single large order, the biggest the mill had ever handled, for a prestigious spinning factory in Manchester. The whole year's revenue depended upon it. The proceeds would also pay for the new waterwheel, which my uncle had commissioned from a famous wheelwright. Until then, my uncle had taken on debt to finance the waterwheel. No one dared speak of the debt, as if to voice it would bring about the thing we were most afraid of.

'Three feet thick?' Billy had said when he heard about our new wheel, which would be forty-two feet in diameter. 'If you lay me on t'ground and roll that wheel o'er me, I'd only just be able to peep out and shout that you was crushing me bones.'

We'd all laughed heartily. In truth, it wouldn't take a forty-two-foot iron wheel to crush Billy. He'd nearly done it himself when he fell through the delivery hatch into a cart, bringing a sack of bobbins down on top of him. We'd all laughed then too, though it was cruel. There seemed no way to save Billy from himself.

As I approached the drying-shed, the invigorating rush of the river grew louder. I let my mind fill with the shushing sound. The shushing, shushing, and nothing else.

For almost a minute I managed it.

Then the argument with Tom flooded back in. My skin crawled at the recollection of how petty and resentful I'd been. I didn't want to feel this way about my closest friend. But I did. More and more the mill came between us. Tom was welcomed further in, and I was pushed out.

I collected a swill of bobbins from where they'd been drying above the kiln. I went back into the yard.

The river, in its angry, constricted state, was so loud I didn't hear Pope until he stepped out from behind me.

'Ahh, li'l Lizzie, lost again,' he said.

Startled, I dropped the swill from my shoulder. The bobbins spilled out onto the mushy ground. The dark mud of the riverbanks could stain unpolished bobbins and ruin them. I scrabbled on the ground to pick them up.

Pope laughed.

He was one of my uncle's 'Accounts Men', though he had nothing to do with keeping the books. He, and the other one, Shaw, usually appeared only on payday, to prevent disputes between hours worked and money paid.

'What do you want?' I said, juggling the slippery bobbins. A sharp flint stone got mixed up amongst them. I put it in my pocket to examine later. 'I'm busy.'

'En't ye always?' Pope said. 'Ne'er seen a person keep turning up to work and slogging on and on when it's not their job. When they don't e'en get paid. What sorta divvy does that?'

'I don't need to explain myself to you,' I said.

'Ah-ha,' said Pope, as if he'd caught me out in some misdeed, 'but I'm yer uncle's bailiff, his representative, so ye *do* need to explain.'

'I'm putting bobbins back into the swill because someone made me drop them.'

'So?' Pope said. 'Oh, yeah, reet. Well, hurry up about it, yer uncle wants to see ye.'

'Got to drop these off at Packing first,' I said, with the swill full at last.

'Leave 'em.'

'If you explain to Mabel…'

Pope grunted. 'Get on with it then. And nay jumping out the winder. I seen ye already, there's nay hiding from me.'

I thought I could easily hide behind his own broad back, because he'd never be able to turn quick enough to catch me. But I went to drop off the bobbins without another word, then duly returned. He wasn't worth fighting today.

'You can walk behind me, if you're going to walk anywhere,' I said. 'I know the way to the office.'

Pope snorted. 'Not the office. He's up at the house.'

I marched across the yard without hesitation. I didn't want anyone to see Pope leading me from the mill, as if I'd done something wrong.

The *cheeep cheeep cheeep* of the circular saw grew louder. Beside the main workshop, Mr Ivison was cutting poles into short lengths, through the haze of pipe smoke that had tinged his moustache yellow. I didn't wave because I didn't want him, while distracted, to lose his good hand to the spinning blade. I had critical questions for Mr Ivsion, but I'd have to talk to him later.

Halfway along the entrance road, Pope caught up with me. He might think me an idiot, but I knew why I was doing what I was doing. To run the mill you needed to understand how everybody did their particular jobs. To run the mill you needed everyone on your side. The mill was the people. Not the machines, the land, the bobbins, as my uncle insisted.

Pope strutted beside me all the way to the manor drive, no matter how much I sped up or slowed down.

4

If the mill was forbidden to me, the manor house was even more so. It was where I should have grown up.

My father was born here, and before him, Grandpa William, who'd added the round turrets at each end of the three-storey, limestone house. The exotic gardens were also Grandpa's creation, though our northern climate had long since killed the palm trees, cacti and five species of passionflower, including the one named after Gran.

Grandpa was known for being overly romantic, and therefore sometimes a little foolish, but I understood his need to break with tradition, to do something radical. He'd made the house, and mill, truly his, and my father had lost it all to Robin.

Uncle Robin himself couldn't stand the folly of the gardens, with their winding paths, curious statues and secret enclaves; he'd gladly let them go to ruin. But he primped and preened the house and the carriage drive, which he'd widened – felling ancient oaks and elms in the process – as if the Queen and her retinue might arrive at any minute.

Pope headed up the drive. I turned into the wooded path that ran parallel. After a couple of minutes, he must have noticed I wasn't beside him. He was slightly out of breath when he reached me on the path.

The manor house was across the road from the mill and elevated up a slope, thus the name, River View. Unfortunately for my aunt, the view was obscured by the bobbin mill, which she despised for being mercantile and common. Happily for my bored and nosy cousins, their bedroom windows provided the perfect spot from which to watch the mill's activities through a telescope.

Gaps in the tree canopy revealed the top storey windows. I thought I saw the glint of a telescope lens, but it was gone before I could be sure.

In the kitchen garden, we surprised the butler smoking amongst the towers of runner bean plants.

'Gotcher,' Pope said, clapping his meaty hands.

The butler scowled at us, then blew smoke onto the little red bean flowers.

We went into the house via the scullery, where the maid who always had a rash on her face was scrubbing a blackened cauldron. I said hello, and she said hello back.

In the main kitchen, Pope jostled past the other servants, who ignored me. He pinched some cheese from a plate and crammed it into his mouth, then paused to tear the crispy skin from a steaming roast chicken.

I overtook him and went straight to the house's central foyer, which doubled as a portrait gallery. When I got the house back for Gran and me, I wanted every trace of my uncle and his family gone. The pompous portraits would be first on the fire.

Pope entered the foyer with a greasy trail of chicken fat across his bristly chin.

'What does he want me for?' I said.

A month ago, my uncle had forbidden me to 'trespass' on mill property. He'd seen me once and instructed Mr Kirke to send me home. He'd seen me a second time and threatened to dock Tom's wages, for working alongside me in the woodshed.

'Dunno,' said Pope. 'What ye done wrong recently? Prob'ly be that.'

I knew, just knew, I'd brought some dreadful judgment down upon Tom. That I'd been summoned here to be told of it, because my punishment would be to deliver the news. I said, 'You can go now, Pope, I know my way to his study.'

'I know ye do, but I en't letting ye wander off like last time. Yer trouble's yer own, and y'en't bringing it on me.'

He walked heavily across the tiled floor, which had once been laid with the blue and white patterned tiles of Portugal (that Grandpa never got to see), and turned into the corridor that led to my uncle's study.

My uncle admitted Pope to his study.

I waited in the corridor outside, ageing into Gran – each minute seemed a year. The mill bell started ringing in the valley, so it was now dinnertime, but I felt too sick to eat. Not that anyone would offer. Last time I was here, I'd just finished eating an apple and had put the core into a nook in the mahogany wall-panelling, with the daft wish that a tree would sprout inside the walls, to engulf the house in its monstrous limbs, squeezing, crushing, crumbling... Then I'd build the house anew.

I looked for the apple core now (for curiosity's sake, not for eating). It was gone. Perhaps the mice had made off with it. I felt mildly better believing that. At least the mice got to move freely around the house.

The study door flew open, just as I was disarranging the porcelain ornaments on a side table – adjusting the positions of the figurines ever so slightly in order to infuriate my aunt, who'd notice, but wouldn't be able to blame the housemaid without seeming to be disarranged herself. I span around to face the open doorway.

'Don't fret, busy Lizzie, yer uncle's got good news. Whatcher doing there?' Pope said, thumping towards me along the narrow corridor. He squinted at the figurines. He paired a tiny shepherdess with a soldier, then lay one on top of the other and said, 'Ha. Yer wicked through and through, dizzy Lizzie. But school'll sort yer out.'

'Elizabeth,' my uncle called from his study.

'Huh, huh, huh.' Pope pounded away.

The floorboards boomed, raising two-century must from beneath the planks. It smelled of an earthen cave, of the deer den.

The study was sparse and dimly lit. Aside from the desk, at which my uncle was sitting, there was a plain teak cabinet containing his personal files, and a low stool with one short leg, which was the single joke he allowed himself. The heavy drapes were drawn against the daylight. He preferred to work by lamp- or candle-light no matter the hour.

'Sit,' he said.

I stood tall and snapped my heels together in my big stomping boots, as I'd once seen a militia man do. Sit upon demand, I never would.

My uncle sniffed. 'As you like.' He leaned against the high back of his chair.

His dark brown hair was oiled and tied neatly, in the fashion of twenty years ago. His cheeks were hollow, from eating meals for a person half his size, about which he made a great performance, so the scullery maid told me. But his clothes always fitted perfectly. Not a month went by without the tailor arriving from Avandale to deliver a new item, and take more measurements.

In today's plain black coat, my uncle's shoulders were level with his chin. For as long as I could remember, he'd not been able to turn his head side to side without also turning his body. His cravat was cream, as always, and tied so tightly his stiff white collar had puckered.

He drew his head back, bringing his chin into the papery folds of his own neck, which wrinkled over his collar. He said, 'This won't take long.'

I stepped towards his desk, trying to loom over him like a ceiling shadow. 'Good,' I said. 'Because you've still got those paraffin barrels stored below the packing loft, and they need moving.'

'Is this today's crusade, Elizabeth?'

'You said you'd move them–'

'When the new waterwheel has been installed.'

'But it's dangerous now.'

'A few more days won't hurt.'

'Hurt what?' I said. 'Whom, I mean.'

My uncle made no move. No emotion flickered across his face. I suspected him of having none. He stared. I glared. He stared, and sucked his hollow cheeks in further.

I willed my eyelids not to blink. His cheeks blew out, then depressed again. I felt a tickly cough rising in my throat and swallowed it. I tensed all my muscles, trying to hold firm. But the corner of my eye began to twitch and my left hand wanted to fly up of its own accord.

The bobbin part of me – the weak stem that was Greenwood – whirled and rattled inside. The threads of my confidence unspooled within.

Some things skip a generation, don't they? Green eyes, wild copper hair (club feet too, but I don't have those). But within a generation? I don't understand why my father let Robin take the mill and himself be exiled.

'There'll be no more running around in breeches.' My uncle sneered with the special disdain he used for my favourite woollens, patched and darned on the knees and seat. 'You're fifteen,' he said, 'and a disgrace to the family name. Must I alone prevent us all from ruin? And no, I don't want your answer to that. No more building dens, dropping from trees, digging holes, sleeping out with the Herdwicks, as though you're a common shepherd–' He listed my further crimes.

Was my highwayman thus accused, when they ambushed him abed? Did he confess, or protest that it was all so long ago?

I didn't flinch. I let my uncle say what he wanted. He meant to insult me, to throw words shaped as knives. Later, I could describe the assault to Tom with this part of my conscience clear.

'I know you think this a contest, Elizabeth. Some war you're waging.'

He intended to provoke an outburst from me, to prove his cause. I saw it in the gathering tightness around his eyes.

He stood up. He placed his pale veined hand on a piece of paper that lay on his desk.

'Whatever you think is happening between us, this is the end.' He tapped the paper. 'This is your admittance to the Mungrispike School for Constant Young Ladies. You leave in two weeks.'

5

'Constant Young Ladies?' Gran said. 'Whatever does that mean? *Constant* young ladies? Are you in danger of turning into something else? That man– that– I'm sorry you were on your own, love. He'd never do this in front of me. What's he up to, I wonder...' She paused. 'Rabbit or squirrel?'

'Don't care,' I said.

'Rabbit then.' Gran took the squirrel by its tail and passed it to me. 'Hang him up, he'll do for tomorrow.'

Numbly, I went to the outdoors cupboard we used for storing the game Gran caught. I tied the squirrel's tail with twine and hung him on a peg.

I returned to the stone block in the yard behind our cottage. Gran had already skinned the rabbit.

'What'll we do with his jacket?' she said, folding the long edges of the empty rabbit skin over the glistening red lining. 'D'you need many more for your den blanket?'

'I'm too old for that.'

'And Tom?'

'Much older than me, apparently.'

Gran started removing the bones from the rabbit carcass. 'Where's this daft school then?'

'Keswick way. Mungrispike.'

'Never heard of a school up there. Lonely place, Mung-rispike.'

'That doesn't help, Gran.'

'Just meant, odd place for a finishing school. How're you going to practise your new airs and graces when there's nowt but Herdwickys and grouse for miles around?'

'It's not funny.'

'There's something funny about it. A school in Mungrispike. And Robin wanting to send you there suddenly.'

'I suppose it's not that sudden,' I said. 'He mentioned boarding school when he told me to stay away from the mill. Thought it was just a threat, that he'd never spare the expense.'

Robin's five children went, or had been, to boarding schools south of Fairy Cross, nearer to the big market towns and industrial cities. Not north towards Keswick. Even on business, he'd never travel that way himself. Barbarians lived north and east of Fairy Cross, and by that he meant people who feared storms and sickness more than they feared his god.

'Ah,' said Gran, scraping the sinews from the rabbit's thigh bone.

'Should I have said?'

'Prob'ly.'

'Why?'

'Don't worry about it for now, duck. Let me think about this. In the meantime, don't do anything rash. I won't make you promise, you'll only break it the quicker. But stay put, please.'

'No fear on that account, Gran, I'm not budging a quarter inch. If he wants me at Mungrispike, he'll have to cart me there like a side of butchered lamb.'

'That's what I'm worried about.'

'What? Why're you worrying about that? Now you're worrying me.'

Gran laid her knife down beside the rabbit. An hour ago, that handful of purple-red meat had been a live fluffy bunny flashing his bobtail, hopping and snuffling towards the juicy grass at the woodland edge.

'There was a lunatic asylum once, up at Mungrispike,' Gran said. 'Awful place. Closed up shop, I forget why. Robin nearly sent his sister, Sarah, after her wee laddie died, you've heard about that, but–'

'She drowned herself in the lake instead.'

Gran cleared her throat. 'A fine woman, Sarah. Never understood why she did it.'

'Was it the thought of Mungrispike?' I said, grimly.

'Hmm. Might well have been.' She reached out and squeezed the fleshy part of my shoulder. 'Lizzie, you're a good lass, but you don't know everything–'

'Never said I did.'

'–just like I don't. Asylums, and schools for inconstant young ladies – the wayward type, that is – you don't get a choice, Lizzie. You get locked up all the same. I need to find out more about this so-called school–'

'Before you let him send me? Gran, no!'

'No. Before I send you elsewhere.'

'But I don't want to go elsewhere, I can't. If I leave, he wins. This is–' I paused and looked beyond the drystone wall of our scrubby yard. The grassy slope bloomed yellow with gorse and purple with heather, and ascended quickly to the high fells and dark mountains.

This cottage was where my uncle had grown up, before he took River View and banished Gran. If he'd ever played childhood games – if he'd ever been a child, which I really couldn't picture – he'd played them here with his sisters.

How far beyond the wall had Robin been during his growing-up years? To where the moor began to slope steeply upwards? Further…to the rocky outcrop I climbed on dry days… Or all the way to the ridge, from where you could see Avandale, the nearest town in the next valley.

He didn't know when he was a child that he'd end up owning the mill. Or did he? Had he always been seething at Grandpa's broken promise to his father, who'd looked after the mill in good faith? Had Robin been scheming, even as a boy? Waiting for his chance to seize everything.

'This,' – I swept my arm towards the mountains – 'is all and everything to me.'

'I know,' Gran said. 'Me too.'

I couldn't speak without imitating a kicked puppy so I sat on the ground next to the pail of rabbit guts. I put my hand in my breeches pocket and rubbed the smooth surface of the flint with my thumb.

I'm woven into this place. To leave, to tease this thread loose, would unravel my whole world. I'm land and lake. Mountain and cloud, tree and leaf. And, whether I like it or not, bobbin.

Then a strange thought occurred to me. Strange but not outlandish. Now I'd thought it, I wondered why I'd never considered it before. It had an instant ring of logic. Was my father somehow faced with such a choice? Not about an asylum or a school to make you obedient, but something…

'Gran…'

She looked at me along the line of her nose. Her weathered skin was taut over her bones. But etched in the wrinkled folds were all the years she'd been fighting for me, and all the years beforehand, when she'd been never-plain, never-old Hephzibah, living her own full life of adventures. Tom's mother said Gran had been beautiful in her day, but Gran would never admit it. She'd stalked these hills for longer than I'd been born, and found every nook and hollow before I made my discoveries.

She said, 'Yes, duck?'

But I couldn't revive her past pain to try to soothe my own. 'Nothing. Just that– I don't know, er...' I couldn't help but wonder anew where my father might be and why Gran had never heard from him. And whether it even mattered, because I'd never met him. 'When you leave home, can you ever come back? I mean, in body, of course you can. But, in yourself? And what if people change while you're gone?'

I thought of Tom. He was growing up quicker than me. He knew his path and was eager to get on with it, while I had nothing to grow into. I belonged here, in Fairy Cross, I was sure of it. But also, I didn't. I could only see my past and present selves: in the cottage with Gran, helping at the mill, roaming the fells and forests. I couldn't see my future self at all. The landscapes and local families would be the same in five, ten, twenty years. But I'd be different. If I didn't fit in now, it would only get worse.

I said, 'What if you change when you go away?' I hesitated. I wasn't sure whom I was talking about anymore. 'What if you change so much you don't want to go back, even though you know you have to?'

6

Next morning, before sunrise, Gran dropped my boots onto the floor beside my bed. The thump woke me, and I burst from a dream about a vicious beast chasing me across the moor.

Gran was in her walking clothes: Grandpa's black frock coat, many years past its best; loose pantaloons she insisted were the latest fashion; and boots the same size as mine, which I'd inherit once she'd charmed the cobbler in Avandale into making her a new pair. Locks of her white hair had escaped yesterday's bun, and she moved awkwardly, as if she'd slept in a chair.

I lay tangled in the coverlet, after my nighttime tussle with the dream-creature, and groaned.

Gran bent slowly to pick my shirt, breeches and jacket off the floor, and flung them on top of me.

'Come on,' she said, stooping again to tuck her pantaloons into her woollen socks. 'I've got breakfast packed, and you've got no excuses.'

'Excuses for what?'

'For anything.'

'I would if you'd let me,' I grumbled, and grabbed my shirt to get dressed.

Gran marched us through the heather and gorse onto the rocky moor. She took us along the tracks made by the Herdwick sheep of long ago. After the sheep, people had worn these muddy tracks to the rock beneath. Some of these people were the nation's new mountain explorers wanting to see the wildness of our lands for themselves, and some of them were just Gran and Tom and me.

We reached the high ridge and surveyed the valley. Our cottage sat alone at the end of the lane leading to the mill and village.

The mill's chimney puffed smoke into the sky, making its own dark clouds. Behind us, the sun had risen above the mountains. Though the Norsemen believed the goddess, Sól, drew the sun across the sky behind her chariot, there was nothing heavenly and divine about this particular morning, nor my stinking mood.

Gran went to the other side of the ridge. She called me over. I picked my way across the uneven ground to join her.

From here we could see the town of Avandale far below. By road it was twenty miles, but across the moor you could walk there in half a day.

'You know how to get to town minding the bogs,' Gran said.

'As much as you.'

'Good girl.' She sounded both pleased and sad. She unrolled her jacket sleeves against the chill.

The wind swirled, disrupted by the ridge; it created different weather on each side. It was how I felt – one foot on the calm protected side, and the other in the gathering storm.

'Am I going now?' I said, in a quick fright at abandonment or exile.

We'd eaten bread and cheese on the march, but I had no other provisions, nor my knapsack of odds and bods. It was just like Gran to spring this sort of test upon me. She left me overnight in the tumbledown hut once, the shepherd's shelter in the lee of the ridge. But I'd had a flask of sheep's milk then.

I wondered suddenly whether she'd brought up my father this same way, though he'd grown from a bairn to an adult of nineteen at River View, with all the comforts and expectations that came with it. Then I thought of myself as him, standing here on the ridge with Gran, after my uncle took the mill. The weight of my predicament seemed to double. I swayed on a wobbly rock.

'Don't be daft, Lizzie.' Gran turned from the valley that cupped the town of Avandale, its dwellings rising up the slopes like suds rinsed in a tub.

She set off towards home. Her long scarf rode the wind, flapping and rippling in the gusts.

'That's it?' I jumped off the teetering rock.

'No, that's not it,' she said. 'I've an urgent letter to write.'

'A letter?' I trudged after her. 'That's me saved from Mungrispike, just like that, with pen and ink?'

'And paper. If there's time.'

'For paper?'

'To write to Bath and receive a reply.'

Bath was where my mother's family lived: the Beaulieus. That's Bew-leys to you and me. They'd owned plantations on the islands of the West Indies, growing sugar cane for import to Britain. The nation's sweet-tooth had made the Beaulieus rich a century ago, though the slaves and plantations were long gone.

When I was younger, I'd read in one of Grandpa's romance books how to wreck a cargo ship on the rocks. I

31

pictured Tom and me hunkered on a howling beach, waving our lanterns to lure the Beaulieus' ship to destruction. Once the ship had smashed to smithereens, we'd swim out to fetch the barrels, hallooing back to shore with our prize.

Was sugarcane packed in barrels? Would it spoil in the salt water? I didn't know. I didn't know anything about the Beaulieu or their sugarcane or ships. Only that my mother, aged seventeen, had met my father while she was on holiday in the lakelands. They'd caused a scandal when they married in Gretna Green, just over the border with Scotland. My cousins liked to remind me of it at least once a month.

I said to Gran, 'Why would the Beaulieus want me now, if they didn't want me when I was born?'

'Because you're older now. Easier to explain when events are long past.'

'I'm not a 'past event'. Nor easy to explain.'

'I know that,' Gran said. 'But for your mother's family…well, the passing of time may've helped.'

'Will it? Seems like it'll be harder. More things have happened since, people get more complicated.'

'May well be. All the same, Lizzie, it was tidier you grew up here.'

'Tidier?' I stumbled over a hummock of grass. Gran caught my arm. I said, 'What am I, the cat's sicked-up hairball?'

Gran threw her head back and guffawed to the sky. 'I'm going to miss you.'

'But I'm not going anywhere.'

'You would have gone anyway, eventually.'

'No.'

'Well, I'll try to make some sort of arrangement. But there'll be a wait, while the post goes to and fro. In the meantime, and I'm sorry, duck, you won't be able to say any goodbyes. Not even to Tom, however hard it'll be. Robin mustn't get wind that we've our own plan. I'll have to correspond with Bath via the Mount, so I'll go visiting tomorrow.' Gran's poet friends lived a day's walk away, so if she wanted to send a private letter she delivered it to them first, and then picked up the reply later.

'You'll stay away from the mill tomorrow, won't you? Just while I'm not here.'

'It's the waterwheel party tomorrow,' I said. 'I've no interest in Robin's folly whatsoever.'

'Does that mean you'll stay away, Lizzie?'

'Don't ask me to promise, I'll only break it the quicker.'

'Then I'm not asking, just trusting you've got more wits than patience.'

We stood side-by-side looking down the rocky slope. I didn't move or speak and neither did Gran.

I had no intention of letting my uncle bundle me off to the school at Mungrispike, nor be delivered to relatives in Bath, like last Christmas's unwanted present. Fairy Cross was my home.

When I could no longer bear the void of silence, I set off down.

7

The waterwheel party was too important to miss. I had to be there when the new wheel started turning. More importantly, I needed everyone to see me there, marking the new beginning, so they'd be ready to stand with me, when the time came.

The mill yard had been set with long tables and benches. Mrs Ivison and some of the other wives were laying out plates and cutlery. Their younger children were pinching the posies of meadow flowers from the tables.

I had urgent questions for Mr Ivison, but he wasn't in the yard as far as I could see. His saw, like all the other machinery, was off while the new waterwheel was being installed.

'Lizzie, love,' Mrs Ivison called, 'would ye help me shift this table?'

I bounded across the yard towards her.

'We're gonna spin that end,' she said, 'so these tables are in a T, instead o' all these rows, like we're having lessons rather than a party.'

We moved the benches away. I lifted the table, and side-stepped round.

She said, 'Aye, aye, a bit more, aye, keep going, stop. There. Thanks.'

We set the table down and Mrs Ivison straightened the cutlery.

'Surprised to see ye, love, thought ye would be, ah… Me mister said your uncle had– Ach, never mind. Glad ye're here, Lizzie, ye should be, no matter what else is happening.'

'I'll always be here,' I said.

'That ye will.'

'The mill's mine after all.'

Mrs Ivison paused with her mouth open.

When I wasn't wondering if Mabel had appointed herself my mother, I wondered whether Mrs Ivsion had. But neither one of them ever told me when I went too far.

Hurriedly, I said, 'Is that for the band?' I pointed to the low platform which had been built in the centre of the yard.

'No such luck,' Mrs Ivison said, too cheerfully. 'Seems the band aren't coming anymore, they're busy preparing for the festival in Avandale. They say.' She raised an eyebrow.

When Grandpa had installed the previous waterwheel, over twenty-five years ago, a brass band came from Avandale. They'd trumpeted Gran's ascent to the stage, where she gave the speech to inaugurate that new wheel. (It was Gran who'd run the mill day-to-day, while Grandpa designed garden mazes.)

'Hmm.' I knew my uncle had never intended to pay for entertainment. The senior craftsmen were hosting the party themselves because my uncle had refused to pay for it, and their lost wages while the wheel was being installed.

'What's the stage for then?' I said.

'Miss Greenwood, will dazzle us on the piano instead.'

'Sophia?' I said. She was the only cousin who could play, sort of.

'The same.'

'And my aunt is letting her?'

'Ooh, don't know about that, love. I don't ask those kinda questions. Mr Greenwood said that's what's happ'ning, so that's what's happ'ning. They're bringing the piano from the house.'

'They're not?'

'They are. Oh– that'll be them now. Listen…'

Above the chattering of magpies, which had come to investigate the party preparations, I heard cursing from the direction of the entrance road.

'Pope?' I said.

'Not like him to miss a chance to put everyone in their place, is it?' Mrs Ivison smirked.

'And my uncle…?'

'Was here earlier, with that fancy chap he's trying to impress. There was a bit of a bother, so your uncle whisked him up to the house. Mr K was hoping to cancel the demonstration, see, because of the high water, worried about the wheel running too fast and all. But that was before your uncle's special dignitary produced a very special piece of exotic wood for the commemorative bobbin. And how could Mr K tell him nay?'

'What did he tell him?'

'Said, 'That's the hardest, densest wood in the world, sir, not suitable for– ah…well, it'll be the first time anyone's made a bobbin out of it.' Never seen Mr K flummoxed like that. Then the Extremely Important Gentleman said the wood was from his family's estate in the West Indies, and it'd mean the world to him to have it carved into a bobbin for his old gran to use. Or some other tale, didn't quite catch it, the mister ushered me off. So now there's a panic on, though don't tell 'em I said that. Mr K's trying to work it out, it's more than his job's worth to disappoint your uncle in front of this dignitary. Best not to interrupt.'

'Actually, I'm looking for Mr Ivison.'

'He still owes your grandma for that partridge?'

'No, nothing like that. I want his help with something.'

'Well, don't let him get ye into Mr K's bad books,' she said, smiling, and then, as if a contrary thought occurred to her, she frowned. 'He's in the workshop with the others.'

If there was a panic on, they were hiding it well. Inside the workshop, Mr Kirke and the other turners were standing in a crescent around Edgar, Tom's elder brother. Edgar was working the hand-boring machine, drilling the hole so the blank would fit onto the lathe for shaping.

Just watching Edgar work, surrounded by the master craftsmen, made me nervous. I could never work so calmly with an audience, but Edgar was as steady as his father. Tom worried this family trait had passed him by; his father joked about it too often.

Mr Ivison was lingering at the back. I went to stand beside him.

Over the rattle of the lathe, which Edgar was operating with the foot pedal, I said, 'Is that the special wood?'

'It is. Ironwood,' Mr Ivison said.

'From the West Indies?'

'Believe so.'

'So it's the type used in old marine clocks?'

'Ye know your materials, love.'

'It's the business, isn't it?'

'Certainly is.' Mr Ivison turned back to watch Edgar.

'So if Mr Kirke or Edgar can work that wood, we could make pulleys and blocks for the ship industry.'

Mr Ivison took a deep breath. 'Far as I know your uncle's got no plans in that direction.'

'When he's gone, I mean.'

'Ah…'

I let the moment hang, then said, 'But why's Edgar using foot-power?' I said. 'It'll take forever.'

'Don't worry, we've got two hours– nay, less than that now, but it's plenty for Edgar to bore the hole and rough the blank, and get everything else ready. Mr K wants the prep done slow to be sure of the accuracy, they've only got that one piece of special wood.'

'But Edgar knows what he's doing, he doesn't need to go so slowly.'

'Nowt for ye to worry about. Mr K's in charge.'

'And why is Mr K's finishing lathe unhooked from the power?' I said, scanning the workshop for anything I could help with so I could stay. If there was a panic on, I wanted to be part of it.

'What do I know, Lizzie?' he said, irritably. 'I'm only the sawyer.'

'Shall I hook it up?'

'Nay, don't touch it.' Then, more kindly, he said, 'Now, what's it ye're after? Or mebby it can wait till later…'

It wasn't like Mr Ivison to try to get rid of me. Nor be so abrupt about Mr Kirke's lathe; it was perfectly normal for me to connect machines to the power. I was bursting to ask how Mr Ivison had organised his strike years ago, how he got everyone on his side. But the mood in the workshop was oddly intense.

'It can wait,' I said.

He nodded. 'Mebby help Tom monitor the water level? Mr K wants a beady eye on it, telling if it gets too high.'

'Alright.' But I didn't want to be alone with Tom just now.

8

The workshop was an awkward, dangerous place with this many people crammed between the machines, with the belts crisscrossing at head height. I tried to keep people from leaning on the machines, in case someone accidentally turned one on.

Everyone wanted to see Mr Kirke make the first bobbin with the ironwood. The children had crowded forwards to see. Impatiently, they were now wriggling through and jumping around the tool-laden workbenches.

Mr Kirke was sharpening his tools at the far end of the workshop. My uncle and his guest – a portly factory-owner from Manchester – were watching the process. The guest kept interrupting, and Mr Kirke, out of politeness, had to keep pausing to answer.

Tom and Edgar were assisting with the whetstones, exchanging glances each time the guest distracted their father. Sharpening required concentration or you could easily round the blade, which could bounce or catch, instead of cut, when the bobbin was spinning at high speed. With a wood as hard as this type of ironwood, Mr Kirke had no room for error.

Pope saw me amongst the audience, and swiped aside two small children on his way over. I was standing next to

Mrs Ivison, and she groaned as he approached.

'Yer uncle's seen ye,' Pope said.

'I know,' I said. 'And I've seen him.'

'Being smart don't suit ye.'

'How would you know?'

By the crinkling of Pope's big-cheeked face, two thoughts may have collided inside his brain. But if they had, they didn't seem to have produced a third, insightful one.

Mrs Ivison snorted with suppressed laughter and bent her head to dab at her eyes. She whimpered slightly.

'Terrible cold, I've got,' she said. 'Terrible.'

'Never mind, Pope,' I said. 'I'm here because I know he's forcing Mr Kirke to do this demonstration when he knows it's not safe. You can tell him I said that. Are you moving people out?'

'What for?'

'Because it's not safe with this many people in here.'

'Do us a favour then, lonely Lizzie, and clear off. It's thou yer uncle wants gan.'

'I'm not going anywhere,' I said.

To the side of Pope's close-up head, I could see Mr Kirke discussing something with Edgar and Tom. I leaned into Mrs Ivison so I could see better. She put her arm around my waist. Edgar was gesturing with his arms, as if mimicking the drive shaft spinning. Mr Kirke was shaking his head and demonstrating something else with his arms.

I said, 'They may need my help.'

'Nobody needs yer help, Lizzie,' said Pope. 'Nobody ever needs yer help.'

Mr Kirke spoke to Tom, who nodded. Then Tom waded through the birch shavings towards us, tipping his head now and then to duck under the belts. He walked straight past me.

'Tom,' I called as he slipped out of the workshop, but he didn't seem to hear.

I followed him out into the yard, though I hated to give Pope the satisfaction of seeing me leave.

Tom was jogging in long, bouncy strides towards the mill-race, where the water level was high after days of heavy rain.

'Tom,' I called again.

He looked over his shoulder and waved me away. He picked up his speed.

Behind me, the power within the workshop started up. The cogs cranked into motion, the power shaft whirred, the belts slapped.

I sprinted after Tom, and caught him as he reached the river bank.

'What're you doing out here?' I said.

'Lizzie, I haven't time.'

'Water's very high.' I gazed at the torrent because he wouldn't look at me. The water tumbled over itself, making foamy white caps on the surface. 'It's going to send the new wheel whizzing. Good job the new cogs are in, or all that power'd be–'

'Everything's fine.'

'Course it is,' I said, wondering what wasn't fine, such that he needed to cut me off. 'Your da's in charge. What was the panic about then? The special wood?'

'He's fine. We're fine. Just checking something.'

'What about the belts? They're very worn, I told my uncle, s'pect your da's mentioned it too… Is it the belts you're worried about?'

'It's fine, Lizzie. Mr Greenwood wanted to hold off replacing them till the new wheel was in, so it's just for

41

another week…but I really haven't time, I'm checking the– er, the…'

'Water level. Mr Ivison said. The worn belts'll be alright with the increased power?'

'Don't worry, tis our problem.'

'But the new waterwheel is much more powerful than the old one, Tom. If the belts are already near breaking, there's more risk of one snapping and flying off–'

'Lizzie…' Tom growled. His face was flushed. He walked away from me, along the bank towards the waterwheel housing, watching the river all the while.

I went after him. 'Even with the new cogs to manage the speed, that's a worry–'

'Leave it, Lizzie.' He kneaded his shoulder and neck as he walked.

'What sort of other adjustments did you have to make?'

'None! Alreet. I told you to leave it, Lizzie. There are nay new cogs, your uncle delayed them. Don't ask why, I don't know. Because of the expense probably.'

'What about the demonstration?' I said, turning to look back at the workshop. 'Is it safe with everyone in there?'

'My Da knows what he's doing.'

'You mean, he's got no choice.' I grabbed Tom's arm. He threw me off. 'Tom, this is a bad idea, you've got to say. Or I can, if you can't–'

He looked at me at last, anxious, and trying to hide it with a stern expression. It had only been three days since we were in the deer den together, but I had an odd feeling that years had passed and I hadn't noticed, or somehow I'd been elsewhere while the change was happening. Tom and I were the same age, but he already seemed to be the man he'd become. Had he grown up in an instant, just like that, upon being made a bobbin turner?

Why's it taking me so long to find my place? Sometimes I feel like a child of ten, and sometimes I know things that make me as old as Gran.

Tom said, 'Lizzie, I–'

But he never finished because a crashing sound interrupted him.

We span around. Chunks of metal burst through the workshop roof. Screams and shouts followed.

Broken slate tiles slid off the roof and shattered on the ground. People spilled out of the workshop into the yard, and still the metal chunks soared until they were lost against the grey of the clouds.

Tom and I pelted back without another word.

I reached the workshop before him. The people streaming out were met by those who'd remained in the yard, and the confusion doubled. Sophia, perhaps in panic, struck up a cheerful tune on the piano. I made for the door into the workshop but Pope blocked me.

'Get out of my way!' I tried to barge past him but he seized me around my waist.

It was the first time he'd ever laid hands on me, and I was startled at his boldness. Tom wheeled around us and into the workshop.

I kicked at Pope's fleshy thighs with the heels of my boots. He gripped me tighter and it took my breath. I elbowed him right, left, right, in the ribs. He grunted. His torso was packed with dense flesh and I couldn't hurt him.

I flung my right arm, bent, backwards over my head and my knuckles found his eye socket. He roared in pain and dropped me. I ran in after Tom.

Inside, the workshop was still, as if it were a Sunday and everyone at rest. The power was off but something unusual caught my eye. Midway along the room, a snapped belt was tangled in two other belts, with one end trailing on the floor.

The air was thick with the dust knocked off the belts. I coughed to clear my throat.

'Who's that? Get out o' here,' Edgar shouted.

I couldn't see him, but he was somewhere near the far end of the workshop.

'It's just,' – I coughed again – 'me.'

I walked towards Edgar's voice.

Beside Mr Kirke's finishing lathe I stopped. His prize machine, which he'd inherited from Grandpa's first foreman, was broken. A cog had shattered. Two small jagged pieces of iron dangled from the axle. The rest of the cog was, presumably, what had shot up through the roof.

'Grab some clean rags,' Edgar said.

On Mr Kirke's lathe, a half-finished bobbin was speckled with blood. I took a handful of cotton rags from the box beside his bench.

Around the bench, the frilly shavings, which were so good at soaking up the workshop's grease and grime, were splattered red. The fibres of the wood, like tiny straws, had drawn the blood outwards from the spots. Each droplet was transformed into a dainty blood snowflake.

'Hurry up, Lizzie.'

I kicked across the length of the littered floor, ducking the motionless belts out of habit.

At the far end, and lying upon a bed of wood shavings, was Mr Kirke. Edgar and Tom were crouching over him.

Tom stood up to let me in. His nearest hand jerked at his side, as if he were about to reach for me but stopped himself. He kept his grey eyes on his father.

'How is he?' I held out some rags. Edgar snatched them.

I caught a glimpse of Mr Kirke. A pad of folded cloth obscured his left eye. A red rose of blood marked the white cotton. In the mill, it was always thus: the romance, and the brutality.

9

Pure and uncomplicated admiration: that's what I wanted to feel about the mill.

I wanted to love it, simply and purely, but it had neither begun that way, converted from a weapon-making forge, nor did it end with a beautifully-crafted bobbin, perfect in form, isolated from function. Our bobbins were used in the big cotton spinning factories in Manchester, and that cotton was picked by slaves in America.

Tending to Mr Kirke's right hand, I tried to think of what this injury meant for him – and Tom and Edgar and Mrs Kirke – and not how it added to the weight of everything. Nothing was pure and nothing was simple. Especially not love.

'YOU! Out, now.' My uncle boomed from the other end of the workshop.

I knew he meant me, but in this moment I had to, had to, show whose side I was on.

'No,' I said loudly, to be sure he heard.

I continued to wrap a clean rag around Mr Kirke's palm. The metal had sliced through his skin, muscle and tendons. I doubted he'd be able to use this hand again with the control and skill he needed for turning bobbins. But his eye was of more immediate concern.

'You've no business here.' My uncle now stood behind me, his voice cold again. He thought it a weakness to let anyone see his anger.

'I was here already, unlike you,' I said, without moving from where I knelt. I tied the bandage, but the blood was already seeping through the layers.

'Alreet, I'm alreet,' Mr Kirke murmured. 'Wotcher fussing like hens for? One good eye's enough to supervise yous layabouts when we get the speed fixed. We'll replace the belts and–' He tried to sit up. Edgar gently pushed him back onto the bed of shavings.

'Up you get, Kirke,' Pope said, pounding his fist, once, twice, on a workbench. 'Mr Greenwood wants things tidied up, back to normal.'

Tom and Edgar looked at one another. They began to rise from where they were crouching over Mr Kirke, who tried to sit up again.

'Not yous, him,' Pope said. 'Old man Kirke. Fella, ye got all them ninnies out there scared for nay reason with that stupid stunt.'

Tom stooped back down to attend to his father.

'Stunt?' I said, standing up to face my uncle. He looked shaken, his mouth more pinched than usual. He particularly hated to be confronted in front of his employees. I said, 'Mr Kirke didn't want to do it, you made him. You knew it was dangerous.'

'Nonsense. It was a minor risk, calculated,' my uncle said in a flat voice, as if he were talking about coppice poles cut too early in the season. 'You can go now, Elizabeth, you're no longer needed.'

'What did you calculate? Mr Kirke's eye–'

'And hand,' Edgar said.

'–for your, what?' I said.

'That's enough, Elizabeth. This is no place for you.'

'This is my place. It's not yours,' I said, jabbing my finger at him though I knew I looked stupid. 'It's mine, it's always been mine. I would never have let this happen. Never. You stole this mill from me and now you're hurting people and ruining the business, you–'

'Get out of here. I won't ask again.'

'I'm not leaving here, and I'm not leaving Fairy Cross. Not for Mungrispike, not anywhere.'

Tom teetered where he was crouching with his back to me. He put one hand on the floor to steady himself.

'Take her home,' said my uncle.

Pope stepped behind me. He circled one beefy arm around my upper chest, pinning my arms, and with his other he clinched my waist and wrists. Shaw had grabbed my feet and lifted me off the floor before I realised what was happening.

'Hold on–' said Edgar, but a glare from my uncle silenced him.

As they carried me out, I kicked and struggled, thrashed and shouted. And though it was undignified, I carried on doing it so everyone in the yard would see.

No one helped, of course. How could they? But they saw. Even Sophia's piano-plinking faded and finally stopped, until the only sounds were me, the rushing river and the magpies cackling, as they picked over the feast that never was.

The sensation of being carried by Pope and Shaw brought on a feeling of nausea. The pressure of their fingers squeezing my flesh. The touch of their coarse hairy skin when it brushed against mine. The smell of Pope's breath in my face. Shaw's eyes lingering on my body too frequently.

They carried me sideways up the track, as if I were a rolled-up old carpet, sagging in the middle. I'd stopped struggling once we were out of earshot of the mill. I thought I should save my strength, I might need to run.

Were Pope and Shaw taking me, perhaps, into the woods? To feed me poisonous mushrooms so I could die a natural death. An inconvenient heir dispatched.

I'd come across a tramp picking mushrooms in the woods, years ago. The first time, I watched from afar. His sweet-smelling odour seemed to belong in the woods, but I could see he didn't know his mushrooms; he was nibbling the fungi with no care for which were edible and which were not. The second time, months later, I tripped over him: a soft bundle half-buried in leaf mulch, and softening into mulch himself. I thought it was a sodden, rolled-up old carpet until I saw his cracked leather boots.

The vision of the tramp in his final resting place made me feel tired suddenly, so tired. How could I fight my uncle and ever hope to win? He controlled everything and everyone in Fairy Cross. I wasn't even allowed to use my own legs to get home. Perhaps in this current pose, that of the sagging carpet was how I'd arrive at Mungrispike too.

I began to struggle again, throwing my body up and down. I screamed. Pope and Shaw cursed. As I paused for breath, I heard rapid steps on the gravel path that led up to our cottage.

'Whatever are you doing?' Gran yelled. 'Get your filthy hands off her.'

Shaw dropped my feet without further encouragement and – urff – Pope let go of my arms. The gravel spiked my fleshy bits as I landed.

Pope and Shaw retreated a few steps.

'GET OUT O' MY SIGHT,' Gran said, 'or you'll find yourselves in the pit like the galumphing bears you are.'

'We don't have a bear pit,' I said, stupidly, as if this were the important thing.

'As far as you know. What d'you think happened to Robin's last set o' thugs?'

She stomped over and hoiked me off the ground. Her pantaloons were covered in floury handprints – she refused to ever wear an apron.

To Pope and Shaw, she barked, 'Think you can treat my lass like that? Blew in on the last rotten wind, din't yous.'

'We been in Mr Greenwood's employ near four years, ma'am,' said Pope.

'Like I said. Last rotten wind. Now, go on, get.'

'But we're to see her yam and make sure she stays there,' Pope said.

'You're not coming into my home and leaving with that fat head upon your neck, so take your pick.'

Pope shuffled on the spot and turned to Shaw, who offered a shrug.

'We'll wait outside,' Pope said, 'to see she don't escape.'

'Escape? From her own home? It's called 'going out', and it's none o' your business.'

'Mr Greenwood says–'

'Young Robin can say what he likes, and I'll say this–' Gran unleashed curse words such as I'd never heard. She must've learnt them in Paris.

I couldn't help but laugh. Pope began to laugh too, nervously, but more cursing from Gran shut him up.

Eventually, he and Shaw lumbered down the hill. Gran yelled her final, most personal insults after them. And I swear a wood pigeon plopped from the sky, dead from the shock. Well, something landed in the undergrowth beside the path.

When I stopped laughing and could breathe again, I said, 'Where's the bear pit then?'

'Not a bear pit, a snake pit, and you're already in it, Lizzie. I'm not going to ask how you got yourself carried up here, I'm guessing I'll hear soon enough. But that's for later, because there's more to this school at Mungrispike. We can't wait for letters to trundle their way to Bath and back.'

10

'Seems that very few young ladies are admitted to Mungrispike. Unusual criteria, apparently,' Gran said, ushering me indoors. She closed the door softly, and steered me towards the mildewed armchairs.

I could smell baking bread. Dreamily, I circled through our shabby parlour and back towards the kitchen, confused by what had happened at the mill. It didn't seem real now I was home, comforted by familiar smells.

'Is it currant buns?' I said. 'Hope so.'

'Never mind the blethering buns, Lizzie. Come here. I need to tell you something you don't want to hear.'

'Then don't tell me. Will you glaze them with sugar?' I said. 'I like sticky buns the best.'

'*Lizzie.*'

I wandered back to the parlour, sat upon the hearth rug, then stretched out flat on my back. The plaster on the ceiling above was cracked. A chunk the size of my fist was missing, where once, while dancing with a broom, I'd put the handle through to the cavity above.

'This house'll fall down around us, won't it? And we'll be buried beneath. Will anyone dig us out, I wonder?'

'Lizzie, for pity's sake, what's the matter with you? Sit up, and listen.'

'There was an accident at the mill,' I said, and sat up. I told her everything.

When I'd finished, Gran said, 'I'll deal with Robin in time. And I'm sorry, but we can't do anything about Mr Kirke this instant. You have to listen to what I've found out about Mungrispike.'

She didn't wait for me to agree. 'Samuel and Mary,' – her poet friends at the Mount – 'heard from a journalist who came to stay once. A friend of their friend, up from London. He said– the journalist, that is, I forget his name…well, he was investigating lunatic asylums, or writing a history, or maybe searching for will-o'-the-wisps on the moor, something of that nature–

'Anyway, he found the Mungrispike place'd closed because there weren't enough inmates. Seems us lakeland folk aren't mad enough to need our own asylum, or we're all so mad no one stands out. Anyway, the lock-up closed, but the premises were never sold. They're owned by the same family still. Who've an interest in – what did he call it now? – 'the inheritance of moral depravity'.'

'What does that mean?' I said, only half-listening, picking loose tufts of coloured wool from the red Turkey rug. Grandpa had longed to see the mystics of the Orient too, but he'd bought the rug in London, and paid ten times its worth.

'Means they think a person's born bad, or mad, or both… Lizzie!'

'Yes. Listening. Mad, bad, both.'

'And that it's every family's duty– which includes this one, Lizzie, which includes Robin, who, let's face it, has a vendetta against you…'

'I've my own vendetta too.'

'The wee blind moles asleep in their tunnels know that. Lizzie, shush up, I'm still explaining. These Mungrispike people believe it's every family's duty to identify their wrong 'uns and put them away before their 'disease infects society', or some twaddle. And all the better to do it, allegedly, when they're young so they can't have kiddies themselves, and thus perpetuate the cycle. It's all cobblers, but some'll believe anything that gives them an excuse for something they want to do anyway.'

I stopped picking at the rug and dreaming of the Orient, wishing the carpet would fly me away.

'Uncle Robin wants to lock me in an asylum? That's ridiculous. They'd never take me, it's obvious I'm not mad–'

'Or bad.'

'But what's it got to do with the school?'

'Right, well– Glad you're listening at last.' Gran came to sit cross-legged on the rug with me. 'This same family, who still own the mansion and hundreds of acres at Mungrispike, has opened this school so 'wayward' young ladies can be made into 'constant' ones. And by that they mean obedient, loyal, quiet. Just how most men want their ladies, young or old, coincidentally. Not your Grandpa, thankfully. He might've been lacking sense in some departments, but not that one. He knew a good woman when she rescued him from certain disgrace.' Gran cackled. 'So…the school's very small, though it's been open for near fifteen years. But the thing is, and this's what got the journalist wondering, no one has ever heard of a young lady leaving the school. Girls are admitted and then…'

'What happens to them?'

Gran shrugged. 'The journalist suspects the asylum is still there, they've just got a different way of finding patients.'

'I don't understand.'

'Course you don't, why would you, it's evil. But this is

what he thinks happens: Families send their girls, the disobedient or outspoken ones, or the ones a bit slow in the head that'll never get married off, to be made into respectable young ladies. And then, during their 'education', the school denounces these girls as bad through and through. Nothing can be done to change their characters, they'll be a danger to society if ever they're let out. But don't worry, fretful folk, Mungrispike has the solution.

'You don't get admitted to the asylum,' Gran continued, her hazel eyes taking on the sparkling look of all her best stories, 'and this is the clever bit…you enter the school and it's your own behaviour that condemns you.'

'Behaviour like what?' I said, listening intently to her words, searching for their meaning, not fooled by the bewitching eyes.

'Speaking back to people in authority, questioning notions that most people take for granted. Running around in breeches, probably.'

'That's not madness, or badness.'

'To some it is. To Robin it is.'

'Gran, you're not saying I've already condemned myself…with my own behaviour?'

'No. No, Lizzie, I'm not saying that. You haven't. And neither have the other girls at Mungrispike, poor lasses. It's all a fiction. But a terribly convenient one. And who's going to speak out, when the lasses have no one to tell?'

'He can't do this!'

'No, he can't. I won't let him. Oh, he'll try. But I'm working on it, Lizzie. I am. Lay low for a time, will you? I won't make you promise, you'll only break–'

'I promise, I do, Gran. Anything, I'll do anything. Just don't let him–'

'S'alright, Lizzie. It's been done before.'

55

11

That night, I couldn't sleep for fear of waking to find I was already locked up at Mungrispike. I lay in bed with the covers thrown off. Then later rolled up in them, freezing, though the night was warm.

I wanted to believe Gran could save me from Mungrispike. I ran through, step by step, every possible plan she would think of. But they all ended with my uncle discovering me – living with her poet friends at the Mount, or hiding out in the deer den, or in Bath, where he'd snatch me while I was sipping tea in a fancy establishment, and everyone would gossip that they'd always known I had a shifty look about me.

And thence to Mungrispike, where the teachers and doctors would discover I was bad and mad all the way through. There'd always been talk about what my father had done, that he'd fallen in with an infamous highwayman. I'd never believed it. But with the mill lost to me, was this my true inheritance?

I was afraid to ask Gran about her plan in case I saw the flaws in it. While events were uncertain there was hope.

Eventually, I got out of bed and padded to Gran's room.

She was breathing heavily, fast asleep. I cleared my throat a few times. She didn't stir. She'd slept through the storm of the decade once, while I'd woken at the first flash of lightning. When the back chimney crashed through the roof of the woodshed, I'd had to wake her.

Evidently, Gran never worried about being drugged with laudanum and kidnapped in her sleep. I was sure this was how Robin would steal me away, sedating me with the potion his wife used for her mysterious pains.

I went back to my room, got into bed and pulled the coverlet up to my nose. I counted a fast minute. Then I jumped up, put on my clothes and boots, and crept down the stairs.

Outside, the moon was plump but not quite full. The night noises in the trees and shrubs were some comfort, for a few minutes. Then I became agitated again. Standing still was as useless as lying in bed. I needed to walk.

Round the back of the cottage, I could see the faint contours of the hills. Walking on the moor always made me feel better. I could wander there now. But also, this was a good way to slip into a ravine, break a leg and not be found for three days.

I circled back to the front and pleaded with the moon. If the moon was Manì, of Norse legend, then he wasn't a very attentive god because nothing happened at all. I began to panic about Mungrispike again, imagining how I'd beseech Manì from the barred window of my room, and get the same response as now.

I didn't notice where my pacing had taken me until I was halfway there. When I realised I was nearing the mill, I paused. But the path led down, it seemed the natural way to go.

I levered open the loose window at the far end of the workshop, my secret way in. I climbed through onto a workbench and slid to the floor.

I dared not light a lamp, which would be seen from River View. If anyone there was awake, spying and plotting.

Further across the yard there was a faint glow in the packing loft. Billy was burning a lamp, though he knew he shouldn't. More than once I'd warned him not to. I seethed at his stupidity. But I knew it was because he was scared of the rats.

At night, the rats came to nibble at the grain lodged in the corners of sacks, which we bought from farmers who'd used them for livestock feed. One of Billy's main jobs was to thoroughly empty the grain sacks before we filled them with bobbins. He had only himself to blame.

How long would Billy last at the mill? I couldn't think of any other lakeland trade he'd be useful at, not coppicing, not smelting, not quarrying. He was too scared to speak up when he didn't understand, too scared to learn. I suppose it was because he was used to being humiliated and beaten in the workhouse. But sometimes it made me want to shake him. I was ashamed at how often my pity turned to contempt.

Inside the workshop, all the drive belts had been taken off the cogs and laid flat on the floor, to check for wear. I was glad to see this; it meant someone with sense had persuaded my uncle. Why won't he listen when I tell him the same things?

I wondered what had happened to Mr Kirke, and how his eye and hand were. I wondered why only Edgar had stood up for me, and why Tom hadn't. He would have done once, he'd have done anything for me, so he said. We'd almost had a moment, several months ago, of complete togetherness, but I'd interrupted the moment. Since then it felt like Tom and I were waiting.

But for what? For something to change, become less complicated…? I knew that would never happen. Tom didn't want anything to change, unless it was something that brought him closer to becoming a master craftsman. Nothing was pure and simple.

The workshop floor had been swept clear of birch shavings and all the surfaces dusted. This happened once a week anyway, or the shavings became so deep it was dangerous to work. It always made me sad to see the workshop so bare – when metal surfaces gleamed and sounds echoed, when traces of the forest had been banished.

I'd come to the empty mill to feel it as mine and mine alone. But there was no comfort here.

I climbed out of the window and flitted across the dark yard towards the drying sheds, and the rushing, shushing river.

Lying on my belly on the soft dewy bank, I ran my fingers through the cold water. My fingertips quickly numbed.

With closed fingers, I resisted the force of the water until I could no longer hold them together, and my arm muscles were trembling. Leaves and twigs then snagged in the fork of my hand. When autumn came, Tom and I would scoop mats of fallen leaves – gold, russet, flame – from the millrace to prevent them from clogging the waterwheel.

No, not Tom. Just me. No, not me even. One of the other apprentices would have to cajole Mr Ivison into lending them his net – the one he used when Mr Kirke wasn't looking, for trout or salmon that swam into the millrace by accident.

The water gave off a fresh, mossy smell. I sniffed hard,

trying to remember it, to catalogue it with the smell of the peat bogs on the moor, the forest bed after rain, of freshly gouged birch wood. And of Gran burning a stew: forgetting she'd put it on and going for a walk, then returning to scrape the burnt bits off the pot, and joke about serving them as a garnish.

It felt like everything was ending. But there seemed to be no beginning queued up behind it. Gran always promised: 'No ending without a shiny new beginning. But the beginning doesn't appear, duck, until the ending's had its way. Be brave enough to wait.'

But what if sometimes there's just an ending?

I distracted myself with the thought of Gran's burnt stew, which had a deep smoky flavour all its own. My stomach grumbled, though I knew it was the comfort of food I sought, not the food itself. I was transported to the warm kitchen of the cottage, where Gran was scraping the pot, laughing and cursing at her forgetfulness, and I was trying to waft away the burning smell with a cloth, instead flapping it into my own hair and clothes.

Then I realised the burning smell was real.

Rolling onto my back, I sniffed again. Definitely smoke. It was too late for the stoker to be at work in the kiln room, and too late for a hearth fire in one of the cottages on the riverbank.

I took a sharp intake of breath, thinking I'd left a lamp on the workshop, then remembered I hadn't lit one.

My next thought was of Billy and his lamp.

Then, the barrels of paraffin recently moved from the waterwheel housing into the shed below the packing loft.

And the one hundred and eighty sacks of finished bobbins upstairs waiting for delivery.

There'd once been another bobbin mill further down river, now abandoned and decaying. The owner had been too optimistic about repaying his debts. After the mill's collapse, the owner had gone up onto the fells, and shot his dog and then himself. (Why the dog?) His family had been forced into the workhouse.

None of us knew how much my uncle had wagered on the big order and the new wheel. Mr Ivison had estimated the costs, but when Mr Kirke found out, he forbade him to tell anyone.

Where I lay behind the drying shed, the rest of the yard and buildings were hidden. I stood up from the bank, slowly, wanting to be wrong, and went around the shed.

But I wasn't wrong. The packing loft was glowing brightly from within. Smoke was seeping out from the gaps in the wooden cladding. Flames shimmied across the inside of the windows. The loft was a hazy orange nest, a welcoming perch for a devilish bird.

12

I ran towards the burning loft before I'd decided what to do.

Sparks sizzled into the black sky. I tried to shout for help, but only managed a husky bark between breaths.

I reached the shed below the packing loft. Inside, smoke was rolling down the ladder. Along the dark walls were the twenty barrels of paraffin. By myself I could never roll all the barrels out in time. Neither could I carry the full sacks of bobbins down from the loft. Can I lower the sacks through the delivery hatch?

'Billy,' I shouted up the loft ladder. 'Billy! Are you there?'

I hoped he wasn't, that he'd fled when the fire started. But knowing Billy, he'd fallen asleep with the lamp on and knocked it over without waking.

My eyes began to water from the smoke. How long until a spark reaches the barrels?

I leapt onto the ladder to climb, but in my haste my feet slipped off the bottom rungs. Splinters pierced my fingers and palms as I slid down. I scrabbled back up.

Cautiously, I poked my head above the level of the loft floor. The heat dried my eyeballs and seemed to stick my lids open.

'Billy,' I shouted, coughing from the smoke. I thought I heard a whimper.

The smoke and flames made a mirage of the loft. But beneath the illusion the layout was familiar: loft hatch in the centre; Billy's bed and the delivery hatch in each corner of one end; the stored bobbins at the other end; the sorting table running the length between.

Billy's end was a forest of fires. His straw mattress was already gone. Remnants of his sheet and pillow fizzled as the floorboards began to burn. Around his bed were dozens of small fires – splashes of paraffin which apprentices had spilled over the years. Mabel flew into a rage when anyone did this, and Billy was the clumsiest. The whole loft was dotted with soaked-in paraffin.

The pitched roof at Billy's end was alight, the fire creeping along the wooden beams, turning the wood to smouldering ash, dropping embers onto the floor, weakening the whole structure of the shed.

'Bil–' I choked on the smoke. Ducked back down and leapt off the ladder onto the solid floor. Biting and tearing at the front of my shirt, I ripped off a large piece, and tied it over my nose and mouth as a mask.

Back up the ladder, I crawled onto the loft floor. The smoke was thinner here. The smooth ridges of the floorboards were hot beneath my hands. I thought I heard a mumble over the crackle and hiss of flames.

A burning chunk of wood landed in front of me and set alight a pool of paraffin. I swung my leg round to stamp out the miniature inferno.

'Billy,' I shouted again, crouching to try to see beyond the smoke. 'Where are you?'

'Here,' Billy cried. 'Here!'

Through the smoke I saw a solid form, an arm, waving. Billy was cowering in the nook between the roof and floor.

Separating us were clusters of fire, which were spreading towards, but hadn't yet reached, the delivery hatch. Billy first, I thought, then the bobbins.

'You've got to come through here, Billy,' I said. 'To me. Come on.'

'Lizzie?' He began to crawl closer to the barrier of fires. Then a section of crossbeam broke from the roof and hit the floor in front of him. He yelped and shot back. The flaming beam divided us.

I wrenched off my jacket, wrapped one sleeve around my arm and bounded forwards. I wheeled my arm again and again, thrashing at the wall of fire to dampen it.

'Billy, come on!' I cleared a narrow gap to the blackened floor. 'Through here, now.' But he wouldn't come.

I wheezed and fell back. The flames sprang up again.

My jacket was singed and smoking. I slapped out the glowing wool fibres, then tightened the grip of the sleeve coiled around my arm.

I jumped up and thrashed at the fire between Billy and me. If he stayed much longer in the corner, he'd be overcome by the smoke and never get out. The flames sprang back to life in seconds.

'Lizzie!'

I slapped the flames again and leapt through the gap towards him. I hoisted him off the floor.

'Follow me. I'll beat the fire down and you jump over.'

He wouldn't budge. Flames billowed on the roof above our heads. The gap I'd come through closed. I tried to pull him with me. He flailed his free arm and punched the back of my head. I grappled with his elbow, and caught his skinny wrist, then locked my left hand around both his wrists. I crouched, leaned under his chest and stood up with him my over my shoulder, my right arm securing the crook of his legs.

He screamed and wailed, as if I were about to throw him into the fire, and writhed on my shoulder.

'Stop it,' I hollered. 'You'll bring us both down.'

He flipped like a caught fish, weakly, then stopped. I turned to face the wall of flames. I had no free hand with which to beat them down. I was already singed head to foot, and couldn't jump over with the weight of Billy on my back. So I took a long, searing breath and did something which would now doubt condemn me to Mungrispike forever more. I walked straight through the wall of flames.

Staggering to the loft hatch, the weight of Billy pulled us forward. We toppled. I landed half on Billy and he half on me, but at least we'd cleared the fire.

Billy groaned. I got to my feet and dragged him towards the hatch. Behind us, a loud crack... Some of the burning floorboards fell through to the shed below. I flung Billy to the hatch and dangled him through the hole.

'I'm going to drop you. Land on your feet.'

I lowered him as far as I could, then let go. I skittered down the ladder, found him crumpled at the bottom, threw him over my shoulder again and stumbled out of the shed.

Ten yards from the door, my legs buckled. I collapsed, with Billy, into the mulch of the yard. Behind us came a whoosh and a bang as burning floorboards tipped into the paraffin barrels. I dragged myself along the ground with Billy's weight on top of me. Raw flesh of my legs scraping on woodchips and stones.

And then...Billy's weight was gone. I strained my neck to lift my head to where the air smelt different, sort of sweet, like pipe smoke.

Mr Ivison was leaning over me. 'Ye're alreet, Lizzie love, ye're alreet.'

13

'That's it then,' Edgar said.

We watched the shed and loft burn. Edgar, Tom and some of the other men and women had doused the outside of the shed and the surrounds so the fire wouldn't spread. But they couldn't get inside to put out the fire, nor retrieve any bobbin sacks.

'Looks like it,' said Mr Ivison.

No one said anything for ages, there was nothing to say. We were all thinking of what the lost bobbins meant.

Mrs Ivison put her arm around my shoulders and whispered, 'What were ye doing here at this time o' night, Lizzie? Your gran's gonna kill ye, and me, and the mister probably. Ours is the closest cottage...we shoulda seen– ye shouldn'ta been the one to go in.'

'No one should,' I said. 'I told my uncle about the paraffin being stored there.'

'Us too,' said Edgar. 'But seems like when ye tell him he's wrong, he don't correct it. Tells ye, *ye're* wrong. That he knows best. Tells ye–'

'–it's not your place to decide what's right or wrong,' I said. 'It's your place to do as he says.'

Edgar sighed.

'Ye oughta skedaddle now, Lizzie.' Mr Ivison pointed

towards River View. A procession of lamps was bobbing down the road towards us. 'That'll be his lordship on his way, with them hoodlums. Me and Edgar need to work out how to explain all this without ye in the picture. That alreet? For your own preservation.'

'Thanks, but I'll stay anyway.'

'Reet ye are,' Mr Ivison said.

Mrs Ivison hugged me tighter. Then Mr Ivison whispered to Edgar.

A couple of minutes later Tom was at my side. I smelt the woodsmoke on his clothes.

Mrs Ivison let me go and began to talk loudly to her husband. Tom tapped me on the arm, then walked slowly away from the group. I followed him in silence.

I didn't want to be the first one to speak, I thought he owed me that. I wanted to ask why he hadn't stood up to my uncle on my behalf. I knew why. But I still wanted to ask.

'See what he's done now,' I said, when we were alone in the middle of the dark yard.

'I'll walk you home,' Tom said. 'Your grandma'll be worried when she hears.'

I ignored this obvious attempt to get me out of the way. 'I told him about the paraffin being stored there, I told him. I'd never be so stupid if I was in charge.'

'It was Billy who knocked over the lamp,' Tom said, quietly.

'You know he's scared of the rats. And he only sleeps in the loft because my uncle won't give him proper lodging.'

'Billy's nay good, he isn't learning.'

'He's trying,' I said, though I wasn't sure he was.

'He's dragging the rest of us down. Mebby he should've gone back–'

'To the workhouse? You don't really believe that, Tom, you sound like my uncle.'

'I don't know. Nay. Nay, I don't think that, but– all those bobbins, everyone's hard work, and me Da's most of all. It's for nowt. He won't get paid for his work, none of us will.'

'It's only a week's wages.'

'Only a week? Lizzie–'

'I know what you mean, *Tom*. Think I wouldn't prefer a lamb chop now and then, instead of Gran's rabbit and squirrel and rabbit again? We depend on the mill's fortunes too, and my uncle's goodwill most of all. He makes me wait till everyone's done bagging up shavings before I'm allowed some for our fires, and it's mostly just sawdust by then. And we've still got that hole in the roof, where the chimney fell down, he won't fix it, we can't use that room for Grandpa's library anymore–'

'*Library*? Puh.'

'What about it?' I said, but Tom didn't reply and I was too angry to bother seeing his side of the matter. 'I'll walk home by myself, if you're so keen for me to be gone. S'pect you're needed, being so indispensable and all. If the mill were mine–'

'But the mill's not yours,' he shouted. 'Never has been, never will be. Let it be. I'm sick of hearing it. We don't need saving, just to get on with our jobs. Put the fire out, tidy up, build a new shed, get on with things.'

'*When* the mill is mine–' I said, stubbornly, then forgot what I was going to say. Or maybe there was nothing more to say, I just needed to declare ownership again and again.

The truth was I had no real plan. I'd thought I could persuade Mr Ivison to help me organise everyone to stand against my uncle. But why would he do that? He'd been laid off from his previous job for being a 'troublemaker'.

Not even his wife knew he'd told me. And they'd had to lie about his references, otherwise my uncle would never have employed him.

I wanted to reclaim the mill more than anything. But I had no idea how to make it happen.

'Say the mill is yours, Lizzie, just for argument's sake–'

'This's an argument we're having, is it?'

'What else would you call it?'

'I thought you were lecturing me on things I already know.'

'Call it what you like,' Tom said, emboldened by the anonymity of the night, 'but if the mill were yours, then now, tonight, you'd be in your uncle's position. The bobbins are gone. The packing loft's gone. What would you do with Billy?'

'It's not fair to ask me that, I'm not my uncle, nor in his position.'

'But you would be, if you were running the mill. And if you were, then I'd be working for you.'

Somehow I'd never considered this. I'd always thought of us working altogether. I didn't want to be in charge of anyone, especially not Tom. 'You wouldn't be working for me, like you do for my uncle. You know your job so well, everyone does, no one needs telling. Except Billy.'

'Exactly.'

'Exactly what?'

'There's always a Billy.'

'I don't know what you mean.'

'You don't understand because you don't really work here. You turn up, do what you fancy, none of it matters.'

'It matters to me, you know it does,' I said.

'But it's not the same. You're not one of us, you're a Greenwood. Greenwoods own all the land we can see, have done for centuries. And we – me, me Da, me brother, me Mam, and everyone else – we're the people who work on Greenwood land, and in your mills.'

'Not my mill,' I mumbled.

'You think you're hefted to this land like the Herdwicks, but you're not. Generations of Greenwoods have lived in Fairy Cross. Kirkes too, but Kirkes don't have a choice. I've got to learn bobbin-turning quick as I can. Look what happened to me Da, he canna– he's not going to be able to–' Tom paused. 'It's me and Edgar now.'

There was so much binding Tom and me, and now so much getting in the way. Had he always thought like this? Of me as an outsider, even to him, and all the while I thought we were on the same side.

The packing loft's remaining beams cracked and fell. A cry of 'Ooh, aaahhh' came from the gathering of workers and villagers, as if they were watching Guy Fawkes burn on a bonfire.

'That's it then,' I said.

14

Tom and I stood inches, yet fathoms, apart.

We watched the fire as it began to subside. I almost wished the packing loft would burn forever so there'd never have to be an after, never have to be a time when Tom and I would go our separate ways across the yard – he to his brother and Mr Ivison and the heart of the aftermath, and me…me up the lane to the cottage, alone.

Then Pope found us.

'Nay good at sloping off, are yer, loopy Lizzie?' He sounded more pleased than anyone should when their employer's business was near ruin. He said, 'Yer uncle wants a word with ye.'

'Course he does,' I muttered. 'I s'pect somehow this's all my fault.'

'Catching on at last. Huh, huh, huh.' Pope left us and disappeared in the direction of the workshop.

I waited a moment before I said to Tom, 'See you tomorrow, maybe,' expecting him to leave.

'What's Mungrispike?' he said.

'Nothing. Nowhere. Just a– just a school.' I should have told him what Gran had found out. But to tell Tom would make it real.

'That he wants to send you to?'

'He'll try.'

'He usually gets what he wants.'

I wanted to say 'Not this time,' but I wasn't sure how much I believed it. Then I heard Pope's heavy breathing coming closer. With him was my uncle, treading silently.

Neither of them had brought a torch, nothing to mark out where we stood. I thought of running then, across the rickety bridge to the other side of the river, and from there to the fells. But what was the point. And Tom couldn't run, he had nowhere to go. His family, his place, was here.

In the forest, sinuous tree roots search underground – when they bump immovable things they turn, twist, knot around each other, always seeking, always growing, yet always connected. But what if some people aren't like trees, don't have roots, only their feet upon a patch of ground and nothing holding them there?

'Elizabeth,' said my uncle.

I didn't need to see his face to feel his animosity. 'Don't tell me,' I said, 'this is my fault because I should've saved the bobbins before Billy.'

'If only you'd learn as quickly when it suits someone other than you,' he said, wearily. 'One worthless life above the hundred people dependent on this mill. What does the world gain by having that boy in it?'

Before I could speak, Tom said, 'Mr Greenwood, sir, I believe it all happened in a flash, I don't think Lizzie, er, Elizabeth could do much else.'

'She coulda thrown shavings on top o' fire and then herself, like ye do on shop floor when a lamp gets knocked,' Pope said.

'The only shavings in the packing loft are– were in Billy's mattress, sir, it was already on fire.'

'Yeah?' Pope said.

'I should've thrown myself on the fire?' I said. 'That's

what you would've done?'

'It's by-the-by what anyone else would have done, Elizabeth,' my uncle said, 'because you were the one there. You still wish to be in charge of the mill, I presume?'

I knew this for a trick. I didn't answer.

'I'll take that as a yes, why change the habit of a lifetime. So tell me, now the bobbins are lost, whom should I lay off first, to make ends meet? Who's most dispensable? The defective boy can return to the workhouse tomorrow, I'm sure you'll agree. Then who? Mr Taylor is old and slow, no one will argue with that. His job can be done by one of the apprentices. We – you and I, in this joint enterprise we find ourselves in – don't need Mabel now there's no packing loft, we'll do the sorting a different way. Because that's what taking charge means after what you've done tonight.'

'That's not what taking charge means,' I said. 'Taking charge means leading by example, admitting your own responsibility. You left those paraffin barrels–'

'I haven't finished, Elizabeth. I expect you know we've got too many bobbin turners. We all know Mr Kirke is retired as of this afternoon. Which of the others is the least skilled, the newest, the one we can afford to lose? I believe it's your friend here. Thomas, is it? You've not yet learnt how to use the finishing lathe?'

'Me father'd just begun to–'

'And now he's retired.'

'Me brother will–'

'I'm afraid we haven't time for your education, Thomas. Perhaps you could take Elizabeth home, if you wish to be of service to me. I hope you won't be too much at odds with one another.'

15

Two days I waited and fretted in the cottage. Wondering what rumours my uncle would fabricate about me, to justify my immediate removal to Mungrispike, and to explain why I'd never return.

Gran had always been convinced that Robin had started the rumours about my father. That he intended to sell the mill and sink his fortune into a gold mine in South America. Gran didn't believe it for a second. Nor that my father been spotted in several locations on the east-west road in the company of a suspected highwayman. Gran knew there was nothing to this.

She also believed – but didn't ask, thinking it preposterous – that he hadn't eloped with a young lady and been secretly married in Scotland. Until a furious gentleman, who'd been on holiday from Bath with his niece, turned up at River View.

Two days I stayed indoors, out of sight. Two days and no one visited, not even Tom. I understood why. But it still hurt.

Tom hadn't said a word to me on the slow walk from the mill to the cottage. I couldn't speak either, my voice was a strangled thing.

Someone must have woken Gran because she was

waiting in the open doorway when we arrived. I went straight to bed, not even pausing for a hug. Tom and Gran stayed up talking softly for hours. I tried not to listen, put a pillow over my head, but the words 'ruin', 'let go', 'Mungrispike' and 'lost', 'lost', 'lost' drifted up to my room and into my dreams.

I hated to hide away like a coward while Gran went politicking, to try to reason with Robin about the lay-offs, only to return with worse and worse news: of Billy's teary departure; Mr Taylor given notice to leave his job and cottage; Tom demoted and his pay cut, just when his family most needed his wages. And Mr Kirke blinded in one eye.

My burnt legs were blistered and raw. I picked at the torn skin during the worst moments alone.

On the third morning my uncle came for me. I was out front in my nightgown, with Gran's old jacket thrown over the top, pinching the big thorns from the rose that rambled over our doorway. Collecting the thorns in a tin cup, I don't know why.

The crunch of the gravel path alerted me to someone's approach.

'Good morning, Elizabeth,' my uncle said. He halted at the end of the path.

I snuck a look at him. He was standing perfectly still, alone.

I was so tired I had no strength to be angry. And foolishly, I thought myself protected at the cottage, as if Gran had woven charms into the rose, as if it were the fairytale thicket around Sleeping Beauty's castle. That daft girl, dozing for a hundred years, waiting for someone to rescue her. If she'd been a lakeland lass, she'd never have pricked her finger in the first place.

Without interrupting my task, I said, 'Try to upset me, if

you like, with how everyone blames me for the loss of the bobbins. I know it's not true.'

'No need for the bravado, Elizabeth, there's no one here but us. Time this was all over, you'll go to Mungrispike today.'

I pricked my finger on a thorn, but it didn't bleed. All my blood seemed to rush to my heart and leave my head empty, dizzy. I gripped the tin cup of thorns for the feel of something solid.

'Go get dressed,' my uncle said.

I reached for the latch on the front door. Press, click, lift. I pushed the door open. I heard the sound of pots clashing in the kitchen at the rear of the house. Gran must be back from her walk.

'No tricks. I know you, Elizabeth.'

I stepped into the house, slowly, as if to move quickly would provoke him into snatching me. I closed the door quietly. Then I lost my nerve.

'Gran,' I hollered, running to find her in the kitchen.

The back door was open, banging on the latch in the breeze that blew me along. But no Gran.

She was nowhere in the yard either. But Pope was. He came from the woodshed, knowing it had been one of my hiding places as a child. He saw me and changed his course.

I hurled myself back through the kitchen. Shaw was approaching from the parlour.

'Gran,' I yelled over his head, and tried to sidestep him with a feint left. But the kitchen was narrow and though he was wiry, lacking Pope's brawn, he caught me easily. 'Gran,' I screamed.

Shaw dragged me kicking into the parlour. I hated being touched by him even more than by Pope.

In the parlour, my uncle was thumbing through an

illustrated journal from twenty years before. I'd fetched it from Grandpa's collection, marked the pages and made my own notes upon them. In particular the readers' letters – I wanted to know what those long-ago people had thought of the Peterloo Massacre in Manchester, when mounted soldiers had cut through a crowd of protesters, demonstrating for voting reform. Gran had first alerted me to the tragedy, and Mr Ivison confirmed it.

'I see where I went wrong with you,' my uncle said, the yellowed paper quivering in his hands. 'Think yourself some sort of radical, some revolutionary? This isn't France, you know. You think you want to overthrow my authority, that I can be replaced with something better? All tyrants start out as rebels, full of noble intentions. But they all end up as tyrants. You've nothing I haven't seen a thousand times.' He brandished the journal, then flung it to the floor. 'But you'll learn your place at school. Get dressed.'

'I'm not dressing for the lunatic ward,' I said. His nostrils flared ever so slightly, and I knew Gran was right about Mungrispike. Yet I was unwisely pleased at him revealing his fears. I said, 'Take me as I am, I don't care.'

'Get dressed. I won't ask again.'

'And I won't–'

'Lizzie.' Gran appeared on the open stairway that led upwards from the parlour. 'Do as your uncle tells you. Upstairs and pack your things.'

'No need for her articles, Hephzibah,' – he'd never call her Aunt – 'they can follow.'

'As you like,' said Gran. 'Lizzie, go.'

Her mouth twitched at the corner where she had a small scar, from a slip with a hunting knife. I read the wrinkle.

I stepped towards her at the foot of the stairs. I breathed a hurricane in and out. My limbs grew so light I thought

I'd fly up through the roof, to cross the celestial heavens with a single breath held in my mouth. The fog in my mind cleared. The sun, in the cavern of my skull, blazed on the single thought remaining: Run.

I put my lightning foot on the first stair and brushed Gran's shoulder.

She whispered, 'Your knapsack's in the woodshed. There's a letter within.' Then she said, loudly, 'Hurry up then. Do as your good uncle says and get dressed for the trip.'

16

Pope and Shaw must have gone back for a dog. I could hear it barking in the distance, behind me on the crest of the hill.

I flew across the lower slopes of the moor taking boulders and hillocks in my stride. I startled pretty skylarks from their ground nests. A red deer, nosing among dwarf birches and juniper bushes, lifted its head to sniff the air. When he smelt my fright he ran too.

I knew where the peat bogs lay. The snowy white tufts of cotton-grass, with which we stuffed our pillows, marked most of the soft patches. But there'd been some hot wild storms of late that would make safe places treacherous. I'd never charted these, preferring to be out in the tempests themselves over the soggy aftermath. Gran would know.

I had a head start. How long did it take my uncle to realise I'd leapt out of the library window and fled? I almost chuckled. But his thugs had a dog, a bloodhound I'd guess. There'd be no hiding snug in hollows for me.

The going grew wetter the lower I tore. My boots shot water from the long grass, polka-dotting my stockings with rich liquid mud. My knees wobbled as I pounded uneven ground, and I lurched. But I felt as a horse, with slick whipping legs, so I never stumbled nor fell. The knapsack beat the running rhythm on my back. I'd no idea what it held – maybe some bread and hard cheese. And the letter.

There was no cover, save a few wind-sculpted rowan trees, and single huge rocks, tossed by giants brawling with each other, perhaps. Folk tales bubbled up through the earth around here, appearing soon as a curiosity needed explaining.

I'd taken the shorter route towards Avandale, directly across the moor, rather than wiggle with the river through the ravine. The river would have given me better cover. But I'd had no time to consider the woes and which-ways of each. Neither had I anticipated the bloodhound, thinking my uncle would bellow from the drystone wall until his dignity could no longer endure it, then give me up as a lost cause. But now I saw he meant to hunt me.

Oh, Gran would scold me how. I should've taken the watercourse and lost the doggie that way. Instead I'm in plain sight, no matter how I weave down the slopes.

How long before Pope and Shaw set the hound loose? How hungry that beast?

I tried not to think of my tiring legs. From the heaving of my breath, it felt I was running swift as Mercury, at the same pace as when I'd begun, haring across the gravel yard, and over the rotten gate, snapping the top rail in my haste. But I knew this for an illusion. I'd been running for nigh on two hours – it usually took four, maybe, five to walk to this point – though my mind saw it as a second and an eternity at once.

What did I do but run? What was my life? I couldn't remember. Running was all. I couldn't stop if I wanted to. Not till I dropped.

The wind shifted as I reached the span of a towering peak. I heard the hound again, closer, loose. No man could outrun me, though the thugs were pursuing still.

This marker of the shifting wind was where town seemed so near, then torturously grew no nearer. Your legs promised they'd carry you, so long as town truly was over the next mound. But the land rippled on beyond each summit, a monstrous serpent advancing beneath.

My legs grew heavy like stone, as if the mountains were reclaiming me, wanting me to stay, stay, in this place. The wind blew hard in my face. Dewdrops poured from my eyes, from the searing wind or fright, I didn't ponder.

Then it was upon me. The beast of the moor, the bog fiend, my uncle's hellhound.

I stooped as I ran, grabbed a rock bearded with lichen. The dog closed the last few yards between us. I hurled the rock with a giant's might. It missed, but the hound blenched and hung back; he knew from his cage that one blow meant many.

He darted to the side. I threw another rock. He dropped behind again, unsure; he needed a chum to bring me down. But he kept after me, his coat damp from the exertion, his mouth foaming.

Then I did fly.

The jagged peaks of the skyline fell as my head jerked up. The marshy slope dropped away from my feet – my boot had hooked a hidden rock I guessed. I thought I could cheat Newton's apple, this force of gravity which drew both apples and feet to the ground. I thought I could use the power of my speed and my terror to keep soaring upwards as I launched. To depart this earthy realm, to escape my uncle, his thugs, their dog.

But the ground reclaimed me.

I plummeted awkwardly onto my side, my left arm trapped beneath me, just short of a boulder. A moment more in the air and my skull would have smashed against this boulder, painting the stone with blood and brain and bone for the hound to lick clean. He leapt on me now I was down, my arm bent and in spasm.

I rolled onto my back, to use my legs and good arm to kick and swipe. I got a handful of coarse hair in his neck. Like this I could keep his snapping jaws from my face for a few seconds more.

I thrashed with my legs and got the tip of my boot up that doggie's arse. He yelped as I sent him to the clouds.

He landed and backed away, growling. He lowered his shoulders and haunches to pounce again. I threw another rock but he'd already left the spot and was above me. My left arm came back into life with a throb. I caught his front paws and flung him backwards over my head.

There came a dull splash, another yelp and a howl.

Flipping onto my belly, I saw that poor doggie scrabble, churning peat in the bog hidden by overhanging grasses. He turned the soft matter with his paws, over and over, but his back legs were gone. Soon he'd be swallowed by the earth, that bog fiend, to suffocate, rot, become peat himself.

I hauled myself off the wet ground. The strap of my knapsack had twisted during the run and the struggle; the tightened loop cut into my neck and underarm. I unwound it. But nothing could be done about my breeches and jacket: they were hanging half-torn. Like I'd been fighting a ravening beast. I coughed, near choked, as I laughed with relief. The dog in the bog gargled.

I can throw him a branch perhaps. He's only a dumb cur, it's not his fault he's vicious, not his fault he's been set upon me. It's just what he's been taught.

The dog whimpered as he sank. I saw a bleached branch at the foot of a rowan tree. I could hold it out for him to grip with his jaws. I could still save him, if I wanted.

'I'm sorry, it's your life or mine,' I said to the dog. 'And

I need mine more, it caused my mother to pass, it can't end with your teeth in my throat.'

I watched the dog, until the decision had been made for me. Then I ran on.

17

I ran until I reached a copse on the edge of the moor. Among the tall, broad-leaved trees of the valley, I was safe from Pope and Shaw. Enough to catch my breath.

The path through the copse took me to the top of a steep cobbled lane on the outskirts of Avandale.

I'd entered town this way before, with Gran. Then, in Gran's company, I'd thought nothing of how the winding lane could make you feel so unexpectedly alone, when you were unable to see more than a few yards ahead or behind at any one time. But I felt it now.

Small workshops, mostly of metal workers, lined the lower stretch of the lane. Over time, smoke from the forges had blackened the workshops' outer walls, making the narrow street a gloomy tunnel. Sooty sludge oozed from between the cobbles; the way ahead was slippery. And the lane was strangely quiet. It felt like a trap.

I whipped around, expecting to see Pope and Shaw hurtling towards me. But the lane was empty. No predator behind. No ambush ahead.

Down and down I trod. Flat-footed, so my heels wouldn't skid on the treacherous cobbles.

The workshops were all closed. It was too still, it seemed the lane had been deliberately cleared.

Where the lane widened into a level street, a stray dog was devouring slimy scraps. A ginger kitten watched from a distance, yowling for tidbits. The only human was a young, ill-kempt boy tapping cobbles with a stick. I hesitated.

The boy stepped side to side across the width of the street, moving slowly down the hill, playing piano on the stones. This odd behaviour made me anxious. His tapping seemed a kind of message.

I waited, flat against a sooty wall, wondering if I had the strength for another fight, with dog or boy, or my own shape-shifting fears.

Then I remembered it was festival time in Avandale, thus the closed workshops. Everyone would be in the town square.

I peeled myself off the wall in relief. No ambush awaited me, yet. But Pope and Shaw would be on their way. Missing one dog. I smiled to myself to think of the fight on the moor. Even without Gran here, my victory made me feel armoured all over.

Dashing down the lane, I swerved around the boy, then leapt over the stick he whipped sideways at just the wrong moment. I slid on the cobbles and careened into a wall. I put my hand out to steady myself, tried to slow my breath.

Then I bounded on towards the town square. I'd try to find help at the festival, from the Bobbin Guild, who'd be taking part in the contest.

Avandale's yearly festival celebrated the King Arthur legends – the town was said to have been an important site during his northern battles.

Out of breath again, I arrived at the market square. A sharp pain was stabbing inside my chest but I had to ignore it. I paused at the mouth of a side street to get my bearings.

Townspeople hurried about their festival activities around the perimeter of the once-grand square. Children, women and men in costumes – knights, mere-maids, warlocks and other citizens of Camelot – fetched and carried, hollering at each other to get out of the way. All this in tribute to a noble king, who was supposedly right now having his thousand-year nap inside the mountain. (Oh Arthur, you're no one's fool. To lie down, to snooze, to struggle no more.)

At the northern end of the square, in front of the clocktower, was the centrepiece of the festival: the stage for the contest. This contest re-enacted the tale of a giant defending a castle against King Arthur and his knights. Sir Tarquin Cesario was the giant, and legend told that he'd been left behind by the Roman rulers to defend the borders of their empire.

Every year each of the Guilds – the associations representing local industries – had a team of 'knights' taking part. Gran had promised one day I could enter the contest, but the day had never come. Winning wasn't about size or power, you had to be quick in your mind and nimble on your feet.

I hoped the Bobbin Guild wouldn't be too busy with the contest to help me.

Cautiously, I made my way across the square towards the clocktower. Weaving around food barrows and stalls where you could get your own heraldry made up, through huddles of gossiping women, dodging the wooden swords of children and men playing at Sir Tarquin and Sir Lancelot. All the while, scanning the crowd for faces I recognised.

My uncle knew many people here. Some of whom

wished to earn his favour. My tattered appearance might prompt someone to detain me. And it wouldn't be long before Pope and Shaw caught up.

Approaching the stage, I saw it was more elaborate than ever. A fake forest sprawled across the platform, with a clearing in the centre front, for the duel with Sir Tarquin. The 'trees' were short and stout, constructed from house-building beams, planks and other odd bits of wood. They were decorated with real branches, and looked half-house, half-tree.

Up on the stage, was the infamous oak of the Sir Tarquin tale. This year's oak was a twisty, knotty creation, made from coppice poles and looped together with vines. Tom and I used to make our own in the yard, then persuade Gran to play Sir Tarquin.

Something stabbed inside my chest again, and I remembered how I'd left things with Tom. I didn't think anyone would blame me for the lost bobbins. But would Tom blame me for his humiliating demotion? He'd warned me again and again not to antagonise my uncle, and I did anyway.

Below the stage was the cloth river, which was strewn with boulders, logs and the remnants of the fallen knights' armour. A group of girls dressed as mere-maids, the vicious creatures of Sir Tarquin's river who 'drowned' contenders who fell off the stage, were getting ready. They'd piled their fishtails beside a boulder and were squabbling about their positions.

A few years ago Gran and I had watched a slender youth unexpectedly win. He'd danced around Sir Tarquin, jabbing the big man's soft bits until the giant collapsed, drenched with sweat in the heat. The youth collected his prize money to rapturous applause.

When Gran told me how much he'd won, I said, 'Is it enough to buy the mill from Uncle Robin?'

'Not quite, duck,' said Gran. 'But it'd pay the week's wages and a bit more.'

18

The Guilds each had a festival tent, festooned with bright banners, ribbons and bunting. I quickly found the Bobbin Guild's tent in the main street beyond the clocktower. The tent was double the size of most others and made of pristine white sailcloth, with a flag on a pole as high as the second storey buildings.

The front flaps of the tent whipped and slapped as the Bobbin team rushed in and out, shouting orders or complaining about them.

I zigzagged through the bustle of contenders and teams, and tucked myself beside the flapping entrance, in the angle of the thick ropes that secured the tent to sand bags on the ground.

From within a man was barking, 'Yous two are the best we got, but yous don't look good enough. This year we've got to, got to, beat Shipbuilding. Ye've nowt to lose except your pride, dignity, family honour, my stake money, any hope of marrying well and mebby the use of your hands, if yous let that brute whack yous on the knuckles.'

'I won't be able to work if me hands're crushed,' said one of the contenders, sounding as if this were the first he'd heard of the possibility.

'Course ye won't. None of us could, that's why ye need

to look lively. The giant don't usually fight hard in the first round, unless he don't like the look o' ye…remember what happened last year…so just get yerselves safely through to the second round, and I'll work out the tactics from there. Got it?'

'But what about–?' said the first contender.

'Good. Outside for practice. Now.'

The canvas flaps fluttered in my face and the two contenders, in white tabards with a blue bobbin emblem, appeared from the tent.

'I'm not risking me hands,' said the first. 'He can fight himself if he's that bothered. Ye seen the size of the Sir Tarquin they got this year?'

'Uh-huh. Brought him over from Whitehaven I heard. But he's not from Cumberland. Came off a ship from someplace in the southern ocean, an island of giants with bronze skin, and tattoos on their faces.'

'Tattoos on his face? His *face*? Is it to bewitch ye, so ye don't see his staff before it's cracked your skull?'

'Don't wanna think about it. Look, I don't know about ye, but I don't give a stuff about beating Shipbuilding. I'm gonna dance around a bit, whirling the staff, make it look like I'm trying, then I'll…'

The contenders disappeared from earshot. In a pause in the to-ing and fro-ing, I slipped into the tent.

The air was ripe with the smell of leftover food and drink – boiled eggs, herring, spilled beer and something else. God, I was hungry. Clothes and other belongings had been dumped along one side, and on the other was a rack of staffs for the contest.

A woman was sitting in the far corner, hunched over the tabard she was sewing. She looked up at me with her smile of brass pins, gazing blankly. Then she turned back to her work, and placed another pin between her lips as she completed a row of stitches.

'What're ye doing in here?' the barking man blared from the corner I couldn't see.

I recoiled into the tent wall and sank into the sagging canvas.

'Well?'

I stood upright again. The man came towards me, in each hand a staff. He clunked the base of one staff on the ground, then the other, in a cross between him and me.

Flinching from the smell of his eggy breath, I stared up into the feathery thicket of his nostrils. I'd imagined a short stocky man to match the heckling voice, but this man was tall and angular like a heron. He wore the emblazoned white tabard over baggy woollen hose. His feet, in his knee-length leather boots, were so long I thought he could paddle there and back to the island of bronze giants and still be home for supper.

I recognised him instantly and my stomach lurched, not only because of his sulphurous breath. I'd seen this man at the mill, last autumn, striding around the yard with my uncle. His name was somebody somebody Johnson. At first, I'd assumed he was inspecting the working conditions, but he'd looked too chummy with my uncle for it to be a formal visit.

'What do ye want?' said Johnson.

'I'm from Fairy Cross Bobbin Mill,' I said.

'That li'l place!' He laughed and tossed one of the staffs into the other hand. 'Greenwood's not sent anyone for fourteen, fifteen, years, and now he sends me thou.'

'I'm not here to fight in the contest.'

'Didn't think ye were.' He glanced over my dishevelled appearance and said, 'Well, it's not clothes-mending or laundry that ye do. What's yer game then?'

'Robin Greenwood's my uncle, and I need your help.'

He thrust his head forward and down to peer at me along his beak. 'Ye asking for him or yerself?'

'For the mill. And the workers.'

'Go on.'

'The mill's in trouble, there was a fire, all the bobbins were lost–'

'Aye, heard about that. Any fool knows to separate his paraffin stores from the dry wood.' He propped the staffs against the side of the tent.

I took this as a sign he was willing to listen.

'But my uncle doesn't,' I said. 'Or rather he doesn't care about doing things properly, only the show of it. But you do, I mean, the Guild does, that's what you're for.' My voice sounded whiny, I don't know why it came out that way. I sounded like a little kiddie complaining about the unfairness of everything, but I couldn't seem to stop it. 'And it's not the fire, well, not only. There was an accident before that, and Mr Kirke lost his eye, and his hand's no good anymore. And now my uncle's laying off workers, says he can't keep everyone on. I've got to stop him before they have to leave their cottages, they've nowhere to go. Tom's been demoted, had his pay cut. And there's Billy, the apprentice who nearly died, he's been sent back to the workhouse–'

'Hold up there, I don't see yer meaning. What's the problem?'

'The workers losing their jobs, having their pay cut. Mr Kirke. Tom. Mr Taylor's been given notice already, and Billy–'

'Who's Billy?'

'The apprentice I just told you about. In the fire.'

'That's it? Doesn't sound like particular trouble to me, just the usual lot of a mill owner.'

Johnson walked towards the woman sewing tabards.

'Done yet?' he said.

'Mnyeh,' she said, through her pins.

'Well, hurry up.'

'But that is the trouble, the owner,' I continued, though he didn't seem to be listening anymore. 'My uncle. He's giving you and the Guild a bad name. The mill's not really his, it's mine. I want you to help me get rid of him, it's the only way.'

Johnson span around and took three rapid steps towards me. 'Now listen here, lassie, I know that red hair o' yers, I know who ye are. Yer father gave up his claim on the mill, so whatever rights ye think ye have, ye don't.'

'What do you know of my father?' I said. No adult spoke of my father in Fairy Cross, as if he'd never existed. But I was proof of his existence, though I wasn't sure who or what was proof of mine. If Johnson wouldn't recognise my claim upon the mill, by right of birth, who would?

Muddled, distracted, I said, 'Do you know my father, do you know where he is?'

'Fairy Cross Mill belongs to Robin Greenwood,' said Johnson. 'It was settled years ago, I'm not getting involved in another o' yer family's games. It was bad enough him bringing those Americans into it.'

'Which Americans? Who brought them?'

'Ye still here?'

'I am until you help me.'

'Ye'll get nay featherbedding from us.'

'But you have to help,' I said, panicking I hadn't much time, that the Guild's tent would be the first place Pope and Shaw would look for me. 'I can't overthrow my uncle without you.'

'Do not,' – Johnson pressed his finger into my forehead and his nail notched my skin – 'speak of overthrowing uncles here.'

I slapped his hand away.

'Or anywhere,' he said. 'The Guild is for bobbin mill owners and master craftsmen. Journeymen and apprentices are on their own. As, me lassie, are thee.'

19

I pushed my way through groups of women, men and children wishing contenders good luck outside the tents. Everyone here was part of a team.

My legs became heavier and heavier until I ground to a halt. It was as if despair had a material form, like granite. I wished my heart would become granite too, so I wouldn't have to feel the hot sickening things rushing around my body, using my blood as a carrier to reach my fingers, my toes and all the weakening parts of me.

The lively well-wishers buffeted me, and I let them.

I found myself in front of the Cotton Guild's tent. It was so tiny the team had to stand outside. Almost all cotton spinning and weaving now happened in Manchester and the other big textile towns in Lancashire; the small local mills were disappearing one by one.

There seemed to be only one contender for the Cotton team. He was a little older than me and very nervous.

A man with a bruised nose, the colour of an over-ripe plum, was squeezing the contender's arms and saying in a strong lakeland accent, 'Nar then, young fella me lad. Yer give it yer best, won't ye? Don't let Sire Tark, thingummy whatsit, wha'rever he calls hisself, pin ye up against them yows and yaks,' – the yews and oaks of the fake forest – 'or ye'll be on them knobbly knees afore ye've a chance to holler yer best battle cry.'

Noticing me watching, he said, 'What's this then, young miss? Are ye Cotton? A late entry for the contest?'

'Me? Cotton, um…err–'

If I told him I was Cotton maybe he'd help. But if I told him what I needed his help for, he'd know I lied. And anyway, what could the Cotton Guild do, being so small? To challenge my uncle I needed people as strong as he.

I said, 'No, I'm not Cotton. I'm…no one.'

'Shame. We coulda done with anorrer laddie to give this 'un some gumption. Under a helmet no one would know yer for a lassie. But ye gotta belong to a Guild, han't yer? Or the whole bleeding lot o' us'll be disqualifi…ah, disqualificated afore we start.'

He turned back to his contender. I blundered on.

Eventually, I was ejected from the stream of people. I found myself in a dead end street. Rubbish had blown in, and half-eaten packets of festival food tossed.

I sat upon a broken barrel and set my knapsack on my restless knees. Time to read the letter Gran had put in my bag. Time for the last resort.

The letter was dated four years ago.

I read: 'Dearest Hephzibah, I am glad to see you honour our agreement at last…'

Then I flipped to the end to discover its author. Miss Vita Moncrieff Beaulieu. I knew this name, she was my mother's sister. But she'd never written to me.

There followed the usual insincere pleasantries – 'How do you fare, after all these years', 'We dearly hope time has treated you well', etcetera.

Then: 'We will endeavour to do what we can with the child, but you must know you have left it a trifle late.'

Too late for what? *Child*? She can't mean me.

Aunt Vita proceeded: 'In my experience, once a child passes a certain age in unsuitable company and a narrow locale, there is little to be done to salvage good character, assuming there was ever a semblance of such.'

Urff. Pummelling fists to the gut. *Dearest* Aunt Vita, Where's the whole-hearted welcome to the family bosom? We haven't even met and you've already damned my moral character. Even aged eleven, was I still too untidy for you?

The letter went on to describe in precise and unnecessary detail Aunt Vita's reasons for knowing me to be the very worst personage in the modern world. My Greenwood nature and upbringing at Gran's hands were to blame.

And that was that. No words of welcome. No apology, no invitation to Bath. No explanation of the agreement Gran was prepared to honour, but Aunt Vita, evidently, was not. Only the address of a Dr Emerson Beaulieu at his business premises in Manchester, to which further correspondence should be addressed.

Had Gran written? If she'd received a reply, it would surely be in my knapsack. I rummaged but found no other clue.

I knew of Emerson Beaulieu too. I wished I didn't. The first time he'd met Gran was on the doorstep of River View. She was wearing her widow's weeds – Grandpa being newly dead. Nonetheless, Dr Emerson Beaulieu had harangued her for allowing her errant son to corrupt his niece. The second time – diverted from River View up the lane, to find Gran in exile at the cottage – he delivered baby-me and left without further word. He was the worst, the very, very worst.

I was so angry I couldn't remember anything about how things were when I was eleven, which might have occasioned this correspondence.

Manchester. And Dr Emerson Beaulieu lurking in it. Manchester was a huge industrial city eighty miles away, another world.

How did Gran think I'd get there? And why would I go? I'd rather stay and fight than surrender my lost self to yet another heartless uncle. I'd never wanted to run away in the first place.

I pondered for a moment. What if the plum-nosed Cotton Guild man was right? Could I hide my identity under a wooden helmet and fight for the Sir Tarquin prize money myself?

If it's enough for a week's wages at the mill, then it's enough to pay the workers myself. Then they could afford to strike against my uncle.

Is a week long enough to loosen Robin's hold on the mill? It's a start. Anything can happen in week.

'You seen who they got as Sir Tarquin this year?' I said to a youth making his duelling preparations in the square. 'They brought him over specially from a land of giants. He's said to have fists of solid bronze.'

It hadn't taken long to find the most frightened-looking contender; he was one of the few who hadn't yet entered the contenders' pen. He was practicing his moves in a far corner of the square, dividing the air into invisible cubes with his spindly staff.

He was seventeen or eighteen, but jumpy as a young deer. He hadn't an ounce of spare fat on his upper limbs or torso, nothing to absorb the blows from Sir Tarquin's staff. Hmm. Like me, I admitted. His long brown hair was tied in a green satin ribbon, which he kept twirling around his forefinger in a nervous tic. Even his fluffy moustache was quivering, each fine hair fluttering in his nose-breeze.

Just then a trumpet blared, announcing the beginning of the first round. The youth jumped. I knew I was about to do a mean thing to this lad who'd never done anything bad to me, but I didn't have time to be kind.

'My, he's really something, that Sir Tark,' I said, coming to stand too close to the youth so he couldn't ignore me. 'He's got the might of Arthur's mountain and all the knights inside. What's your name then, buck?'

He looked at me, bewildered. 'Um, Lewis.' He stopped scoring the air, but kept his staff aloft, as if it'd snagged in a gap between this world and another. His green and black tabard was flopped over a crate beside him, his wooden helmet beside it.

'So, Lewis, d'you think you'll get your helmet bashed in like a flowerpot, or your knees knocked backwards?' I said. 'One of the two always happens to a first-timer.'

'Flowerpot?' he said. 'I'm not Agriculture, I'm from the Gunpowder team.'

'Ah, yes, of course.' I peered at his tabard, thinking it wouldn't be too big on me. 'There'll be sky-high hopes for you then. Are you going on with a big bang, or out with one?'

'I don't have fireworks...what do you mean...? I've only this staff, I thought that's all you're allowed...should I get..?' His pale face turned ashen. 'Oh, nay...helmet bashed in like a flowerpot, I see...I'm going to be...'

I felt sorry for Lewis then. But I needed his place, and the chance to win the prize money, desperately. I hated to see myself goading him, finding his fears then doubling them; it's what my uncle did to me.

'You'll be alright,' I said, in a gentle tone, as though talking to Billy, 'if you're nimble. You've only your pride, dignity, family honour, and so forth and so on, to lose.' I attempted a reassuring laugh. Lewis didn't look reassured. 'Don't mind me, I'm from– ah, Shipbuilding. Just trying to scare the contenders who'll be a threat to us in the final round.'

'I'm not a threat,' he squealed. 'I shouldn't even be here. Me brother took sick yesterday, his boss made me take his place. I don't even work at the 'powder factory.'

'Then you're in luck. If you're not in the Guild you can't fight anyway. Tis the rules.'

'Not really?'

'Go check with the marshal,' I said. 'Then pretend to your team the marshal asked about your Guild. Couldn't lie – could you? – and now, regrettably, you've been disqualified. Not your fault.'

'Shall I do that? Ask the marshal?'

'I'll look after your things here. You won't need them anyhow.'

Lewis nodded, and leant his staff against the crate. 'Canna break the rules, you're reet.' His eyes took on a faraway look. 'Absolutely canna break the rules.' He hurried off, his loosely jointed legs carrying him unsteadily towards the stage.

Lewis didn't look back, but I waited a few moments anyway, to quell my doubts about whether I'd really done him a favour, as I wanted to believe, or just set him up for a lifetime of ridicule by his brother. It didn't work, but I put on his tabard anyway, tied up my hair with a length of twine from my pocket and tucked the full copper nest under the helmet.

The helmet was a sort of barrel with three small round holes: two for eyes and one for your mouth, so from the outside you looked to be permanently saying ooooh. Inside it was musty, woody, like the hollow heart of a rotted tree. It was also stifling. I was as likely to be asphyxiated by my own panicked breath as knocked out by Sir Tarquin. I looked and felt absurd, but at least no one would know me from the next barrel of beer.

I made my way through the crowd, bumping into people because the helmet's eyeholes were too far apart and I couldn't see directly ahead.

As long as Sir Tarquin is kind enough to swing his staff from the left or right, I'll be fine. But if he strikes dead centre I won't see the blow before my helmet shatters and with it my skull.

Stumbling over someone's foot, I trod on another. A man shouted, 'Oi,' and shoved me. I bounced off a man's belly; it was surprisingly firm. As I span and fell, an image flashed across the eyeholes of my helmet. I couldn't be sure, my vision was so impaired, but the man into whom I'd tumbled had the same build as Pope.

I gulped the hot stale air inside my helmet and turned to face the ground. I drew my knees under me and got to my feet, all the while staring down so I didn't have to confirm my fear.

I staggered on through the crowd to take my place in the contest.

20

'Remember, remember,' called the announcer on the stage, sweeping his arm towards the contenders' pen, 'the fifth of November. *Gunpowder*, treason and plot!'

The crowd cheered.

The announcer circled his arm again, then waved impatiently at the marshal guarding the pen. He said, 'Well, it seems someone has forgotten to remember.'

The crowd laughed.

I pushed my way through the front rows of people, with no time to go via the contenders' pen, as you were supposed to.

'Here,' I shouted above the hubbub, thrusting my spindly staff into the air.

The marshal in front of the stage intercepted me. I dodged him, reached the foot of the stage and swung my leg to the platform to climb up.

He grabbed the back of my tabard and hauled me down. 'Nay, ye don't,' he said.

'But I'm Gunpowder,' I said. 'It's my turn.'

'Ye could be anyone, lurching through the crowd like that. Ye have to be admitted to the pen first.'

'I know that. But I'm Gunpowder, see.' I tugged at the green emblem on the front of my black tabard.

The announcer stepped to the front of the stage. 'Are ye fighting or not, lad?'

'Yes, but he won't let me,' I said.

'Didn't come through the contenders' pen,' said the marshal. 'Canna let him on stage.'

The announcer bent down. 'Come on, McCourt, it's only a show.'

'To ye,' said the marshal, McCourt. 'But we got our rules, Kennedy.'

The crowd began to boo.

Kennedy, the announcer, stood up and shouted, 'Gunpowder, treason and...there's a plot right here, me good people. Young Gunpowder's not allowed to face Sir Tarquin. Seems he's broken a minor rule. So, I'm afraid that means the first round has finished. Ye'll have to wait until this evening to see more of the plucky contenders challenging the giant.'

The crowd booed and jeered. Someone said, 'Let him have his go.' Several others said, 'Go on. Go *on*.'

McCourt gripped my arm and began to drag me away from the stage.

'What a shame,' said Kennedy, to the crowd. 'And this lad was supposed to be good 'un. I'm sorry, folks, seems we saved the best for last but now yous won't see it. McCourt,' he called loudly so everyone could hear, 'there's nothing to be done? Ye're denying these good people their show?

McCourt halted. He shuffled on the spot.

Up on the stage, Kennedy said, 'Ah, what a shame, ladies and gentlemen, a terrible shame.'

'I am sorry about not going through the contenders' pen,' I said. I wasn't, but I'd have done anything to get up on that stage. 'But someone tried to rob me of my tabard and staff.'

'Did they now?' said McCourt, pursing his lips. 'What did he look like, this fella who tried to rob ye?'

'I didn't see, I had my helmet on. Look, it doesn't fit properly–'

'It's not been made for ye, that's why it don't fit.'

'No. I mean, yes. But our chief got the measurements wrong.'

'Ye think I believe a gunpowder-maker don't know his measurements. He wouldn't live long enough to make helmets, ill-fitting or otherwise.'

'McCourt,' Kennedy pleaded. 'I'm dying up here. Help me out.'

'Alreet, Kennedy, this once. I mean it,' said McCourt. To me, he said: 'Just get up there and make it a good one. Or I'm coming to find ye after.'

I scrambled onto the stage to a deafening applause.

In the suffocating helmet I breathed heavily. The blindspot in the centre of my vision confused me and I turned slowly on the spot trying to see where Sir Tarquin was.

I saw Kennedy as I rotated, then the crowd...then Kennedy again...the crowd again and again. But no giant. I felt a rush of air behind me and I jumped round...but nothing.

'Here he is,' Kennedy cried, in a different direction to where I thought he was. 'Young Gunpowder, young Guy Fawkes, come to blow up this contest!'

'Ye can't say that, 'blow up',' said McCourt from somewhere below me. 'Sounds like we support treason.'

'It's just a figure of speech,' Kennedy said.

'Well, ye can't say it. Stick to plain speaking and leave yer figuring out of it.'

'Working the crowd into a lather is what I'm here for,' said Kennedy, 'and colourful language is part of that.'

'If ye up and do cursing for all the town to hear, there'll be trouble–' McCourt said.

'Can we get on with it?' I interrupted. 'I'm ready to fight but I don't know where your giant is.

McCourt chortled.

'He's no ordinary giant,' said Kennedy, addressing the crowd again. 'Young Gunpowder doesn't know...but we do.'

The crowd screamed and clapped. A bell rang.

Hotter and hotter it grew inside the wooden helmet. My anxious panting had produced a sort of fog, so now my field of vision was blurry as well as incomplete.

I saw the crowd as a coloured smudge. The cacophony of their cheers, chants and boos appeared to come from all directions. For one lunatic moment I thought the din was actually coming from inside my head, that the wooden barrel was the entirety of my world, and all sights, sounds and smells emanated from me only, that the world outside was my creation. Then I felt a blow on the fleshy part of my calf and knew that if I were a god I wouldn't have hit myself so painfully.

My perception of the world flipped, from inside to out, and suddenly I saw how small I was, how alone, up here on the stage, fighting a fight I couldn't win so I could return to Fairy Cross to fight and lose another.

I reached to take off my helmet, so at least I could prance around, safely twirling the staff as the reluctant Bobbin contender had intended to do, making it look like I was trying. Then I realised I couldn't. If that had been Pope in the crowd, he'd know me at once on the stage. I let go of the helmet and took the staff in both hands. I'd have to dance half-blind after all.

I planted my feet wide and firm, and listened. I heard nothing but the distorted sound of the crowd. I tried again, closing my eyes, but I couldn't pick out any specific noise that would alert me to the giant's position. I opened my eyes, blinking through tears of frustration, ready to call Kennedy and tell him I had to concede. Then beneath my feet I felt the wooden stage vibrate.

A tiny tingle of hope started in my belly. I might not be able to see or hear perfectly, but if I could also feel the giant's moves there was a possibility I could avoid my head being swiped off, like a flowerhead from its stalk.

The vibrations grew stronger and my feet absorbed them, until the silent booming seemed to shoot up through my legs. I jumped to my right and felt the strange rush of air again.

The crowd said, 'Owwooooh,' in delight, and fell quiet for a moment.

Kennedy yelled, 'Didn't I say I had a treat for yous, folks? Young Gunpowder, he's got eyes in the back of his head!'

The crowd cheered, but I let the noise dissipate from my mind. The vibrations through the floor were becoming urgent again. I turned towards the probable origin and a dark shape filled my view.

I ducked without thinking, then rolled to my left. From the crowd, I heard the sound of air being sucked through a thousand sets of teeth.

As I'd rolled I felt a solid rough thing graze my arm. I was quick, but the giant wasn't far behind. There was no room for error, and no time to ponder further. Or change my tactics, because I had none to speak of, only instinct and agility and three thousand days of running, jumping and climbing, and re-enacting the battles from Grandpa's romance novels.

The vibrations again. I leapt, then crouched with my head tucked to my knees.

A blow glanced off my back, catching my tabard, dragging it downwards so it pulled tight against my throat. I gagged, then quickly released the pressure.

The crowd roared and howled. In my heightened state, I imagined the people weren't people at all but a huge pack of predators, waiting for their leader to lame me before they all pounced. I knew I'd been lucky so far, but also that luck never holds. The giant's tactic to rush then bludgeon me was crude, but he had the power of clear sight and colossal strength.

In a crouch, with spring in my haunches, ready as a panther, I moved to face the way I thought he'd gone. Then quickly I pivoted a few degrees as I felt the wooden stage boom.

I hunched with my arms before me, as if I were about to lift a large barrel. As the disturbed air swirled on my hands and bare forearms, I threw myself forwards and brought my arms together in the tightest hug I could manage.

I caught something, something dense and wide, bristly with the dark hair that curled through the eyeholes of my helmet and tickled my eyelids.

I clung onto my catch, this hairy Leviathan. Jumped away and to the side and pulled the caught thing with everything I had. It didn't move. I skidded on the stage now slippery with sweat.

Something clonked my helmet. My head flew sideways, my neck wrenched. I pulled again and tilted onto my heels to try to dig myself in. I pulled until my stretching arms seemed to flatten like hot metal under a smith's hammer; they seemed certain to unhinge from my shoulder sockets, and still I pulled.

Then the Leviathan, this strange land whale, yielded an

inch to my effort. My force was so intense, so all-absorbing, I could neither stop pulling nor pull harder. If something didn't change soon only a lightning bolt from Thor himself could separate me from the giant. I became my own force, the strength of my effort, my arms looped eternal, no beginning, no end. The Leviathan shifted an inch more, and then the lightning struck…I flew backwards, my catch gone.

There was a boom so violent the stage bounced me. The giant had fallen. I thudded onto my back.

Then I heard nothing, or rather everything. The crowd was so loud it became a hum, the sort of hum that really could be inside your head, that you could only hear when all else is silent. I felt elated yet terrified, and confused as to whether the drone of the crowd was actually a sound I was making. I tore off my helmet to see.

A huge man lay sprawled face-down on the stage. He was dressed as a Roman centurion, in crimson cloth and brown leather, with a metal breastplate. I didn't know if he had strange tattoos on his face, his golden cockaded helmet was still on, but the backs of his bronze legs were marked with black lines and mythical symbols. His right foot twitched and he groaned. I couldn't tell if this were part of Kennedy's show, or if I really had hurt him.

The small figure of Kennedy appeared. He jumped onto the giant's heaving back and beckoned to me. Before I could think better of it, I'd leapt up too.

Kennedy held my arm aloft and cried to the crowd, 'Just wait till the second round when Sir Tarquin seeks his revenge!'

I tried to smile and enjoy my victory. The giant beneath me growled. He filled his enormous lungs and sighed the sigh of the ages. His back, the ground beneath my feet, rose and fell.

Kennedy teetered and clutched my arm to steady himself. He chuckled and said, 'He'll remember ye for this humiliation. Don't think it'll be so easy in the second round.'

21

Waiting and worrying in the contenders' pen, I watched the interlude before the finals of the Sir Tarquin contest. It was a skit about the Loathly Lady of the King Arthur tales – a beauty cursed to appear as a hag until the hero saw her true nature.

Gran had told me this tale many times, even when I was far too old for it – she played beauty, hag and hero. Gran was always the hero of her own tales.

But what was happening to her right now? Had Robin punished her for setting up my escape?

I didn't know if I could undo all the years Gran had been punished on Grandpa's account, then my father's, and now mine.

Another contender leant on the wooden railing beside me. He sighed loudly several times and waited for me to look at him. When I didn't, he said, 'Oh dear, yer first time, is it?'

I could see his belly protruding through the wooden railings. It jiggled as he adjusted position. I ignored him, and his belly. But neither went away.

'Don't worry,' he said. 'If you don't hit the giant, he won't hit you back. And just surrender when ye get tired of dancing around.'

'Surrender?' I said. 'What's the point of challenging if you give up without a fight?'

The man thrust his shoulders back and his belly bounced upwards against the railing. 'I beat the Sir Tarquin of sixteen years ago.'

'Sixteen years? I wasn't even born,' I said, irritated by his pomposity.

The man looked as if he were about to burst or maybe fart. 'Ye impertinent li'l– Ye'll get your comeuppance.'

'Had it already,' I said. 'Any other advice?'

'Blth, blth, blth,' the man said in outrage, but at least I was spared the advice. He flounced off. I heard him bad-mouthing me to other contenders.

Afternoon yawned but never seemed to become twilight. It was midsummer, the longest day of the year.

For me, it felt like the longest day of my life. Except when I'd found out the mill should have been mine. My cousin Joseph had taunted me after I'd beaten him in a game. I didn't believe him, until Gran confirmed it. I was almost seven. Not old enough to understand how uncles, aunts and cousins could view the same events so differently to Gran and me. But plenty old enough to be angry that something of mine, in addition to my father and mother, had been taken away.

Before then, Tom and I mostly played games in the woods: building dens in the root caves or tangly nests around forked branches; digging holes for giants' treasure; and searching for roe fawns, left in the safety of the undergrowth while their mothers went foraging. But after that longest day, I drew us to games near the mill.

We tapped the birch trees, as the people of Finland were said to do, to release the sap for drinking. My uncle accused me of destroying his coppice crop. We dammed the inlet to the narrow millrace, and thereby stopped the

111

waterwheel. My uncle lashed me with dry birch branches – the same used for making the besom brooms that swept the workshop floor. Not to cut me, but to humiliate me in front of the mill workers.

Later, I had plans to spirit away the wood shavings, which were burnt in the furnace that dried the finished bobbins. But before I could steal enough grain sacks for the job, my uncle made Tom a junior apprentice, earlier than expected.

It was the first time I noticed how Robin used other people to hurt me. I had to devise other games then, alone. That was how I'd found the old highwayman.

After the Comeuppance Man had gone, I went back to watching the skit.

The crowd was guffawing at the Loathly Lady trying to throw a shawl over her hunched back – she kept missing because she couldn't toss the shawl high enough over the hump. The hilarity of this passed me by. The script and the stage moves were so predictable. Maybe that was the point. People were laughing because they knew what was coming next. I didn't understand the appeal.

Funny things should be a surprise. But scary things…well, I was doing my best to eliminate the un-expected.

After my fight with Sir Tarquin, I'd begun to feel giddy, half-delirious. I felt oddly outside myself. I was both in my body and next to it, watching my movements from a close remove. It was as though I'd acquired a god's omniscience, an all-seeing ability.

I began to observe the other contenders, who were practising in the pen. My eyes fell upon the Bobbin contender, the one who'd said he whirl his staff around a bit to make it look like he was trying. He was sparring with a man in the burgundy tabard of the Quarrying team.

In a game with myself, I tried to predict the Bobbin contender's moves, then those of the Quarrying man. I was right more times than not. It both thrilled and scared me. The giddy feeling took over. I convinced myself I could see the future, actually see it, like scenes in a play; the vivid pictures playing out in my mind's eye, my personal view-o-rama.

Carried away with the thrill, I saw myself win the contest and the prize money. I saw myself return triumphantly to Fairy Cross, and my uncle quaver before me. I saw him relinquish the mill.

I knew I'd only beat Sir Tarquin if I did something completely unpredictable. But what moves would be unpredictable to the bronzed giant, who'd fought fifty men and me, and must have encountered every possible combination? I had to discover them.

In parallel to all this, and frequently interrupting my visions of glory, I saw another set of scenes, just as vivid: all the ways in which I'd be crushed into pieces of eggshell by Sir Tarquin. These scenes flashed into my mind more and more as the afternoon wore on.

As the sun dipped behind the tall buildings of the square, I began to feel sick.

I pushed my helmet down over my face, and staggered to the corner of the pen closest to the audience. Leaning on the fence for support, I lifted my helmet now and then to get some respite from the hot fog of my fear.

'There you are, giant-slayer,' said a man, propping his elbows on the fence. 'Congratulations. I've never seen anyone bring Sir Tarquin down in the first round, and especially not so ingeniously. I could use a warrior like you.'

He meant to flatter me into giving him attention, I could see he was used to it. He was exceptionally handsome – his features so sculpted and skin so flawless, he was almost bland-looking. It was very unusual for a man to have no scar or blemish on his face.

He took off his hat, an old-fashioned tricorne, like the heroes and rogues of Grandpa's romance novels. He ran his fingers through his long raven hair. He looked at me intently from under his eyebrows, one of which he now arched. There was an unspoken question here, but I wasn't falling for it. The creases in his forehead twitched with the effort of holding his eyebrow aloft.

'Thanks, and all that,' I said, 'but I've got to concentrate.'

'Course you have, course you have,' said the man, ruffling his hair again.

He tilted his head back to replace his hat. When his elbow lifted, his jacket did too and I caught sight of a gleaming pistol at his hip.

He said, 'But what if you don't need to fight... You're wanting the prize money, I assume? What if there's another way to get it? Not that particular pot of gold, but another, greater in worth. You'd have to do something for me, mind.'

'I don't doubt it,' I muttered. His price. My labour and sacrifice. Robin was the same. To deter him, I said, 'I'm here for the fight not the money.'

'Ah, that's what I like to hear,' the man said, though he didn't look pleased. 'A fellow crusader, champion of the small people, destroyer of the rich and powerful. Then you're even more perfectly suited to the mission. Want to hear what it is?'

'No.'

'You don't want to know which noble cause you can help with?'

I assumed that from his appearance, pistol and self-

114

assured manner the noble cause would involve him getting rich, and someone else (probably me) getting hurt. 'Not at all,' I said.

'It's related to your duel with Sir Tarquin,' he said, determined that I should learn his purpose whether I liked it or not. 'Or rather, an extension of. That is, another David and Goliath battle,' he persisted. 'You, me and some other noble warriors as David, and–'

'I got it. But I still don't want to know. I've got a Goliath already, and my own reasons for it. I'm not fighting your fight too.'

'Ha, ha, ha,' he chortled, insincerely. He replaced his tricorne hat, wearing it with one point angled above his left eyebrow, as a soldier carrying a musket on his shoulder would. 'Very well, very well. I am dismissed. Well, good luck you won't need, but if you want a tip, that giant's got a number of set moves. They're dangerous, and'll draw you into playing his game, but they're predictable. If you can disrupt his routines, like you did before, he'll be all at sea. Then you'll have him.'

He slapped the fencepost and drew away, leaving his fingers to slowly rake the top of the post.

I was strangely perturbed by this man seeming to confirm my own thoughts. Is he waiting for me to call him back? Does he think me predictable too, which is why he thinks he can entice me into his shady endeavour?

I said nothing and let the man leave. He headed into the crowd without looking back. By the doff of his hat, I saw how he weaved away. Eventually, he disappeared.

The clocktower bell chimed. One hour remained until the final round of the contest.

22

Kennedy called the first contender, from the Iron Guild, to the stage. The Iron man swaggered through our ranks. The other contenders cheered and whooped. I watched intently from the fence, to learn what I could for my turn.

The contender climbed the steps to the stage. He took the first one boldly, then his strides became shorter and shorter until his foot missed the final step and he began to topple.

For a moment it looked as if he'd regained his balance, lunging forward with his front leg, but he wasn't quick enough and his knee struck the wooden boards first. He yelped and crumpled.

I realised I'd been holding my breath, and blew out loudly.

The Iron contender got to his feet saying, 'I'm alreet, I'm alreet,' then yelped again. Sir Tarquin was pounding across the stage towards him.

The fight commenced.

A minute later a squeaky voice said, 'Ye want that staff studding with nails?'

It was a skinny, sallow-faced boy of about ten or eleven. He was dressed as a ragamuffin. Presumably he'd been in the festival parade, which always included a horde of children dressed as peasants, to celebrate King Arthur's conquest of the feudal lords.

The boy was holding onto the top rail of the fence. The backs of his hands were covered in cuts and scrapes, smudgy grooves blackened with grime. It reminded me of the soot between the cobbles in the smiths' lane.

He sang nonsense syllables, 'Buh, buh, brah, buh, bumh,' and twisted side-to-side on his bare heels, like he had nothing better to do than jeopardise my moment of glory, and everything that depended upon it.

'Beggar off, beggar boy,' I said, annoyed by yet another distraction. 'That's cheating.'

At that moment, Sir Tarquin caught the Iron contender with an upwards swipe. The man flew into the fake boulders, smashing them into sticks and scraps of paper, returning them to their raw state. I juddered at the thought of bones and skin being thus fragmented, my own most particularly.

The crowd went, 'Ahh-ha-haaa!'

The contender's helmet rolled off the stage and a group of people grappled for it as a memento. A woman cried, 'Let the mere-maids have him!'

'Ye wanna win, don't ye?' said the ragamuffin.

I tried to ignore him, but couldn't stop myself glancing sideways; his twisting movements kept catching my eye.

'What's that on yer tabard?' he said.

I noticed now he wasn't in fact in comic dress for a re-enactment of the people's liberation. He was a street urchin. We didn't have them in Fairy Cross, they were just plain peasants, or chased out of the hamlet by Pope, because my uncle didn't want them begging near the mill and making the place look poor.

'This is the cannon you'll be shot out of,' I said, of the Gunpowder emblem, 'if you don't get vanished pronto.'

'Suit yerself.' The boy stopped swaying. 'They call me Frankie Flash.'

I laughed, half-cough, half-splutter. It was cruel, I know. He was a sorry-looking thing, but the very thought of it…probably he'd come up with the name himself.

Frankie Flash, if that's what he wanted to be called, began to twitch from his arms to his toes.

'Who does?' I said, absently, feeling a little more kindly disposed towards him, but still more concerned with the action on stage.

'Them that want ye–'

He snatched my staff and walloped the back of my helmet. I slumped forwards over the fence. By the time I was upright again, he'd disappeared with my weapon.

Once you were in the contenders' pen you could neither leave without forfeiting your place nor have anyone pass you additional kit.

Well, that's just prima perfect, I thought. I've voluntarily got my head in a wooden flowerpot, atop my slender five-foot frame, with the county's strongest man to fight and not even a splinter to stick him with. If that urchin, flash Frankie, doesn't come back with my–

Ah-ha.

I spied him at the far end of the pen. He was using my staff as a pole to jump and spin around. The audience nearby clapped and laughed at his circus tricks. I thought him a nuisance, nothing more, so I tucked my helmet beside the fencepost and dashed after him, shouting, 'Oi, Flash-in-a-pan, that's mine.'

He was mid jump when I reached him. I flung out my arm to grab the staff, but he swung away from me and I missed. When he landed, he threaded the staff nimbly through his hands and I missed again. He scrambled through the fence into the crowd. I plunged after him with no thought other than how I must reclaim that staff. My stratagem depended upon it.

I jumped up and down on the spot to see above the bobbing heads of the crowd. The urchin was too small to make out, but on my third jump I saw people's heads moving vigorously along a snaking line. The heads parted from one another, then closed again, and in this direction there also seemed to be more noise. I hurled myself through the crowd, and caught a glimpse of Frankie as he scampered away.

Frankie led me across the packed square and into a side street, beyond where the market stalls reached. Here it was unexpectedly empty and quiet.

He stopped and bent double, panting. I swooped for the staff, but he span around with his back to me and I caught only air. He side-skipped out of my reach. He whistled. Then another three urchins and a little 'un, clutching sticks and tool-handles, appeared from an alley.

They were so scrawny you could drown them all, like unwanted kittens, in a single sack. Their shirts and breeches were either too big or too small, and torn, like mine, but more frayed because the rips were older. Only one of them wore shoes. I could see his hooked, black toenails poking out between the uppers and sole. Another had a nasty oozing abscess on his neck. And the little one was the dusty boy who'd been tapping cobbles in Smiths Lane.

'How'd ye like *our* staffs?' said the biggest urchin. He waved the stout stick he held, and the others joggled theirs too.

'What, those toothpicks?' I said, a feeling of dread prickling my skin. Something wasn't right. 'You couldn't knock down a chicken.'

'We'll see.' The biggest one grinned. 'Looks like ye're our chicken.'

'Five of you,' I said. 'Or rather, four, and that miniature one – is he a pixie? – and one of me? You're making it too easy.'

It was so still in this street you wouldn't know there was a festival on at all. I glanced around, expecting ambush by Pope and Shaw, but there was nothing except paper bills promoting the Sir Tarquin contest drifting in the breeze, snagging on doorsteps and pasting themselves around sticky barrels.

If these urchins are in my uncle's pay, I ought to run, and to hell with the contest. But if they're just messing with me, knowing me for an out-of-towner, and have nothing to do with my uncle, then I'm sure I can get my staff back and return to the contenders' pen before anyone misses me.

The little 'un began hopping on the spot, barely able to contain himself. His hands fluttered, as if getting ready for slapping.

Then I remembered the handsome rogue who'd approached me earlier, calling me giant-slayer. And Frankie Flash saying, 'Them that want ye'.

I said, 'Who's it that wants me then? And what for?'

23

'Ye'll find out in a minute,' said Frankie Flash.

'I don't have a minute, the contest won't wait for me,' I said, to see if that minute would buy me another in which to think.

The urchins circled me in their raggedy way. They had their staffs and tool-handles but it wasn't as if they were Norman spearmen, drilled in battle manoeuvres. I could break through their ranks easily.

And I can run... My legs are leaden from yesterday's hunt, but they're moor-trained and my lungs made for mountain ascent. I can outrun five malnourished children any day, so long as I know the terrain.

I stepped slowly towards the two boys blocking my way to the square, to test their reactions. I still hoped to talk my way out of the predicament and keep my place in the contest.

'If your master wants me,' – I meant the handsome stranger – 'he knows where to find me, I don't know why he's got you believing yourselves bounty hunters.'

They closed in on me.

I held out my arms to keep them at bay, and turned slowly on the spot.

I said, 'Did he tell you I toppled that seven-foot giant,

on my own and half-blind in the helmet? What d'you think you can actually do to me?'

A dog barked somewhere in the alley. It gave me a start. In my personal view-o-rama, I was back on the moor, running for my life.

I realised I'd got it all wrong. That handsome stranger was a nobody, just a chancer. He might have been looking for someone to commit a crime on his behalf, or toying with me for his own amusement, but this was my uncle's trap, it had to be. Who else would want me captured so discreetly, hidden from people who believed him a reputable mill owner?

The little dusty boy bent to claw at his scabby knee. I lunged, shoved him over and broke through their barrier.

I pelted through the alley towards the square, bearing to my left as the alley forked. When I reached the top, relieved that I'd soon be lost in the festival crowd, I found no square. There were three unfamiliar paths before me. I was going the wrong way.

Frankie Flash rounded the turn behind, sprinting on his bare toes. He really was fast. But had he the staying power? Getting lost in Avandale's streets and alleys was a bad plan. But if I was already lost the only thing I could do was run him to exhaustion.

I turned to face Frankie and tore off my tabard. I flung it over his head, whipped around and scorched up the middle alley.

Now I was running for distance I realised my legs were more tired than I'd thought. It was an effort to lift my knees so my toes didn't catch on the cobbles. These legs I relied upon weren't mine, or so it seemed. It was as if I were trying to propel myself using Sir Tarquin's legs, thick as oaks and truly made of bronze.

*

Frankie Flash was screeching behind but I didn't turn, knowing I'd be unbalanced on the nubbly ground. My heart pounded as if it were a battering ram and my ribcage the prison bars it must break. My throat burned with the rapidity of my breaths.

I turned a corner. New smells assaulted me – singed feathers, acrid smoke, putrefying waste. Shuffling people bunched together suddenly, trapping me between their barrows and hand-held loads, urging me further into their midst.

I broke free and turned again, into an alley of tall crumbly buildings, where washing lines made bridges for mice. I skulked low under the dresses and trousers that attacked me with their damp clinging limbs.

Out of the alley, I hurtled past shops selling wares you couldn't get in Fairy Cross – silver goblets, engraved ivory knife sets, hats mounted with tiny stuffed birds. I don't know why I noticed, it was half an attempt to memorise the unfamiliar streets, I suppose. But behind the main streets Avandale was a labyrinth. The narrow, dark ways seemed to stretch and contort around me. Just as I thought I'd found a route, the path closed, in a dead-end, or blocked by a cart unloading.

Deeper in the maze, the evening shadows began to play devilish tricks. Huge beasts crept along passages, then vanished into the brickwork. I knew they were the magnified shapes of the alley inhabitants, who crouched in doorways, or staggered drunkenly and bumped me, hollering curses to the ether. But that didn't help me feel less afraid. In the higgledy-piggledy passages, I saw the fangs and claws and clubs and swords of ogres and other mythical beasts, all of them pursuing me.

To catch my breath, I slowed to a fast walk, looking

over my shoulder as much as ahead. This alley was mostly flat brick walls, where the backs of two streets met. There were occasional high windows and steep staircases down to gloomy basements.

Then I found myself alone in a short stretch of dank weeping brick. I paused in a squat doorway and listened.

There were strange sounds coming from the rooftops, like the tooting of tawny owls on their night hunt. The noises were too regular to be accidental.

Are these alley-dwellers in cahoots with Frankie? These toots and screeches some secret signal?

The calls in the air descended to street level. I heard them in front of and behind me. I very nearly lost my head, thinking I was pursued by aerial sprites, or dryads or naiads: creatures I'd offended while playing games in the woodlands and rivers of Fairy Cross.

I can't go on like this.

I examined the hovel behind me. Rattled the knob but the door was locked. Paint had flaked off in jagged pieces; the grain of the wood beneath was coarse and raised. I guessed the damp had weakened the wood.

Looking left and right, I thumped the door with my heel. A chain rattled. I checked the alley again. No one yet. Then I turned and kicked the door hard; it caved in as the latch ripped from the rotted timber. I fell forwards into the hovel, and flung closed what was left of the door.

24

I crouched in the gloom and stench of the hovel.

The mistakes were mine. I owned them. I should never have entered the contest. I was too puffed up with my strength and luck after killing the dog on the moor, too thrilled to be in Avandale alone, unchained from Gran.

I pleaded silently to the gods who'd helped me in the past – the ancient Greek ones, the Roman, the Norse – even the leprechauns of Grandpa's folktales. I prayed for some sort of deliverance. Anything, anything, other than what awaited me.

I can't go on running from my uncle. There's nowhere to run to. Frankie will be stalking the streets with Pope and Shaw. They'll find me sooner or later. But neither can I fight my uncle. It'll never be fair, one-on-one as against Sir Tarquin. As long as Robin sets the rules I can't win.

In the darkness, my tense body relaxed. Surrender was such an intoxicating thought. What sweet relief to give in, give up, to let Robin decide what to do with me. Rather than carry this burden of choosing what to do, knowing the consequences were mine alone to bear.

I didn't want to make choices anymore, and keep getting them wrong.

'Urrrggh, eeee…' the darkness wailed.

I teetered on my toes with the surprise.

What was it? My brains fizzed with possibilities – a maimed cat, a creaking old loom, a witch? Or perhaps an ancient, irritable deity I'd conjured with my self-serving prayer.

Regaining my balance, I stood slowly, feeling behind me where I thought the wall was. It was slightly wet, gritty. I rubbed my fingertips together; it felt like damp earth. I wondered if I'd entered a cave. The front of the hovel had looked to be rough plaster, but it could have been painted stone. I tapped the ground with my boot. Uneven and gravelly, but that didn't tell me anything more.

'Eeeee, ahhhh.'

I didn't want to investigate but knew I had to. I shuffled forwards. My thick-soled boots loosened rocks from the floor. I sculled the air with both hands, hoping the noise wasn't cranky machinery that would slice off my fingers. Nervously, I laughed at the thought of searching in the dark for my severed digits, chopped like carrots for the pot.

I clutched at the air, trying to knead it into a harmless shape – the fluffy kitten I wanted the noise to be. Still nothing.

'Euraaagghhhhh.' The wail became a shriek, harsh like a crow's. It was just in front of and below me.

I stumbled back, wobbling on the rocks I'd loosened.

'Euraaghh, euraaghh, euraaagghhhhh…'

The door of the hovel inched open.

A small head of messy brown hair bobbed in and out, haloed by the light from the alley. 'I know ye're in there, miss,' said Frankie Flash.

'Euraaagghhhhh, euraaghh!'

'Ye can shut the shrieking, Mrs Maria,' Frankie said. 'It

divn't need doing now I'm here.' To me, he said, 'Ye might as well come out, miss, there's nay door but this one.'

Confused by Frankie's polite tone, I almost went to him, wondering if I'd been mistaken about his intentions. I was so confused about everything, I was seeing enemies in neglected street kiddies, and friends in…well, I hadn't seen any of those.

The door flew open and shattered against the wall.

Light from a gas-lamp illuminated the hovel – the earthen floor, the warped walls, and Mrs Maria, an old lady in a lopsided rocking chair, flailing her arms as if being attacked by bats. I felt nearly as sorry for her as I did for myself. She too had been waiting in the gloom, probably believing me an attacker.

Another gas-lamp bobbed in and lit the first intruder from behind. Pope, and Shaw.

'Ye led us a merry chase,' Pope said, smugly.

'Glad you enjoyed yourself,' I said. 'Your dog didn't much.'

'Li'l lost Lizzie, when will ye learn? Thought ye could get help from the Guild and we wou'nt know. Thought ye could cheat yer way into the contest and we wou'nt see. Thought ye could fight and win.'

'Don't take me back,' I said. 'Help me instead.'

'Help ye?' He came towards me with his lamp. The flickering light made grotesque shadows of his lumpen features. He looked into my eyes, trying to work out my game. But I had none. It was a genuine plea.

'Help me take the mill back from my uncle.' It was desperate, futile, I know. I half-hoped that if I stalled for time Frankie would have a change of heart, and return with a horde of savvy urchins to overpower Pope and Shaw.

'What's in it for us?' said Shaw. He rarely spoke, but he

was always watching.

'Shut it, man.' Pope whirled around with his lamp.

'Before he comes, I want to know.'

'Ye think so, but ye don't.'

'Yeah, I do wanna know. How much'll ye–?'

But Shaw cut himself short, and I never got to offer him the Sir Tarquin prize money.

My uncle appeared in the doorway. His face was in full shadow but I knew his silhouette and his stiff way of moving.

'Come to take me to Mungrispike?' I said, naming my fear, to look it in the eye, stare it down.

Is the beginning of my imprisonment? That can't be! How can that be? I've only just got out into the world.

I let myself feel the panicky fear, but I'd never let my uncle see it.

Calmly, I said, 'You may have me trapped but I'll never go willingly.'

'Elizabeth,' he said, in his infuriatingly patient way, 'this is for your own safety. Look where you've brought yourself.'

'For my safety?'

Safe. As if saying it would make it so. I'd never felt less safe in my life. What do they do to the girls at Mungrispike? If it's a place of experimentation, as Gran had heard, how will they test me? Will they examine my bodily person in intimate ways, then pronounce me mad and bad all the way through?

I said, 'Look where you've brought yourself, dear uncle. How's it you've stooped so low as to find yourself in a stinking hovel, sorry Mrs Maria,' – but the old lady didn't respond – 'kidnapping your own niece?'

'You can save the melodramatics, Elizabeth. There's no kidnap, I'm your legal guardian. Your father made it so.'

'He did not. You drove him from Fairy Cross before I arrived, before he knew about me.'

'Is that what your grandmother told you?'

'It's the truth.'

'Take her outside,' he said to Pope and Shaw, 'I haven't the time or inclination for this.'

Pope made for my arm, but he was still holding the lamp and I was ready for him. His fingers closed on my ripped jacket but caught no flesh. I tugged against his hold and sprang away, leaving him a scrap of woollen cloth.

But there was nowhere to run to except behind Mrs Maria's rocking chair. I didn't mean to use her as a shield, I hadn't time to think, hoping only that I could lure Pope and Shaw further into the hovel, then barge through the doorway past my uncle.

'Eurrraagghhh,' shrieked Mrs Maria, rocking violently. I steadied the back of the chair so she wouldn't catapult herself out.

'What ye gonna do?' Pope lunged left and right either side of the rocking chair, his lamp swinging, the flaming oil spitting. 'Throw an old hag at me? Huh, huh, huh.'

'Get on with it,' said my uncle.

'It's the truth,' I yelled. 'If you've got me anyway, why won't you admit it? You stole the mill, you drove my father out and now you think you can tidy me away, by locking me up in an asylum.'

'Asylum?' said Shaw.

My uncle laughed loudly and oddly, in a rehearsed sort of way. 'You've no idea how much you resemble Kit.'

'Asylum?' Shaw said again.

'You don't call my father that,' I yelled. What's going on? That's two mentions of my father in a day – first Johnson, now my uncle – more than the last year. I said, 'He's Christopher to you, if he's anything.'

'He was a great deal, despite what you've heard. I suppose he thought it for the best too. Running away.' He paused. 'Was it?'

The creeping dread returned. I no longer felt armoured all over, as when I'd killed the dog in the bog.

'You'd know better than anyone,' he said. 'Was it best he fled Fairy Cross, and abandoned you?'

Clutching onto Mrs Maria's rocking chair, I began to sway in a private melodrama. Scenes of my father packing a knapsack like mine. Scenes of him slipping like a fugitive through the village to the crossways, to hitch a lift to who-knew-faraway-where. And another earlier scene, of him leaving squalling baby-me in the box Gran used for her knitting wool.

I knew these were Robin's tricks, he'd say anything to get what he wanted. But also, what did I really know about those times before my birth? Only what I'd been told by Gran. Her usual tales were wildly heroic, magical, hilarious. She always insisted every one was true, though of course they weren't. But on my own I couldn't pick fact from fantasy. What had truly occurred?

Pope seized me, pinning my arms by my sides. Shaw grabbed one of my hands and looped rope around it before I could fight him off, then yanked my hand behind my back to tie it to the other. I swear he whispered into my hair, 'Dithered too long.'

I wrestled and yowled. Mrs Maria began to shriek again. I was grateful for her protest. She carried on screeching as Shaw dragged me backwards into the nighttime alley.

My uncle threw a long cloak around my shoulders so no one could see my hands were bound. I tried to shrug it off. Pope tied the cloak's cord tightly around my neck.

I blinked furiously to dispel humiliating tears, which

ran down my face and neck to soak the cord, which seemed to swell and grow tighter.

When I blinked to clear the last drops, Frankie Flash was in the alley. Not with a horde of urchins, but with a man and a boy, a little older than me.

25

A pistol clicked. Pope stopped abruptly. I bumped into the back of him, and Shaw into me. Frankie slunk out of sight.

The man in the alley said, 'Hold it there.'

My uncle took two steps to the side. The man traced his movement with the pistol. My uncle took another step along the alley.

'Run, if you like,' said the man. 'I always enjoy the sport.'

'Do you now?' my uncle said, but he didn't move again.

'Boss?' said Pope.

The unfamiliar boy drew his pistol too. He pointed it at Pope.

Pope and Shaw moved quickly to sandwich me, fore and aft, between them. If the boy were to shoot now, the bullet could pass through Pope and lodge in me.

The boy moved his pistol arm lower and lower, slowly, targeting Pope's legs and feet. Then he lifted his out-stretched arm to head-height and stepped forward at the same time. From here, he couldn't miss Pope's head. But he'd miss mine.

'Giz it ower then,' Frankie said, his shrill voice piping up from somewhere near the man.

'What's that?' Pope said.

'The coin ye owe me, course.'

'Ye brought these crooks for the sake of yer pennies? Won't be near enough to pay 'em.'

'He's sold us out, ye fool,' Shaw said. He gripped my shoulders tighter, each finger a talon. Then he let go.

'Tis biz'ness, that's all.' Frankie appeared beside the man with the pistol.

The man emerged from the shadow of the wall. I recognised the hat, the old-fashioned tricorne, before I saw his face. It was the handsome rogue who'd called me giant-slayer.

'Hurry up,' he said, 'the kid wants his coin.'

'We never shook on it,' Pope said.

'Hand over the boy's money,' said my uncle.

Pope began to reach inside his jacket.

'Hold it there,' said the man in the tricorne hat. 'The kid'll get it.'

Pope paused with his hand hidden inside his jacket.

Frankie scurried forwards, then stopped a few yards from Pope. 'If ye're thinking about yer knife there, mister, divn't. He'll blow ye a third eye before ye can get yer hand on it.'

'Boss?' said Pope.

'I said, hand over the boy's money.'

Pope withdrew his hand from his jacket and held both arms aloft. Frankie scampered over, grabbed Pope's lapel and fumbled in the pocket. Coins tinkled.

Frankie said, 'Yeaah, money money,' then dashed away to a door alcove with his prize.

The man in the tricorne hat stepped closer to my uncle. My uncle took a half step backwards, almost imperceptible, as if he were willing himself not to retreat but his feet had other ideas. I'd never seen him intimidated before.

The man said, 'Her too. The giant-slayer.'

'Her? What for?' said my uncle. 'She's my niece, you've no claim upon her.'

'We don't need a claim, she's free to choose.'

'Choose what?' I said, removing myself from between Pope and Shaw.

'Go with your uncle,' said the man, 'or come with us.'

'With you?'

Is this a choice, or a trick? Confused, I looked at Frankie. He was whispering to the boy, whose pistol remained an extension of his steady arm, aimed at Pope and Shaw.

The boy was dark-haired, with a slender frame, a few inches taller than me and probably a year or two older. In the dim light of the alley, the state of his clothing – respectable or shabby – wasn't visible, only that he wore no hat. There was nothing else by which to assess him. Aside from his keeping company with the man in the tricorne hat, who was evidently a scoundrel of one type or another. There's no good choice here at all.

Frankie stopped whispering and beckoned to me. 'Come on then, what's-yer-name.'

Does a betrayal of my enemy make Frankie my friend? I've no way of knowing until it's too late. But I know what my uncle intends to do with me.

I said, 'You can untie me now.'

'I'll do that at the inn when you're safe,' said my uncle.

'No. Now.'

I remembered standing on the ridge with Gran a few days before, teetering on the wobbly rock, buffeted by the wind. She'd been preparing me then, I realised, reminding me how to get to Avandale across the moor. How did she know that was how I'd leave?

Ever since I'd fled home I'd thought only of returning to take the mill, to make everything right for everyone – as it should have been, if history had been written differently and my father never banished. But I couldn't go back to undo those events. I could only go forwards. But how far must I go?

'I'm not going with you,' I said to Robin. 'You can't hurt me with your lies anymore. And you can't hurt me with the truth, whatever you think it is. There's no safe for me, and no safe for you.'

I expected him to laugh, to dismiss me as childish for believing myself some sort of Fury, an ancient Greek goddess of vengeance.

But he didn't. No one said anything.

A new era might have dawned elsewhere and left us behind, preserved in this moment of eternal uncertainty, with Mrs Maria shrieking periodically in the background, a siren of impending doom.

Frankie was the first to break it. He was at my bound hands with a blade, telling me to stop wriggling, which I didn't know I was doing. He slashed at the rope, nicked my thumb. He wrenched the rope from my wrists, burning my skin with the rough fibres. 'Let's go,' he said.

He was disappearing round a bend in the alley before my trembling legs received the message.

I took one last look at my uncle.

He said, 'Very well, Elizabeth. You've made your choice, as your father did. Will you fall further? Time will tell.'

Then I hurtled after Frankie. My legs knew how to run, but my mind didn't know what it knew. Doubt kept me alert. But it also kept me perpetually in fear, in fear of doing the wrong thing. What am I hurtling towards?

Seconds later I heard the man and the boy running after me. I turned to check, and check again, that it was they and not Pope and Shaw. We ran through the Avandale streets, which now teemed with nighttime activity.

The man and boy stayed always behind me, as if for protection. Whatever they wanted me for was worth a huge risk.

26

On the edge of town, the moon was high and bright.

We passed the last turning, which led to the convent where Robin had once threatened to send Gran. The convent for her, Mungrispike for me. The cold pebbly lake bed for aunt Sarah.

Beyond Avandale's final dwellings – one-storey shacks for the poorest people – another man waited with three horses. When he saw us, he untethered the horses from a fencepost.

The man, the boy, Frankie and I skidded to a halt on the gravel road in the horses' moon shadows.

'I can't go any further until I know what you want with me,' I said.

'Do what thou like, th'art not coming with us,' said the short stocky man holding the horses' reins.

'Now, Cavendish–' panted the man in the tricorne hat, '–that's no way to– speak to our recruit.' He took a set of reins.

'Recruit for what?' Cavendish said.

'I'll explain on the way.'

'There's no way till thou explain, Florian.'

'Really, Cavendish? We haven't time for this.'

'Neither's there time for thy peculiar fancies.'

'I'm not peculiar,' I said. 'I don't even want to be here.'

'Then get lost,' said Cavendish.

Get lost I could do. But for how long? Gran had dropped a few pennies into my knapsack – all she'd had in the house at the time. I'd spent some on food at the festival stalls; there was probably enough left for a rabbit pie. I could snare my own rabbits and squirrels, however, if I ran now and took refuge in the forest. But how long could I live like that? Someone – hunter, poacher, vagabond – would see me eventually. And it would get me no closer to reclaiming the mill.

'You said I could earn money if I helped you, greater than the prize of the contest?' I said.

'Thought you were all about the fight, had your own Goliath?' said Florian.

'That too.'

'That's what they all say, until their neck's on the line.'

'Come on, man, we haven't time,' Cavendish growled. 'Leave her for t'watchmen.'

'Why the watchmen?' I said.

He grunted. 'Nags'll have been missed by now.'

'The horses are stolen?'

'Permanent loan,' Florian said. 'Just without the owner's permission. Are you with us or not?'

'But what do you want me to do?' I said.

'I'll tell you the first part now, then Henry,' – he indicated the dark-haired boy – 'will tell you the rest when we're moving. How's that?'

I saw it was all I'd get. 'Henry,' I said, with relief to know everyone's name, as if that made them trustworthy, 'you're Henry?'

The boy nodded, but he wouldn't look at me.

'And you'll tell me when we're on the road?'

He nodded again. 'But, ah–'

'Splendid,' said Florian.

'This is a mistake thou'll regret, man,' Cavendish said.

'Is there another kind?' Florian said.

Cavendish didn't reply. He took hold of the brim of his round hat and tugged it down over his ears. He flung a set of reins to Henry, and tightened a saddlebag on his own horse. He mounted, then cantered away.

'Never mind him, likes to think he's in charge,' Florian said, once Cavendish was out of earshot. 'Now, where was I? Ah, yes. We're gathering in the forest, yonder, then riding to Manchester to...' He tailed off.

Manchester. I thought of the letter Gran had put in my knapsack, and the address of my great-uncle. Was Gran planning to meet me there?

I waited for the rest of Florian's plan. But he swung up onto his horse, slapped its rump and galloped ahead of Cavendish.

'Hold on,' I shouted.

'Shh,' said Henry. He was already on his horse, his feet in the stirrups, reins in hand. Everything was happening so quickly.

'Leg up?' Frankie ushered me towards Henry's horse, and linked his skinny fingers.

I put my foot in the bridge of Frankie's hands.

'Frankie Flash,' I whispered, 'I don't know if you've done me a favour bringing them to Mrs Maria's, or landed me in even deeper trouble.'

'Nowther do I,' Frankie said, spreading his bare feet further apart, preparing to take my weight.

'Aren't you coming too?'

'Nay. I'd die if I was like them, on the road. I'm not strong, nay horse. But in toon, I know the ways.'

I didn't know town ways. And neither did I know the road. What did Grandpa know of being on the road when he set off on his travels and adventures? Just what he'd read in his romances. But he had his own money, I conceded. And money meant choices. Robin had taught me that.

'Better get going before yer uncle comes looking,' said Frankie.

'Yeah...' I said, arrested for a moment, caught between one terrible choice and another.

Then I put my weight onto Frankie's hands before I remembered he was half my size. His wrists cracked and popped.

'Sorry,' I said, sliding into the shiny saddle behind Henry.

Frankie shook out his bony hands. 'I'm stronger than I look,' he said, but I wasn't sure even he believed it.

The horse was huge. I began feel dizzy with the thought of travelling so high off the ground. The wooziness flooded my mind and I couldn't remember what I was doing out here on the bleak road.

Beneath me the horse's ribcage heaved. Brass buckles and rings clinked as the horse shook its head.

Henry said, 'Hup, hup, Samson,' and we flew.

I gripped the sides of Henry's waist, too timid to hug him, though it made me unstable in the saddle. My knapsack bounced between us. It felt strange to be this close to a boy I didn't know. I'd only ever hugged Tom, whom I'd known all my life, and even that felt oddly tense, sort of comforting but also unfamiliar.

With a jolt, I realised I didn't have any lifelong friends anymore. Not until I returned to Fairy Cross. And when would that be? I didn't even know what the next hour held. Were Henry and Florian friends? I was sure Cavendish wasn't. And I knew what my uncle was. At least here, now, rushing away from Avandale, things weren't yet decided. There was still hope.

'Hold tight, Lizzie,' Henry said over his shoulder, his voice almost lost to the air. 'We'll stop soon, but we need to put some distance between us and anyone searching.'

I took a deep breath and circled his waist with my arms. Feeling his lower ribs against my forearms, I moved my grip lower, to his taut belly. He leaned forward and kicked our mount into a gallop. I tilted to press gently against Henry's back, and so we rode as one: horse and boy and me. Six eyes, twelve limbs, the same as the beast from my dreams.

The heat of Henry's body felt comforting yet unfamiliar. There was another feeling too. It could have been the speed at which we galloped, and the fact I was disappearing into the night with a band of horse thieves, but my and Henry's closeness in particular felt a little bit...well, a little bit dangerous.

27

It was cooler on the open road than in town. The sweat drying on my skin made me feel colder still and brittle in my bones.

Florian and Cavendish slowed to a canter, a trot, then a walk. They began to argue. Tactfully, Henry reined in Samson, and we dropped behind. Their raised voices trailed back to us, but I couldn't make out their words.

Mist floated above the low spots in the road. The horses' feet disturbed the mist, which swirled then closed behind us, as if we clopped through water, our tracks erased. I felt as though I existed for a single second at a time, bursting into being with each of Samson's steps, and then sort of existing nowhere inbetween.

We passed fields, copses and quiet roadside dwellings. What had gone before was a fading dream. My whole growing-up life in Fairy Cross seemed years ago already. What was to come was so unknowable I felt the future would never arrive, and that I was suspended in this mist, atop a horse of supernatural proportions, forever.

To tether myself somehow, I held onto a feeling of Tom. I couldn't picture his face. It was too indistinct. Not blurry exactly, more like in flux – all the faces he'd ever had, during the years in which I'd known that face would one day perish.

If I did try to fix upon Tom's face, all I could picture was his disappointment and anguish on the night of the fire. Of when we'd arrived at the cottage, and I tried to thanks and sorry and goodbye and sorry and where have you gone because I'm still here, I think. Only now I'm not there, and don't know when I will be again.

When I thought I'd waited long enough, I said to Henry, 'Tell me, what's in Manchester and why does Florian need me so badly?'

Henry didn't answer.

I pondered his reluctance, and said, 'The horses are stolen…'

'Not by me.'

'And who are you?'

'Henry James Brooke.'

I was glad he'd told me his full name without hesitation, though it wasn't what I'd meant. The name told me little but it did make him real – and I was in danger, in the eerie mist, of forgetting this was all very, very real. His name made him a person with parents, who'd chosen it, and siblings and friends who used it to call him or tease him. And all the other things people did with your name to pin you down, to make you knowable, traceable, a unique person in the world. Not a lost nobody disappearing into the mist, never to be asked about again.

'I'm Lizzie.'

'I know.'

'Oh, of course.' I remembered how he'd told me to hold on tight. 'I know you're deliberately not answering my question, about what Florian wants me for–'

'I'm not answering because I don't know, not exactly.'

'But he said you'd tell me!'

'I would if I could. You weren't part of the plan.'

'You're not part of my plan,' I said, 'but I still need to know.'

'You'll have to wait until we stop.'

'Stop now, let me down. I've changed my mind.'

'Too late.'

I let go of Henry's waist.

'Don't think about jumping down,' he said.

I took hold of his waist again. And waited.

Some ten, fifteen, minutes passed in silence. Then, slowly, I moved my body away from Henry's. I coughed to give an excuse for separating further, and fussed with my knapsack, making sure I knocked the small of his back with my pretend rummaging.

In my personal view-o-rama, I pictured how I'd swing my right leg over the horse's rump, let go of Henry and grab the back of the saddle all in one movement. Then I'd drop to the ground, trying not to slide around the barrel of Samson's body and end up underneath his hooves, to have my skull cracked like a cobnut.

I knew I could run and find a hiding place in the woods in under a minute.

To prepare, I shifted my weight ever so slightly onto my left buttock. My hip rotated forwards and pressed into Henry's back. I tried to calm my breathing so as not to alert him with the north wind blowing on his neck.

Samson whinnied, perhaps sensing my fear. I counted to twelve. Then I released the grip of my right heel on Samson's belly, ready to jump.

'Don't think about running,' Henry said. 'Cavendish can hit a moving target while blindfolded, and you're not as subtle as you think. He'll hear you crashing through the

144

undergrowth, if that's what you're planning. And there're worse things than him in the forest.'

I didn't reply straight away, I had to hold a sob with my tongue.

When I almost had control of myself, I said, 'Am I captive then?'

He hooted into the night air. Samson neighed.

Up ahead, Florian whistled a bird-like call. Henry tried to whistle back. He blew feebly, between laughs, and made no noise but a splutter.

Florian trotted back along the road. 'What's up?'

'Nothing out of the ordinary,' Henry said.

He turned in the saddle. His face was so close I could feel his breath on my skin, but I couldn't see his features. I still didn't know what he actually looked like. It was odd to be physically close to someone you wouldn't recognise in daylight.

He said, 'In answer to your question, I'll tell you what he,' – he indicated Florian – 'told me. You're riding a stolen horse in the company of bandits, and no matter your age the law won't be sympathetic. You'll hang before you've a chance to say 'a terribly unfortunate misunderstanding'. But we're delighted to welcome you as our distinguished guest, who's got no other place to go.'

'Ha,' said Florian. 'That was quick. Chose well, didn't I? Cavendish will be delighted to hear she's with us wholeheartedly.'

'You tricked me,' I said.

'No, we saved you,' Florian said. 'The trick's only in your mind.'

'It's not. You're using words to manipulate me into agreeing with you.'

'I can use a pistol if you like.'

One trap to another. I thought I was making my own choice.

'Well, it's a relief to get all that out of the way.' Florian pulled on the reins and brought his horse's nose to face the road not yet travelled. 'Let's go now we're fully committed to one another.' He cantered through the mist towards Cavendish.

Henry nudged Samson to walk on.

Thinking my situation couldn't get any worse, I said, 'So, Henry James Brooke, if indeed that's your real name, if indeed you're innocent of stealing horses, if indeed–'

'You want to ask me something? Then say it.'

'What did Florian make *you* do?'

Henry didn't flinch or speak. We were so close in the saddle that the outline of his back was most of my view. As his silence continued, my anger subsided, replaced by fear. His black outline seemed to change from being a solid thing, a boy's live body, to become a void, a nothingness into which I might fall.

Eventually, he said, 'It doesn't really matter what Florian wants you to do. Trust me, it's better not to know until the moment, because you'll have to do it anyway.'

28

Into the woods. Deeper and deeper.

Darkness wrapped its cloak around us. The pale mist whispered between the trees, carrying secret messages from bark to leaf.

On foot, Cavendish led the procession with his horse. He took us along a path that weaved around trees and dense undergrowth, skirted wide hollows and sometimes appeared to double-back on itself. Henry walked behind Cavendish, leading Samson and Florian's dappled grey. Then me. And Florian behind, to catch me if I ran.

'Sling her over thy nag, if th'art so keen to take her,' Cavendish had said, when we halted on the road beside an opening in the undergrowth.

'Cavendish, my good man, she's a volunteer,' said Florian. 'Volunteers aren't slung over horses like sacks of wheat.'

'I'm not a volunteer,' I said. 'You tricked me.'

Cavendish said, 'Sacks o' wheat don't scream or run to t'sheriff.'

'Sacks of wheat don't help us get rich.'

'They do if you have a lot of them,' I said.

Florian turned his palms to the sky. 'I'm trying to help you here, Lizzie. You want to be a sack of wheat, or a volunteer?'

'No more talk about sacks o' wheat, man. This is serious business. She's just a girl–'

'I'm not *just* a girl,' I said, but Henry elbowed me to be quiet.

'–just a girl thy picked from a parade.'

'Not a parade, dear Cavendish, a contest. A duel against a man three times her size. She's qualified for the task.'

'Tisn't her qualifications I'm doubting, mate. Loyalty, man, loyalty. What are we to her? What's her to us?'

'Nothing, granted. Now. But soon–'

'Th'art too quick to trust, chum, far too quick. Did for thy last chief, I hear.'

'No, that was me.'

Cavendish didn't reply at first. Then he said, 'Mutiny? Puh. That meant to impress me?'

'Merely to inform you. But if your courage is faltering, Cavendish, if you need reassuring like a frightened old biddy, then let me put your mind at rest. Lizzie will be tested first.'

'Tested?' I said. 'First I've heard of it. Tested how?'

'Hff,' Cavendish said.

'And if I fail?' I said. No one spoke. I said again, 'If I fail?'

Cavendish turned off the road, between the spires of foxgloves grey in the moonlight. As his horse brushed the plants the bells nodded, like ancient men in sombre hoods, passing their judgment.

We waded through the mist as if through a spectral sea, our own feet alien, creatures of the ghostly depths. In front of me, the white tail of Florian's horse swished, swished, swished…

I glimpsed a vision of Gran in the mist, as she'd been abed during a long illness, wizened with starvation. It gave me a lingering scare, that sickness, to see Gran nearly gone, as she'd appear on her deathbed with me alone to watch her fade. And I remembered what she'd told me in her delirium – what I'd never believed, being uttered in fever. Of my father's dangerous games in the greenwood.

When we reached a crossways in the path, beside an old oak with a storm-fractured limb, I was reminded of the crossroads of home. This was where fairy folk left the changeling children, their own wicked bairns swapped for human kiddies. For what purpose the folk tales in Grandpa's books differed.

Was it to cause mischief for the human parents, or to give the fairy young a better life?

Or to raise a human child in fairy ways, then swap it back? Use the child, who'd never again fit in, to create havoc in the human world.

I'd always wondered whether I might be a changeling child.

We turned at the oak. Soon after, we approached a clearing lit with small fires, guarded at the entrance by two men.

'Who's there?' said one of the men. He was tall, heavy-set, half-hidden by a low branch.

'Thou knows who's here,' Cavendish said. 'I left this morning and now I'm back, as I told youse I would be.'

'Where's the Chief?'

'Back there,' Cavendish said tersely. His horse snorted.

'Can't see him.'

'Put that gob o' thine to good use and call.'

'Watch it, Cavendish. We don't answer to you. Chief?' the guard shouted. 'Chief, you there?'

Behind me, Florian chortled.

He said, 'Dum diddly dum,' and scuffed around on the path. 'What a fine and splendid evening we're having, Lizzie. The moon, the mist, the thrill of adventure... Wouldn't you agree?' He bumped my shoulder.

'Best kidnapping I've ever had.'

'Ha. Isn't it just? A model kidnapping indeed. You play the game so perfectly.' He clapped his hands. 'Ho hum, better get on then, and put dear Cavendish out of his misery.' He called to the guards, 'Stand down, lads, I'm here safe and well. With a prize.'

The two guards stepped to either side of the path. Cavendish entered the fire-lit clearing without further word. His horse, as if displeased at his master's treatment, stamped its back hooves before walking on.

Henry moved along the path towards the guards.

'Hullo there, lad,' said the second guard. 'Good time in town?'

'In a way,' Henry said.

'What way's that then? Eh? Eh? Aw, come on, a young lad like you, the Chief's apprentice, going to town, while we're stuck here in the dirt. What's happening there?'

'Nothing much, just the festival.'

'The festival! Nothing much? What I'd give to go to a festival. What d'you get up to?'

'Scouting.'

'Scouting? That all? No feasting, no drinking? No dancing?'

'Work to do, boys,' Florian said from behind me. As if stealing horses and tricking people were legitimate endeavours. 'We've all got our burdens.'

'Yeah, and how's about some others share ours. We been standing here all night.'

'I'll tether the horses and take my turn,' Henry said.

'Good lad,' said the guard.

'No,' Florian said. 'I need you. Sort the horses, then–'

He stepped around me to speak into Henry's ear. Then he moved aside, under the low beech branches. He whispered with the guards.

Henry turned to me and said, 'Lizzie, keep close.'

I wasn't going to argue with that. Part of me, the daft part probably, wanted to believe Henry wouldn't hurt me. Perhaps it was as simple as us being a similar age, or because he too had been tricked by Florian. I was searching, foolishly, for any similarity to someone in whom I had faith. I was searching for Tom.

I need one small certainty to cling to. Something to reassure me I'm not going to die tonight.

A guard slapped the body of his rifle; his rings on the metal startled me.

Henry stepped into the clearing with the horses. I knew I had to follow, but I couldn't make myself move. As Henry and the horses turned left, I caught a glimpse of the camp. I tried to take it in as quickly as I could. The rough shelters made of sailcloth. The fires, and cliques of men around them. The smell of woodsmoke and charred meat. The roar of laughter and a gunshot, then another.

'What're you dawdling for?' Florian said, clearly no longer content to enjoy the fine and splendid night. 'There's no place else to go.'

He shoved me in the back and I stumbled over a tree root. My fingertips grazed the ground. In this position, as though a monkey walking on all fours, I passed the guards. They laughed. Florian pushed past me and strode into the camp.

Instead of standing up, I dipped fully to the ground. There's no certainty but this one: I have to get away.

I glanced over my shoulder, ready to dart off the path to lose myself in the shadows.

Both Florian's guards were leering at me.

'Not much of a prize, are you?' said the first guard. His voice boomed, seeming to ball into an enormous fist, summoning power from the night, a punch to the side of my head.

'I didn't ask to be.'

'What are you for then?' he said. 'Come on, scratter, why's the Chief brought you? And why're you walking free? Can't see how you'd have any charm over him.'

I boiled a rage at the suggestion I was walking free, having a pleasant nighttime stroll under the silver moon. I felt I had nothing to lose I wasn't going to lose anyway. It brought relief, this anger. Mostly as a welcome change from being afraid. But it was a risky sort of relief, the devil-may-care kind. I'd felt it before, reckless choices followed.

I stood up and faced the guard. I said, 'I'm not for anything. I'm just me.'

'That en't enough. You gotta be of some use, otherwise you're just eating our food and shitting it out and no one's getting rich inbetween.'

'I'm not helping you get rich. But I'll get rich myself,' – I thought of Frankie Flash's double-cross – 'when I sell the lot of you to the sheriff.'

'Don't joke about treachery.' The guard made a sudden movement I couldn't see. The smell of stale sweat wafted out of his clothes. 'We en't meeting the hangman thanks to you. You'll find yourself with a hole in your head before that happens.'

He nudged my belly with his rifle, but the top of it knocked the point of my sternum. The wind went out of me with the shock. He could break my bones without even trying, shatter me to bits like an old cabinet.

He said, 'Go on, get. You may not wanna to be here but you gotta earn your keep.'

I took two careful steps backwards, then turned into the clearing. I scanned the scene for Henry, but he was nowhere. He'd been reclaimed by the night.

Why didn't he wait for me? Well, I've got my certainty at least. I'm on my own.

29

The outlaws' camp glowed orange, yet I felt no heat from the fires. Or maybe it was the chill of my feverish sweat, now hot, now cold – my anger still burning, my fright paralysing, with no comfortable state between.

In the centre of the camp, about fifty yards away, was a huge fire. The flames crackled up into the night sky. Luminous flakes swirled in every direction, like a swarm of fiery bees protecting their infernal hive. Around the fire, silhouettes reeled and jostled. More outlaws. They may have been dancing, or they may have been fighting. I guessed there were about twenty or thirty men surrounding the pyre, but the shadows doubled everything, not least my fear.

When I saw a solid mass in the blaze, I lurched forward several steps, suddenly transported to the scene of the packing loft fire. The mass a body, a person, needing to be saved.

'Awooooh-ahhh,' a man hollered from beside the fire.

Laughter followed. Someone began to beat a rhythm on an empty barrel. I came back to myself, to the now of the camp and the smell of charred meat. The body in the fire was just an animal: a wild pig or a deer.

There's plenty to panic about, I said to myself, but don't

panic at everything.

'Lizzie, why're you dithering back here?' Florian marched towards me, lit from behind by a smoky orange glow. 'Come on, let's get this over with. Remember, you're a capable, loyal volunteer.'

'Capable of what?' I said. 'Loyal to whom?'

'Loyal to me, of course.' He took my arm. I thought he meant to parade me before the mob of shouting, chanting outlaws, but instead he steered me past the fire. He said, 'I saved you from your wicked uncle and you're forever in my debt.'

'What about Cavendish?' I said.

'Puh. Loyal to Cavendish? He'd have left you there. Wouldn't even have found you in the first place. I don't know why she keeps him around.'

'She who?' I said, but he was too busy muttering to himself.

Away from the fire, in a darker, cooler area, Florian stopped. Here, nestled among a cluster of silver birches, was a well-made tent. Ropes tethered the domed tent to the trees; it looked as if the construction had been in place for some time.

Florian lifted the front flap of canvas and said, 'After you, m'lady.'

'Why, what's in there?' I said.

'If you go in, you'll find out.'

'I'm not going in until you tell me.'

'Walk round the outside if you like, it's not attached to the gates of hell.'

'I'm not playing games, I just want to know what you want me for.'

'And if you go in, you'll find out. Can't talk out here.'

'The tent's got brick walls?'

'Just get in there, Lizzie.' He yanked my arm.

I stooped to enter, then dropped to my sore knees, where the blistered skin hadn't yet healed. I crawled in.

Inside, the tent smelt strongly of the forest bed – of leaf mulch and fungi – and the muskiness of an animal's den. A lamp flickered on the ground beside the central pole. The frame of the tent was visible in the tawny light: a network of branches lashed together, with a forked branch supporting the oilcloth roof.

Hanging from the fork was a dazzling sight: a skein of jewelled necklaces. I'd never seen such a hoard. Not even when my aunt showed me the family heirlooms, so she could once again remind me I'd never inherit a thing. The gemstones on the necklaces caught the light from the lamp, beaming red, blue, purple and green dancing dots onto the canvas, as if forest beasts prowled outside the tent, their fantastical coloured eyes shining through, seeing me, their prey, within.

The tent was empty save a woman, sitting cross-legged at the far end, her back curved into the slope of the canvas. I wondered if she was a fortune-teller. I didn't need reminding that this was my unluckiest day.

'Who are you?' she said.

'This is the new plan,' Florian said, from outside the tent. He slapped my burnt leg to chivvy me in.

'How so?' she called.

'I've got it all thought out,' Florian said. Then: 'Ah, Cavendish, my dear man. No, no, it's for me to explain. No,' he said firmly. 'No…'

I heard Cavendish mumble. Then they fell out of earshot.

The woman leant forwards and onto her hands. She uncrossed her legs and crawled slowly towards the centre.

The reflections of the coloured gemstones marked her face and neck; she appeared to be a strange sort of leopard.

She drew close to the light to examine me. She had golden skin and amber eyes. Her chestnut hair was tied messily and a long frizzy ponytail fell over her shoulder. She was slim, between thirty and forty years of age, and dressed in shirt, jacket and breeches, like me. Only hers weren't in tatters and plastered with peat from the moor.

'Christ, what an ordeal.' Florian crawled into the tent. 'You have to set Cavendish straight. He's been nothing but the voice of doom since we left. He wants to disagree with everything I say just because I've said it. Shove over, Lizzie. Urgh, and that town. The festival puts everyone on edge, couldn't get a decent price anywhere...' He reached into his jacket pocket and took out a gold and emerald necklace. He held it up in front of me, cocked his head to one side and said, 'Hm, maybe. It'll help you look the part. Anyway,' he said to the woman, tucking the necklace back into his pocket, 'I got her instead.'

'Florian,' the woman said, in a displeased tone.

'I know, I know, change of plan. But I've thought it through. Now there's no need for you to risk going to Manchester at all.'

'No?' said the woman. She sat on her heels, withdrawing from the light.

'Don't you see?' He lifted his tricorne hat by the crown and placed it carefully on the ground. Then he stretched out to lie on his back. He raised one knee, brought it across his out-stretched leg and with his hand pressed his knee to the floor. 'Lizzie, you're in the way still.'

He kicked me with his toe. I shuffled.

Things popped and cracked in his spine. 'Aahh,' he said, letting his bent leg relax. 'She can take your place. It'll have to play out a little differently, of course, and I'll need

157

to wait close by. But she's got the pluck and I've seen her strength, if it comes to that. She could probably carry a man, certainly a girl. It'll work, Kit, I know it will.'

I took a sharp intake of breath. Florian didn't notice, but the woman, Kit, did. The outline of her head whipped from his direction to mine.

Kit: my father's nickname. It wasn't unusual, Kit short for Christopher, Kit or Kitty short for Katherine. I tried not to read anything into the coincidence. Not to be piqued by the link and invent a connection that didn't exist.

'No,' said Kit.

'It's better this way. You'll stay here out of sight until it's time.'

'No, Florian. If it really has to be done, I'll do it.'

'But there's no need now we've got her.'

'Needs must when the devil drives.'

'To hell with the bloody devil, Kit. You're a fool to even consider it.' He rolled over to kneel in front of her.

It was intriguing to be on the inside of their disagreement. I was nobody to them. No one in Fairy Cross talked this way in front of me, no matter how much it was about me. Particularly when it was about me.

'You're too distinctive, Kit, too well-known there. If you're caught, then it's all off.'

'No concern for poor little me rotting in jail?' Kit laughed.

'You won't be there long enough to rot, you know that.'

'And she knows what'll happen if she's caught? She's agreed to it all, has she?'

'He tricked me into coming here,' I said. 'I don't know anything.'

Florian turned to me and said, 'The bank in Manchester is due to transport its deposits to London soon–'

'Florian,' said Kit, 'don't.'

'We need to know when, and what route they'll take – they change it every time.'

'For God's sake, Florian, shut up. If you tell her–'

'There's a man at the bank who devises the routes. Only he knows until the very day.'

'Lizzie, go now,' Kit said. 'You don't need to hear this.'

'That man has a daughter–'

Kit reached for Florian's mouth. He leaned out of her reach and brought his too-handsome face close to mine.

'Then it's your responsibility,' Kit said. 'I'll have nothing to do with it, the plans are getting shakier by the minute.'

'This is going to work,' said Florian.

'You've already changed the Manchester scheme twice, we don't have time to test this.'

'He has a daughter, yes…' I said, in spite of my better self. 'What's that got to do with it?'

'You're going to lure her away from her chaperone so I can, ah, look after her for a few hours,' Florian said. 'Just until we get what we need from her father.'

'You're going to kidnap an innocent girl?'

'Well, if you put it like that, we all are.'

'Kidnap?' I said, stuck upon the word. I wished he hadn't told me, I wished I hadn't asked. Because now I knew, and could never not know. 'Kidnap? Kid–?'

'Close your mouth, Lizzie, you look like a fish,' Florian said. 'Repeating it thrice won't get the deed done. That's your job.'

30

Outside the tent, in the chilly night air, Cavendish and Henry were waiting, several paces apart.

When I emerged, behind Kit and Florian, Henry stepped forwards and gave me a blanket; it was as rough as a pig's bristly hide, and smelt the same, but it was Henry's gesture that I noted. I bundled the blanket and hugged it to my chest.

'I've not agreed to it, and neither has she,' Kit said, throwing off Florian's arm as he tried to take her aside.

'She doesn't need to agree with it, she just needs to do it.' Florian bounded in front of Kit.

'You know that's not what I'm saying. If she doesn't want to do it, she'll sabotage it. Not deliberately, maybe, but by being timid or nervy, or trying to be overly confident. Any number of ways.'

'I'll be there the whole time.'

'No. She's not doing it.'

'Have it your way, Kit, you always do. I'll get Henry to take her back.'

'Th'art not letting her go, man,' Cavendish interrupted. He went to stand between Kit and Florian. 'Thou brought her here, thou deal with it.'

'Cavendish, good God...' Florian said. 'What are you saying?'

'Playing the fool suits thee well, chum, but that don't get thee out o' t'task.'

Beside me, Henry clashed his teeth together, then turned away to face the dark trees. I remembered what he'd said to me on the road, about not wanting to know my mission beforehand because I'd have to do it anyway. It was too late for that. Too late for me. Henry knew I'd never leave the woods alive.

'I want to do it!' I blurted, before anyone could state the nature of the task, and commit themselves to an irreversible act. 'I mean, I don't really want to, but I will. Florian, you said you'd pay me...'

'Naturally there'll be some small compensation for your time,' said Florian, reaching for his hat, then realising it wasn't there and raking his hair instead. 'If all goes well.'

'But if it goes wrong, she's on her own...' Kit stepped out from behind Cavendish.

'Seems like I am anyway,' I said.

'Without any of us to stop you talking, I mean. How do I know you won't tell the sheriff about this camp, or give descriptions of us–'

'I thought you were known in Manchester already,' I said.

She laughed. 'Well, that is true.'

'Not just Manchester,' – Florian shook me by the shoulders – 'the Valiant Lady Kit is known from here to the Middle Lands.'

'I've never heard of you.'

'We move in different circles.'

'I'd rather yours than mine,' I said.

'Then you should know the full consequences,' said Kit. 'Getting caught will earn you a noose around your neck.'

'Ever seen a man dance upon the gallows tree?' Florian said, gleefully.

'Yes,' I said. 'Once.'

The retired old highwayman, who was hanged from the charred elm at the fairy crossroads. Lynched upon Robin's orders. I'd followed the thugs, then watched from beside the rutted road. I couldn't not watch. It'd been me who'd let the man's secret slip.

'Oh,' Florian said.

'Then I cut him down and buried him.'

'I see.'

'I was eleven.'

'And?'

'Just so you know,' I said, 'that I'm not afraid.'

'But you are a little sinister, ' Florian said, and laughed. 'Now I'm afraid! Very well, then how about a girl? One just like you, too bold for her boots, swinging from the gibbet, her pretty green eyes bulging from her head, fair skin turning purple. Can you picture that, little lost Lizzie?'

The words 'little lost Lizzie' stung the most. I said nothing. I stared back at him, fixing upon the space between his eyes so mine didn't flicker in looking from one to the other. Tom did this to me when he didn't want his wavering gaze to suggest he had doubts.

This man, Florian – horse-thief and highway robber – had seen me at my strongest, beating Sir Tarquin. He'd seen me at my weakest, captured by Robin. And he'd only known me for half a day and a night. He knew my most personal yearning: to reclaim the mill. He believed I had a lot to play for, a lot to lose.

'I don't want paying, at least not with money,' I said. 'I want your help.'

'Our help?' said Kit.

'Yes. I want some of your men, Florian, to come with

me to Fairy Cross–'

'What's a fairy cross? I can't spare anyone for magical purposes.'

'Fairy Cross is a place, a hamlet. It's where I'm from. I want you and some of you men to go there with me. There's a mill, which should be mine. I want you to help me drive out my uncle.'

'A mill?' Kit said. 'A cotton mill?'

'Bobbins.'

'Oh,' she said, sounding almost disappointed.

'Splendid,' said Florian. 'See, Cavendish? We all have a common cause. Liberation! For bobbin, er, manufacturers, and all the other poor unfortunate folk, whoever they may be. Lizzie, why didn't you just say so, instead of encouraging all this bothersome disagreement?

'Well, that's settled. Kit, I've seen the uncle and his fellows in action, they're not up to much. Not even armed. A day's travel, there and back to this mill. Half a day, in and out, I reckon…some strategic beatings, whatever's in the till–'

'There's no till,' I said, 'it's a workshop, not a shop.'

'What's the difference? Anyway, whatever's in the locked box, the safe, wherever he keeps his money. Then torch the site–'

'No!' I said. 'You can't burn it, you can't damage anything at all. I just want my uncle to go, to give up the mill, give it back to me.'

'Ah, well, that sort of job's not really my speciality. But naturally, let's parley after Manchester. When you've proved your worth, we'll come to some arrangement. I'll give anything a go once. Actually sounds rather intriguing, doesn't it, Kit? Probably you've the patience and cunning to drive a man from his property. Lord only knows you've separated me from mine enough times.'

'Is this what you want, Lizzie?' Kit said. 'You care enough about the mill–'

'And the workers,' I said, forming a hunch about Kit's interests.

'–and the workers…I see… You care enough to help us in Manchester? Whatever it may mean for you?'

'Yes–' I began.

'Fairy…what did you say?' said Florian.

'Cross,' I said. 'Fairy Cross.'

'I see,' he said, thoughtfully.

'You know it?'

'No, no. Not in the slightest. Sounds very pastoral, very inconsequential.'

'Well, anyway,' I said. 'I care enough, yes, to help you in Manchester–'

Kit said, 'Still not sure about this. There must be another way.'

'–whatever it means for me,' I said, and paused. Getting to Manchester meant finding my great-uncle, and a safe place at last. 'Yes, more than anything. I'll do it.'

'We leave at dawn tomorrow,' Florian announced.

'Day after,' said Cavendish.

'Not tomorrow?'

'Can't be in town too long.'

'Have it your way, Cavendish,' Florian said. 'Is this a Manchester quirk I should know about? Everything's got to be on your terms. Fff. Henry, a word….'

He and Henry walked away a few paces to confer.

Kit and Cavendish exchanged some muted words, then she went back into her tent. Cavendish slipped away. I stood there, dumbly, wondering if I'd been dismissed, and if so, where I was supposed to sleep.

Henry returned alone. 'Florian wants you to share my tent tonight.'

'So you can keep an eye on me?'

'Yes.'

'What if I try to escape?' I was only half-joking.

'Don't do that,' Henry said, and led me quickly to the edge of the camp.

The perimeter was ringed with bracken and brambles. I patted the tips of the plants, as if they would recede at my touch and with them all barriers to my escape. It was dangerous to let my guard down, I knew that, but I was starting to feel at home amongst the trees. I knew the ways and the tricks of the forest. I'd studied them all my life.

'Is there where you tell me what's worse in the woods than Cavendish?' I said.

'No, you can imagine that for yourself. It's where I show you why you can't escape.'

He began to walk around the perimeter of the camp, then seemed to change his mind and took a different route through the clustered tents to the other side. I followed.

'There,' Henry said. 'See that, up ahead, half in the bracken.'

'I don't see anything. A rotting tree trunk, maybe.'

'It's not a tree trunk. Come on.'

Beside the tree trunk that wasn't a tree trunk, he stopped. 'Smells like it's rotting,' I said, putting my hand over my nose and mouth.

Henry bent down and said, 'Not asleep, are you there, Morris?'

'Blth, blth, what? What?'

The not-tree-trunk became a ragged, stinking man. Chains clinked as he struggled to sit upright. He said, 'Sleep? Who? Me? Noooo. No, no, no. Tis you, is it, lad? It is. How's about some scraps for poor Morris?'

'You know you don't get fed unless you keep watch,' Henry said.

'I'm keeping watch, I'm keeping watch,' Morris protested. 'Not asleep. I saw you, o'er there, waiting outside the Lady's tent. Saw you and this lass whispering. Saw you– Hm, then you was right here. Maybe a few seconds, lad, alright, maybe nodded off for a few. But only seconds, seconds! I been watching everything else, all night, I swear it. I'm starving.'

'What about the others?'

'What about 'em? Oh, *they'll* be asleep. Useless. How about some scraps from that hog? Must be some left over. Me first, mind. Them others're asleep–'

'I'm not asleep, I can hear everything you're saying,' a voice called from further round the perimeter.

'Shut it, Pike. Not heard a peep from you for hours. You—'

'Alright,' said Henry. 'I'll see what I can get.'

'Me first,' Morris said.

'He was first last night,' Pike shouted.

'I'll bring you something,' I said to Morris.

'Ohhh, no, no you don't,' Morris said in a low voice. 'Don't think you can bribe me, lassie. Got my eye on you, got my eye...' He laughed hoarsely, then descended into a choking cough. When he recovered he said, 'Just the one, mind. The other one don't see much from inside that damn dog's belly. Eh, lad, eh? Morris knows. You want me to look out for this one in per'tickler. Got it. Morris can't be bribed.'

'Come on, Lizzie,' Henry said.

'You'll keep me fed, won't you, lad?' Morris shouted after us. 'You're a good 'un.'

As we picked our way between the small tents, Henry said, 'Florian calls them Traitors Watch. Don't expect that needs much explaining. Most of them are from the old chief's gang, before Florian took over. He keeps them around to remind everyone.'

'So no one thinks of betraying him?'

'Yup. And to keep watch.'

'How long for?'

'All day and all night.'

'I mean, days, weeks…months?'

'Depends,' he said. 'On when the others want some target practice.'

31

There'd always been a target on my back. I just didn't know it until Robin came for me that morning at the cottage. Gran knew. And she tried to warn me. As did Tom, in his way, though he must have tried to disbelieve it. Would I have listened if they'd told me plain? Your uncle wants you dead.

But why had Robin lynched the retired highwayman? The old gent's daring deeds were long past; he wasn't bothering anyone, alone in his cottage on the east-west road, after his wife died. He was kind to me. Indulged my lonely games. I tried not to think of him, but he was always there, thrashing in the glare of the moon. There was so much that needed remembering, and so much I wanted to forget.

Henry stopped in front of a small, lopsided tent.

'After you,' he said.

I crouched, lifted a corner of the canvas, and slithered in on my belly. Inside it was completely dark. A giant batwing wrapped around my face. 'Argh,' I cried. I slapped and writhed and fought it off.

'What are you doing? I just put that up,' Henry said.

'Put what?'

'It's a drape, sort of, you know– to go down the middle between us.'

'Oh, sorry, it was all leathery and clingy…what do we need a drape for? It's totally black in here.'

'Well, I'm putting it back up. Stay where you are.'

'I don't know where that is.'

'Just stay still.' He came in after me, and began fumbling with the oilcloth drape. 'You're sitting on it,' he said, 'go that way a bit, and then…up…and, no, stop, you're rolling up in it. Just…'

I laughed until the oilcloth and me were separated eventually, and Henry did whatever he'd done with it before.

On the bare earth, I lay still like a pencil. The drape rippled along the length of me as it caught the breeze sneaking under the shelter. 'Where's the groundsheet? I'm not on it.'

Henry sighed.

'You haven't got one? What do you do when it rains?'

'Get wet.'

A minute passed, then I said, 'I can't sleep.'

' 'Cause you keep talking.'

I tried to be a pencil again and not speak, to make my point. Beside my ear, the one away from Henry, something tiny scratched, pic-pic-pic, on the canvas. Another tiny something crawled onto my thumb. I tried to count its legs as it crept through the fine hairs on the back of my hand.

Is this what it's like to be in a coffin? I wondered. When the worms and other beasties come for you. And if you're buried next to someone, as I lay next to Henry, would you know? And if you did know, would it feel companionable, or even more lonely because you thought you should feel safe but you didn't.

Was there any part of the old highwayman that knew

what was happening when I'd buried him? Did he know it was me who'd given him to the worms? The only way I had of saying sorry.

It wasn't my way to fill every waking second with idle chitter chatter, but tonight I couldn't help myself. If I didn't talk, I felt I might vanish – pouff – into the black nothing.

I said, 'We made a deer den, Tom and me, in the woods at home. A proper one, dug into the root cave of a big oak, like foxes do. We lined it with moss and covered the entrance with birch branches. But the deer came nibbling when we weren't there and ate all the leaves. We left it open after that. Then we built a stove, more of a fire pit really, cooked a bunny–' I stopped myself.

'Then what?' Henry said.

'Then nothing.'

'Carry on if you want to.'

'I don't.'

'You did a minute ago.'

'And now I don't.'

'I want to hear,' said Henry.

'Why? Has he told you to befriend me?'

'Who, Florian?'

'Who else?'

Henry was silent in the dark. Then he said, 'Honestly, yes, he has. But I want to know anyway. About you, your life. It's really different to mine.'

'How so?'

'Don't want to talk about it.'

'Then you don't get a piece of my life,' I said, 'to use against me later.'

He was quiet for so long I thought he'd gone to sleep. I knew I wouldn't be able to sleep. I couldn't stop thinking about Morris, and Pike, and the others I hadn't seen. Over and over I fretted about Traitors Watch and myself a part of it. I had to make Florian and Cavendish believe I was going to help them in Manchester.

'I had an apprenticeship, before. A good one,' Henry said, out of nowhere. I'd almost forgotten he was beside me. 'To a draughtsman in a shipyard, learning to draw the ship designs...'

'Go on.' I wasn't letting him off that lightly.

'I was thirteen when Florian, er, found me.'

'And now you're...?'

'Sixteen.'

'Go on.'

'You first.'

'No. You already know too much, you've met my uncle and his thugs, you know about the mill, you saw me in the contest.'

'That's not a fair trade,' he said. 'Anyone could've seen those things.'

'Suit yourself.'

'Alright,' he said, with irritation in his voice.

'It's you who wants to talk.'

'I said, Alright.'

'Alright then.'

He didn't speak. In the void I thought again of Traitors Watch. If things went wrong for me in Manchester, how long would I last on the Watch, chained and starving, before I was used for sport?

Then Henry said, 'I wish I'd been older, or no...I wish I'd been more sure of myself when Florian approached me. Sure enough to say no. I didn't believe what he was promising me, course I didn't, but I wanted to believe, so much...and I convinced myself.'

'What did he make you do? Was it worse than what he wants me to do?'

'No, you don't get that yet. Why did you agree to their

171

plan?' He spoke quietly still, but with a hard edge, almost angry. 'Why? I thought you were better than that.'

'I am.'

'No, no, you're not. You're as bad as the rest of us.'

I couldn't tell him why I thought I wasn't, because I had no intention of going through with the plan in Manchester. Instead I said, 'So what's the problem between Florian and Cavendish?'

'Don't know exactly, but Florian doesn't like how close Cavendish is to Kit.'

'Is he really in charge? Florian. Because sometimes it seems like–'

'Don't let anyone hear you say that,' Henry said quickly. 'I didn't hear you say that.'

'Then...er...' – what could I ask about? – 'what about the previous chief? What happened to him?'

'Before my time.'

'And?' I said.

'And no one talks about it.'

'Alright then,' I said. 'So...are they together, Kit and Florian?'

'Huh, he wants them to be.'

'She's not with Cavendish?'

'Not as far as I can tell. But they arrived together, already an *alliance*.' He let this hang in the air. 'Before they joined with Florian. They *trust* each other completely.' Another pause. 'Florian doesn't get it, he's too caught up in himself to see. But Kit and Cavendish...I'm not sure...they've got a common cause but it's more than that, they've shared something that *binds* them together.'

I pondered in the darkness of the tent, but my mind began to slow with tiredness. I found myself drifting into a waking dream.

The pause must have made Henry nervous because he

spoke abruptly. I snapped awake.

'Florian's got the men,' he said, 'and they've the plan to ambush the bank's coaches. But I don't think they're in it for the money, or not only. Florian is, of course, and his men.'

'And what are you in it for?'

'In for a penny, in for a pound.' He laughed in an odd way. 'In it up to my neck. Just like you.'

I didn't reply.

Then he pushed a bulky object under the drape. 'You can use this as a pillow if you want,' he said. 'It's just my jacket. Sorry, it's not the cleanest. We don't get much laundry done out here.'

'Er, thanks.' I was confused by his ever-changing tone towards me. Friendly, then bitter, then considerate, then angry. And now considerate again.

In it up to my neck? I suppose I was. But only until I got to Manchester. Then I was running as fast as I could away from Florian and Cavendish, and Henry. Once I'd broken free I'd never think of any of this again. In the dark of the tent I actually clutched my neck.

'Deer don't make dens,' Henry said, quietly.

'I know. We built it to watch them.'

I put Henry's jacket under my head. The wool was scratchy at first, like the blanket. But there was comfort in the gesture. In spite of myself, I drifted off and fell, fell, asleep.

Waking in the dark, I couldn't remember where I was.

I breathed short shallow breaths through my nose, trying not to give away my hiding place. Twigs snapped nearby, leaves rustled, an owl hooted and another replied. Closer still, someone breathed the long breaths of sleep.

Then I remembered. I hadn't escaped – that was a dream.

Disappointment, bitter and deep, replaced my fright. For a moment I'd believed myself free. I couldn't shake the thought, the dream had felt so real.

I listened to Henry's uneasy slumber. He murmured, then almost squeaked, and his elbow or fist nudged my arm through the drape he'd hung between us. But he slept on.

The cloak of darkness made me bold, too bold. The part of my mind that understood consequences didn't seem to have woken. I patted my clothing, checked my pockets and tapped my toes together. Fully dressed and booted. Even my knapsack was still strung across my chest.

Silently, I removed the small logs that held down the canvas of the tent. The chilly breeze flapped the sailcloth and Henry groaned. I paused. Henry didn't stir.

'Traitors Watch isn't for me,' I whispered. I rolled out of the tent.

32

Morris was my best bet. He was certain to be asleep again, despite his insistence otherwise. But his sentry post was on the other side of the camp.

Go around or go through?

Henry's tent was in the outer ring of the camp, though not on the very edge. The glow from the central fire was faint. But there could still be men awake there.

Moonlight beamed on and off as night clouds drifted and merged. Perhaps the moon was Maní after all, but like all the gods he made you earn your luck. The outline of the closest tents appeared for a few seconds. I memorised their positions. I decided to pick my way through the outer ring, concealing myself from the men on Traitors Watch until I reached Morris's post.

The silver light dimmed and I bent low, taking my first cautious steps towards the rough shelters. When Henry had brought me to his tent, the men who slept nearby had eyed me attentively. I didn't want to attract their kind of attention, not now, not anytime. I moved slowly, mindful of dry twigs.

The moon disappeared and I waited.

Someone snorted inside one of the tents, then began snoring. My eyes adjusted a little more to the dark.

I crept on.

Past the first cluster of tents, I paused again before a short stretch of open ground. If a sentry on Traitors Watch were awake, he'd see me dash across. The clouds glowed brighter and a sliver of the moon peeped out. I saw the sentry, and the sprawled figure of a man between me and the next tents. I tried to remember where the sprawled man was, and not panic about tripping over him or others I couldn't see.

The clouds swallowed the moon again. I flitted across the open ground, around the man and away from the sentry.

Here, I was much closer to the centre of the camp. Beside the fire, three or four figures were hunched. One of them stood up and began to walk. Around the fire at first, then several strides towards me, and back again. He said something to his fellows, then disappeared between the tents beyond the fire. Is he going to bed, or patrolling? I don't have time to wait and see. How long until Henry wakes to find I'm not there?

Before the man had a chance to patrol my side of the camp, I made my move.

Scuttling between and around tents, I dodged the barrels, sacks and other obstacles strewn around the camp. Behind an upturned barrow I rested, to gather myself for the last surge. Through a gap between tents I could see Morris's solid form against the feathery bracken fronds. Further round the perimeter Pike was humming to himself. Morris's other neighbour was a man I'd never seen, nor had the measure of. I'd have to pass as close to Morris as I dared.

The horses, tethered in the central clearing, whinnied. I listened for the bark of the dog Morris had mentioned, but heard none.

'Who's there?' called one of the men around the fire. 'Who's there?' he said again, coming closer.

'No one, you idiot. S'just the nags sniffing a wolf in t'woods,' a man shouted from somewhere near me.

'There en't no wolves. But I gotta check,' the first man said. 'Could be rustlers.'

'No one's gonna steal t'horses, man. You'd've heard 'em coming from t'trees. If you been awake, that is.'

'I'm awake and don't wanna be,' said a third man. 'Will youse shut up? Or we may as well all be keeping watch.'

The three of them bickered and others joined in. I heard Pike welcome the company and Morris's other neighbour holler curses. But nothing from Morris himself.

I fumbled on the ground and found a few small stones amongst the leaf litter. I gathered them in my hand.

In the tent next to me someone growled. A man emerged and stumbled to the bracken. There was the sound of water splashing on leaves.

'Aargh, you effing–' said Morris's neighbour.

'Thought you was begging for a drink? Huh, huh,' the man said, and lumbered back to his tent.

I waited until the man had crawled into bed. I waited some more, breathing slowly with the night breeze. Then, without standing up, I flung the handful of stones as far behind me as I could.

'What's that?' the first man yelled.

I dashed to the edge of the tents. With one last look at Morris's sleeping body, I shot across the border land and into the bracken.

'Rustlers!' the first man shouted from where I'd just been. 'Told youse.'

33

Through a grove of birches I ran, directed by their white peeling trunks. Onwards into the deep forest.

My first plan was to find the path we'd come in on. But wading through the undergrowth, hooking my feet on roots, vines and brambles, I knew I'd be lucky to find any path at all. My next plan was to head in a straight line away from the camp, for as long as my courage would allow, then climb a tree and wait until morning to find my way to the road.

After five, maybe ten, minutes, I brushed the thick trunk of a tree – beech or oak – and felt the wide ridges of its bark. I stopped. Here would do as anywhere. I didn't know if I was going in a straight line away from the camp. I could just as easily be circling.

I searched the girth of the trunk for boles, anything I could use as a foothold to explore higher up. There was one, about waist-height, slippery with lichen but flattish on top.

Stretching to reach the bole with my right foot, I pinched the ridged bark between my fingers. Slowly, I hoisted myself up to balance on the bole, clinging on with my right hand. I searched for a branch.

There was a low bough above my head. I nearly cried

out with relief. How lucky I'd been to sneak past Morris. And now I'd found a tree, the right tree.

I reached for the bough, felt along and across. It was too thick to grip with one hand. I'd have to grasp it with both at the same time, then swing my legs up, to hang upside down securely, then pull myself around the width of the bough to sit astride the top. I saw exactly how I'd do it.

Holding my left hand against the side of the bough, to keep it within my touch, I took a deep breath and pushed myself up off the knobbly ledge.

I caught the bough, but my hands were too far apart and the bark was damp. I tried to dig my fingernails in but I began to slip. Before I fell uncontrollably, I pushed against the trunk with my foot and jumped backwards into the undergrowth.

My landing was soft and I yelped quietly with joy. On the next attempt I knew I could do it. I faced the tree again, found good holds for both hands, stretched for the bole with my foot and…heard the undergrowth swish and crackle.

I froze, and waited. Nothing emerged. I put my weight on the bole and began to pull myself up. The rustling again, closer. Silently, I lowered myself to the ground. I hugged the tree and pressed my cheek to its rough skin, as if it would share its ancient wisdom. But I didn't need the tree to tell me the rustling was not a foraging badger, nor a rogue dog with Morris's eye in its belly, or any other four-legged beast. I hesitated no more.

Blundering through the undergrowth, I drowned out the man-sized noise with the sound of my own desperate crashing.

I heard a voice, getting nearer. I ran faster. Straight into a bramble thicket. I tried to retreat but my clothes, skin, hair and even my bootlaces were snagged. I twisted and wrenched, and fell further in. It was a fairytale thicket this.

Then the voice caught up with me. A hand grabbed my jacket and hauled me backwards to the ground.

'What're you doing, Lizzie? You'll get yourself killed.' Henry stood over me.

'Let me go,' I cried, jumping to my feet.

'I wasn't joking about who else is in these woods, you'll never get out on your own.'

'Then come with me!'

He missed a beat, then said, 'Don't say that out loud.'

'Then let me go.'

'Can't do that, Lizzie, you know I can't. Come back with me to the camp and no one will know.'

'What does it matter if they do?'

'Don't be stupid, this was the test.'

'What test? Oh.' I remembered Florian and Cavendish arguing on the roadside. Florian placating Cavendish with the promise that I'd be tested first. 'To see if I'd run?'

'Yes.'

'And I've failed?'

'Only if they find out. Come with me now and they never will. They need you, you're safest with them. Out here, alone, miles from the road...you won't be so lucky. Those that hunt, hunt at night too.'

'You're just trying to scare me. I'm not afraid to take my chances.'

'Your chances haven't been good so far.'

'I got past Morris.'

Henry said nothing.

My stomach chose that moment to growl. Henry blew out through his nose, almost a wry laugh. I waited for him to remind me that Morris was hopeless at keeping watch, that he wouldn't even notice the two of us re-entering the camp. But he didn't.

'How far would I get?' I said.

'Before you were caught by someone else?'

'No, before you shoot me down.'

'I'm not going to shoot you down,' Henry said.

'Then I'll run.'

'There are other ways to tame you, Lizzie, don't push your luck. Florian needs you.'

'And after I've done what he asks, he'll let me go?'

From Henry a sniff, and a long exhalation.

'Henry?' I said.

'I thought that once.'

Uneasily, I passed the next day in the camp, confined to Henry's tent and the patch of scrubby earth around it, with a different outlaw to watch me every few hours. To my relief, it seemed I was tedious sport. No one bothered me. They were all too busy with what had happened to Morris.

He'd been found dead at his post on Traitors Watch. The camp was in uproar, but none of the horses had been stolen, nor anything else disturbed. Florian and Cavendish were interrogating the men who'd been on watch around the fire. Everyone was baffled. But I wasn't.

When it came to Henry's turn to supervise me, the man who'd grilled Cavendish upon our arrival at the camp sauntered over.

'The lad's sick o' the sight o' you already,' the guard said. He pretended he was going to kick me, but sprayed dirt over me instead, and laughed.

34

We set out from camp the next day, in the small blue hours before dawn. Florian, Cavendish, Henry. Florian's man, Porter. Cavendish and Kit's man, Gaunt. And me.

Only nature spoke as we padded in single file along the forest path to the road. The still-dark trees shook with birds awakening. Blackbirds, robins and warblers sang raucously for the new day. As we approached the road, wings whooshed low over my head, followed by a baleful cry: an owl lamenting lost mice, perhaps. The bracken, nettles and foxgloves beyond the path twitched, and dry twigs snapped, as hidden creatures returned to their dens.

The forest was no longer eerie to me, as it'd been in the mist. The true danger marched with us, inescapable; the true danger was us.

When we reached the road we prepared the horses in silence – tightening saddle bags, lengthening reins, adjusting stirrups. Perhaps the others were adrift in thought as I was. I tried not to think of 'us' and 'we', but there was no other way to describe it. To an outside observer, we were together, of a single purpose.

On the inside, however, I was separate, going my own way. Maybe the others had their own motives and plans too, but watching Florian, Cavendish and their men I didn't think so. This morning there'd been no bickering nor joviality, only quiet determination.

And Henry? I didn't want to think about him at all. I knew he'd killed Morris, to cover up my escape.

Florian mounted the grey, Porter his own bony old nag. Cavendish and Gaunt climbed onto Cavendish's horse. Henry climbed atop Samson. I planted myself on the ground.

'No use being coy, Lizzie,' Florian said, 'you'll ride with Henry, naturally. You two have quite a bond.'

'Can't I ride with one of you?' I said, not quite believing I was saying it. 'Samson's too big for me.'

'Th'art holding us up now, lass,' said Cavendish. 'There's no time for flirting with thy lad.'

'Flirting?' I said, trying not to look at Henry. 'I've no time for romance when you're all conspiring to get me hanged.'

Florian roared with laughter. Even Cavendish appeared to chuckle, silently, his shoulders shaking.

'Enough banter. Let's get on with t'task. Get saddled up, Lizzie.' Cavendish kicked his horse into a walk and left us.

'Chop, chop,' Florian said, and clicked his tongue. His horse followed Cavendish's.

Reluctantly, I put my foot in Samson's stirrup. Henry reached down to pull me up.

'Get off,' I said, 'I'm perfectly able by myself.'

'I know you are,' Henry said. 'But I want to help.'

'Your help is poison,' I hissed.

'My help saved you,' he hissed back.

Warily, I took his arm and let him lift me onto Samson. Trying to settle in the saddle without touching Henry, I said, 'I haven't forgotten.'

183

Porter's decrepit horse set an unbearably slow pace for our party.

I wanted to arrive in Manchester in an instant, from here to there in the click of my fingers. Not plod heavily along the waking road, terrified something within me would snap and I'd blurt out my plan to abscond, just to relieve the uncertainty of whether I'd manage it or not.

Farmers driving carts laden with grain sacks, cabbages and mangelwurzels now trundled amongst us. Processions of people and donkeys going to market overtook us. Our dragging pace was intolerable.

I tried to distract myself with my plan for Manchester. But the problem of how I'd escape kept unfurling itself every which way like the tongues of a fern. For every answer, it seemed, you had to pay for your knowledge with at least five even more difficult questions. There was no end to them.

Astride Samson's sleek warm back, I began to wonder if the horse missed his former life, grazing innocently in a rich squire's paddock. If a horse is used for an illicit deed, can it ever go back to being an ordinary horse? Then I wondered why I was being so stupid as to contemplate this about a horse, when what I meant was: Can I go back to begin an ordinary person?

'How much longer?' I said.

Henry shrugged.

'Can we at least join the others up ahead?'

'We have to stick with Porter.'

'I'm going to shoot that tiresome nag,' I growled, 'with the pistol from your belt.'

'Don't do that.'

Henry's pistol was tapping my leg as we rode; it had such a pleasing weight. I'd never shot a pistol but I'd held a rifle once. I found myself picturing a scene in which I snatched the pistol from Henry's belt and blew a hole in the back of Florian's head, then Cavendish's, before anyone realised what was happening. I couldn't decide what to do about Porter and Gaunt, but I supposed they couldn't be left alive to seek revenge. In my mind's eye, Henry and I then galloped onward to Manchester and found my great-uncle, who promised to help us reclaim the mill from Robin.

Hold on. How did Henry wheedle his way into this picture? Henry was out.

I re-dreamed the vision without Henry in it, but it lost some of the heroic camaraderie.

It took me some time, plodding, plodding, to remember to be appalled at murdering two, maybe four, men in cold blood. And when I did remember, I found I wasn't as sickened as I should be.

A few miles out of Manchester we turned off onto a narrow trail. At the end was a small shack with a tin roof, which was bowed and dented as if someone had jumped up and down on it. Porter dismounted his horse. Gaunt dismounted from Cavendish's horse.

The two of them disappeared into the trees behind the shack. Then they returned, stumbling through the undergrowth with a cart. They hauled it down and up over a boggy ditch, cursing at one another.

They harnessed Porter's old horse to the cart. We set off again. Even more slowly.

'What's the cart for?' I whispered to Henry.

'Provisions maybe.'

'It's to put the...the girl in, isn't it? Is Florian going to take her back to the camp?'

'First question: Don't know. Second question: Still don't know.'

185

I turned to look at the cart behind us. 'And what's under the sacking? Chains? Or no, not more guns?'

'And again: don't know.'

'You never ask what's going on?' I said.

'Try not to.'

I was infuriated with Henry's refusal to ask the questions that were bursting out of me. I'd hardly slept and I felt irritable about everything. The lack of sleep had made me jittery, just when I needed to be at my most composed. I doubted my plan, my nerve to go through with it and my ability to keep up the pretence.

'For god's sake,' I said. 'You just sit around waiting to be told everything?'

'It works eventually.'

'Does it really?'

'Yes. Florian told me something this morning. He said, 'I'm right about Lizzie, she'll join us I'm sure.' '

'He said what?'

'You heard.'

'What does he mean?'

'Work it out for yourself,' Henry said.

This enraged me more than anything. What is it about me that makes Florian think this? I have to change it. And yet, in spite of my better self, I had to admit I was also a little bit flattered.

I said, 'He knows full well that I'm only helping him because...' – for a second I forgot why – 'because I need his help to get the mill back from Robin. Why would he think I'd ever join his gang?'

Henry sighed.

'I don't even know why I asked. Just because it's not your idea to kidnap this girl, Henry, doesn't mean you're innocent. Don't tell me you're only following orders. You've got a choice, you've *always* got a choice.'

He was quiet for a moment but I felt his back tense against me. Then he said, 'Remind me of that when we're done in Manchester. Tell me then about your choices.'

35

In the hard black heart of the city, we turned into the courtyard of a rundown inn.

A thick, undulating layer of horse droppings covered the cobbles. Ahead was the soot-stained brick inn, where several bedraggled men and women were loitering. To our left were the stables. And against the right-hand wall of the courtyard were some raised troughs of stunted and withered leaves.

'Is someone trying to grow vegetables here?' I said. 'You've got to admire their optimism. And prudent use of the dung.'

Everybody – Florian, Cavendish and Henry – laughed.

Uneasily, I laughed too. Only yesterday I was a captive, fearful for my life. Today my captors and I were sharing a joke. My joke. I wasn't sure if I was still a captive, or was becoming the volunteer Florian insisted I'd always been.

'Cavendish, you brute, what sort of place have you brought me to?' Florian circled the yard on his pretty grey, trying to find a dry spot on which to dismount. 'Do I look like a tosher to you?'

I glanced down, instinctively. He was referring to sewer-hunters – the bands of men who sifted refuse and sludge in the labyrinth of sewers beneath the streets, searching for coins, silver cutlery, bones and other scraps that could be cleaned and sold.

I reminded myself to keep an eye out for dropped things I could scavenge. I didn't know how long it would take me to reach my great-uncle in St Ann's Square. I thought it wise to earn my own money if I could.

Then a cry, from the sky or a high window, made me look up. But there was nothing to see in the yellow-grey sky above the courtyard, only the single blank cloud which smothered the whole city of Manchester.

This cloud had been drizzling upon us for hours. Millions of tiny water beads wobbled on the surface of my 'borrowed' jacket and breeches. I thought I was probably carrying five extra pounds in weight. And that was before I counted the burden of knowing about the kidnap plan, and of a man murdered on my account.

Manchester was Cavendish's home city.

At first, when we reached the city limits, he was tight-lipped and rode apart from the rest of us. To travel between the thoroughfares and busy shopping streets, he took us along shortcuts through quiet back streets and dingy passages.

Impressed at his command of the city layout, I'd asked, 'How do you know the routes so well?'

'Lived here all me life, lass. And before you think o' some joke about how I advised them Romans on building t'first roads, I'm only in me fourth decade. It were mostly as a lad o' about thy age that I got familiar with t'back routes.'

'A pickpocket, were you?' Florian said.

'Needs must.'

'Don't they always?' Florian sighed. 'Started on house-breaking myself. Family trade. Not much need for a naval fellow like my father after Boney got his island paradise.'

I supposed he meant his father couldn't find work after the wars with France ended, and our King didn't need so many men to serve on the warships. The French Emperor Napoleon was imprisoned on an island, for the second time, though this time he didn't escape.

Florian said, 'Then my old man, the fool, fell in love with a tavern wench, set up home on the same highway he used to rob. Ah, well, tis all over and done.' Then, with his usual nonchalance: 'Not everyone gets to swagger in at the top and skip all the hard graft, Lizzie.'

'Are you saying I should think myself lucky?' I said.

'Well, don't you?' Florian swept his arm to the sky, the dense smoggy cloud of coal-fired factory smoke and every other foul vapour imaginable.

'Paradise lost,' I said.

'Isn't it just.'

'This is me home th'art slandering,' Cavendish said, scratching at his unshaven face.

'At least you've got one,' said Florian.

I felt suddenly, hugely sad. I fought the urge to wallow.

Remembering something from Grandpa's library, and wanting to change the subject from that of home and not having one, I said, 'Are there two rivers that join here?' Roman settlements were often chosen for their navigational connections.

'There art,' said Cavendish, slowly, as if surprised. 'Th'ast an interest, lass?'

He didn't give me a chance to answer. He began to talk, taking us all by surprise. He knew so much; you wouldn't think it to look at him.

We clopped along chaotic thoroughfares of trolley buses, carriages and all manner of heavily-laden carts.

Pedestrians, seemingly with a wish to experiment with their luck, darted and weaved between the moving carriages.

In cramped neighbourhoods, women in shawls and headscarves spilled out of crumbling tenements, dragging little children onto the damp streets. We saw these children, here and there, scouring the gutters for pieces of coal.

And the backdrop to these frenetic scenes were the industrial buildings, bigger than any cathedral. I bristled to recall how Robin used to describe Manchester's factories with such irritating reverence.

These vast factories belonged to the rich men of Lancashire, the modern-day barons, who profited from this concentration of humanity and all its grubby misery. The factories were like the poet Blake's 'dark Satanic mills'. The chimneys, as cannons, fired poisonous vapour into the heavens. In a battle with whom? I wondered. The people of Manchester were surely losing.

'Which crime is it that'll be overlooked by the law?' I said quietly to Henry in the coaching inn's yard.

I was grimly amused by the name of the coaching inn in this slum of Angel Meadow. The sign was freshly painted and hung low over the doorway from an ornate iron arm. The Amnesty.

I nudged Henry, pointing to the sign, which depicted a poor man stealing an apple and a policeman smiling benignly. 'The crime we're going to commit tomorrow, or you lot holding me hostage?'

Henry took a sharp intake of breath. 'That's not funny.'

'Isn't it? Ooh, d'you think the sign's a bad omen?' I laughed. At myself, I think. Someone was mocking me, though I didn't quite know whom. 'Are we only safe while we're inside the inn?'

He turned in the saddle to look at me as he'd done when I'd quizzed him on the road out of Avandale. I thought he was going to deliver a similar speech, with the same bitter tone in his voice. It was the first time I'd studied his face in daylight. I'd expected a sullen, brooding face, but his skin was sun-browned and healthy. He had no one dominant feature; altogether it seemed a friendly face. Yet it was full of anger and resentment, directed at me.

He said, 'You think you've had a tough life, do you, Lizzie? Growing up with your grandmother who loves you. Reading your romances and re-enacting battles like you're a golden hero of old. Wandering the hills, building your dens in the woods, like you've nothing better to do than daydream about what a saviour you are, and how all the little people will cheer when you return to that stupid mill...'

Well, the bitter tone was the same. I didn't know what to say, and said so.

'Lost for words, Lizzie? First time for everything,' Florian said. 'Buck up, old chap, you'll have your own little people one day, when I'm grey or, ahem, gone...and you've got the run of the camp.'

Henry turned away and said, 'This's all a game to you, Lizzie.'

'A game?' I said. 'I don't think this a game–'

Cavendish dismounted into the squelch of manure. The sound of it arrested me. I leaned over in the saddle to peer at the quagmire of horse doings. Samson tensed in reaction to my imbalance.

On the ground, bits of hay – softened and split on their way through horses' innards – stuck out of the grassy, pungent mush. The squelch of it, the thick soupiness...with a shudder and a daft giggle, I recalled the boggy moor of home, across which I'd fled to Avandale.

There was something about that chase I'd enjoyed, I was ashamed to admit. Not enjoyed exactly. A cold thrill, perhaps.

When I'd fought the dog on the moor, that thrill had spiralled into a dizziness, a sort of delirium. Watching the dog suffocate while I breathed the full breaths of life, I'd felt a strange power, as if the dog's strength and viciousness had left him and entered me. At that moment, I felt I could do anything.

With a jolt, I remembered how much I'd enjoyed defeating Sir Tarquin in the contest. I'd entered to win the money but also…I had actually enjoyed the test, the puzzle of how to beat the giant.

Is this what Henry means by 'game'? Saving the mill from Robin, and reforming his practices, is my purpose. But does Henry think I'm also a little bit, dangerously, in love with the struggle itself?

'Enough squabbling,' said Cavendish, taking Samson's reins. 'If either of youse falter, or risk t'mission, there's a game I'll play with thou.'

'It's not by any chance, target practice?' I said.

Cavendish grinned for the first time since I'd met him. I knew he had some teeth missing, I'd seen the gaps when he talked, but I'd never noticed how jagged they were. With his mouth stretched in a smile it looked as if some teeth had been deliberately chiselled to a point.

He went on grinning. I kept staring. I couldn't help it. Those shark teeth were so perturbing. I imagined him tearing raw flesh with them.

I realised I'd become too comfortable in his, and their, company. If I didn't wake up, be alert to what was really happening, it would cost me.

Behind me, Florian's horse was prancing on the spot. Florian said, 'This is absurd. Henry, get the stable boy to lay down some boards.'

'I'll go,' I said, sliding down off Samson. I plopped ankle-deep into the manure.

This was my chance. Start by investigating the stables for other exits to the surrounding streets. I hoped to abscond tonight.

The manure sucked at my boots as I glooped to the stables. On another occasion I would have enjoyed this sensation, but Cavendish's grin had shaken me.

Escape was urgent, none of this was a game. These men wanted me to help kidnap a girl. If I didn't, they'd kill me, no matter that they'd laughed at my jokes. And if I did help them, they'd hold this secret over me and I'd have to live outside the law forever, like Henry.

The name of the inn wasn't funny at all. No sheriff or judge would hold an amnesty for kidnappers.

36

The stables were surprisingly clean.

I took a few steps inside, then looked back at the mess of my footsteps – swampy islands amid the curls of fresh wood, which were so reminiscent of the birch shavings of the mill, where the clean fresh smell made everything seem new, and everything possible. And so very far away.

'Think I've nothing berrer to do than slop out after the likes o' you,' said a boy.

He backed out from a stall, bent double, raking with a large pitchfork. He stood and shook the rake's prongs at me and…oh, it was a girl.

She wore a floppy cap and I couldn't see her hair, only that it was brown, from the wisps curled below her ears. Her face was pale, with blotchy freckles all over. She was dressed in black breeches and a burgundy velveteen coat too big for her, with a stiff dirty apron over the top. She was probably about twelve or thirteen.

'Sorry,' I said, 'but there's no way to avoid the muck.'

'Yard's not mine. Only t'stables.'

'Right. Well, the guv'nor out there wants some boards laying down. You got anything I can use?' While she paused to consider this, I leapt to her side and said, 'Do you know St Ann's Square?'

'What?'

'St Ann's Square. Shh. Do you know it? Yes or no?'

She frowned and leaned the fork of the rake towards me. I sidestepped the prongs. She said slowly, 'Yeaah, I know it.'

'Where is it? Tell me quick.'

She pursed her lips and chewed the inside of her mouth. She scrutinised my face. Then she looked off to the side and began making movements with her free hand, as if cutting an invisible cake into quarters. She closed her eyes and snaked her hand side to side, then pointed with one finger, left, right, left. She opened her eyes and scratched at her collar, pulling a nest of straw from beneath it.

'Nope,' she said. 'I can't describe it, can only show you. My legs know it, but innkeep don't like my legs taking me places farther than t'scullery no more.'

I thought for a moment. 'What if I can persuade the innkeep to send you on an errand somewhere? Could you show me then?'

'Pah. Damn 'keep will know you're up to sommat straight off, and think me part o' it. You are up to sommat?'

'No. I mean, I need to–'

She began violently raking the straw between us, scraping the metal prongs over the hard ground. I flinched at the sound. She flung straw over my boots, where it stuck to the wet manure.

'What's it you want, lad?' she said loudly.

I span around. The opening to the yard was dazzling against the dimness of the stable. I saw no one there.

'You bringing them nags in, or what?' said the girl.

'The guv'nor out there,' said Henry, repeating my words exactly, 'wants some boards laying down. You got anything–'

'S'what this one just asked,' – the girl flashed me a wide-eyed look – 'and I've not had a chance to consider it yet. Are there any more o' youse to pester me before I get looking?'

'Just us,' Henry said in a flat tone, his face hidden in shadow. He came further into the stables.

He must have heard me ask about St Ann's Square. Had he repeated my exact words to warn me that someone would hear? Or to threaten me? He'd guess I had a new plan to escape. But he'd be mad to cover for me again, as in the forest. What had he to gain from risking himself for me?

'Come on then,' said the stable girl. 'The two o' youse are gonna carry them boards out, if I can find any knackered thing to use.'

I followed her, nervously, with Henry at my back.

At the far end of the stables, she said, 'Hold this,' and thrust the rake at me. I took it. She began to rummage behind crates and under coils of thick rope.

I wanted to know what Henry was doing behind me, so I turned and walked the length of the stalls, poking at bundles of straw with the rake, trying to appear casual.

Henry wasn't doing anything. I don't know what I was expecting – to discover his true intentions in his expression, or by his movements? Instead the stabled horses made me wonder how things were at night. Half the stalls were occupied with tired-looking horses, nothing like Samson, or Florian's grey.

'Sleep out here, do you?' I said, returning. 'Only our horses are finer than these old mules. The guv'nor will want to know there'll be no rustling of his horses while he's a-kip.'

'Dontcha even...' The girl stood and glared at me, furious.

197

'Sorry. It's not that I don't trust you or anything, just that, you know, the state of the yard and the inn...it all looks a bit, well...'

'We don't like too many visitors here,' she said, conspiratorially. She grinned like a wicked imp. 'Ah, now I remember.' She bounded into the final stall, and reappeared dragging a rough, splintered plank, then went back for another. 'These'll do for your precious prince, will they?'

'Yes, thanks.'

'Good. And when you come back for your nags, don't ask for no one but Theo. That's me. Before you ask, it's short for Theodora, but if you call me Dora, you'll find yourself face down in t'yard, fighting for your last breaths, gobbling muck like it's smash potater. Aw right?'

Henry and I nodded.

'Right-choo are,' Theo said. 'Got some rags too, if your Supreme Highness out there wants his dainty slippers buffed.' She went off to raid a barrel.

Out of the corner of my eye I saw Henry staring at me. Theo scrabbled in the barrel, leaning further and further in. Her top half disappeared into the cask, which began to teeter. I glanced at Henry, trying not to laugh. He smiled.

It was a genuine smile, of that I was sure. But was it one of amusement at Theo-not-Dora? Or to let me know my secret was safe with him? I owed him double now.

37

I hoped to find Theo that evening – to ask if she could draw the route to St Ann's Square, or whether she knew another landmark nearby.

Downstairs in The Amnesty's tavern, Cavendish showed Henry and me to a table in the centre of the noisy room.

'Stay put, both o' youse,' he said. 'And while we get our work done, don't draw no attention to thyselves.'

I drew a rickety chair a short way back from the table so as not to bump anyone, and slid onto the rough wooden seat. 'What is this place?'

'A meeting place for like minds, lass, that's all thou need to know.'

'Like yours or like mine?'

'They're one and t'same, art they not, Lizzie?'

I didn't want to reply. Instead, I began idly scratching my thumbnail across the wooden tabletop, which was soft with soaked-in beer.

'Thy initials and his, nowt else. No secret messages,' Cavendish said.

I looked up at him in surprise. 'Initials? Why would I do that?'

'Why indeed?' Slapping Henry on the arm, he laughed.

I had to look away. To my relief, there across the packed room was Florian. He picked his way towards us through people and tables and thrust-out chairs. He hesitated where he'd have to brush bottoms or bellies to squeeze through. I watched him hold his breath more than once. The smell of people's woollen clothing drying slowly gave the tavern a farmyard whiff. Pipe smoke, stale sweat and braising meat added to the heady scent.

There was a sort of animal comfort here, until you looked more closely at the women and men: how their eyes were never still; how they constantly shifted position, standing up, sitting down, standing up again, as if preparing for a quick getaway.

Florian reached us. He set his shoulders square and held his chin high. Cavendish pressed his thin, whiskery lips inwards, but he couldn't hide the upwards turn of his mouth. I knew he'd deliberately chosen a table in the centre of the room in order to perturb Florian.

'Unsavoury bunch, t'Amnesty lot,' Cavendish said.

'I'm quite at home, thank you, Cavendish,' Florian said. 'Quite at home. Let's go then. You two stay here.'

'But not *here*,' Henry said. 'It makes me uneasy not being able to see what's going on. I'd prefer to sit with my back against the wall.'

'Wouldya now?' Cavendish said. 'Makes sense, th'art Florid's boy after all.'

'I'll thank you kindly to not call me that.'

'Well, I'll not be seen with a 'Florian' in a place like this. How'd thou get such a name?'

'Same way everyone gets their name.'

'Seriously, man? Seriously? That's thy born and baptised name? Takes all folk, I s'pose.'

'Has this some relevance, Cavendish, to our mission?'

'Nah, man, nah. Just don't be Florid while th'art here.'

'Florian.'

'Him neither.'

'Am I still Lizzie?' I said.

'What sort of stupid question is that?' Florian said.

'Just asking, you know. So I'm playing my part properly. So you don't have a reason to go back on your promise to me.'

Florian looked up to the smoke-filled corner of the room, as if he might locate the promise there, some pesky flying creature that had slipped his grasp.

'Her uncle's mill,' Henry said.

Florian thrust his finger in the air and nodded.

I knew he'd never mean to help me. 'My mill. And am I still Lizzie?'

'For today, Lizzie lass, aye,' said Cavendish. 'But tomorrer thou'll become someone else. Go sit yerself over there by t'wall then, lad, if th'art worried about a knife in thy back. Me and me man Florid've got our preparations to make.'

'*Thank* you, Cavendish. If my name's too much trouble, you can call me Chief.'

Cavendish smirked, and twitched his flattened nose. 'Th'art not a chief here, man.'

'What do you mean by that, dear Cavendish?'

'This's a working man's place.'

'And?'

'Like a Guild?' I said.

'Nah, not quite,' Cavendish said. 'Them factories are too big for guilds to be of any use. And course, guilds are only for skilled menfolk, and many o' t'workers in Manchester are kiddies and wenches. But someday, maybe. There's plenty o' folk working toward it. Th'ast a keen eye though, Lizzie, lass.'

'Enough of the wistful longing, Cavendish. We've a job

to do.' To Henry he said, 'Don't let her out of your sight. Anything she does, you're responsible for. And that goes for whether she breaks a plate or takes a man's eye out with a spoon. If there's a cost, Henry, you're paying. As you're already heavily indebted to me, I'll–'

' '–let you imagine how payment will be extracted', ' said Henry. 'Understood.'

'And don't talk to no one else.'

'They're my attendants, Cavendish,' Florian said. 'They can talk to whom they like.'

'Don't care whose flunkeys they are, tis my town.'

'What if someone talks to us?' I said.

'Tell them th'art with me. Anyone here'll know what that means.

'What does it mean?' I said to Henry, once Cavendish and Florian had gone. 'That we're with Cavendish.'

'Ask if you want, but the message is clear to me.'

'Course it is. Sit down, shut up, look the other way.'

We sat in tense silence with our backs against the wall.

Then Henry said, 'What's so special about the bobbin mill that you're willing go along with all of this?'

'Why do you care?'

'I want to know why it means so much to you. What it's like to care about something. As much as you do,' he added, quickly.

'Oh, what does it matter?' I said to some higher being that ought to have been watching over me, but evidently wasn't. Henry could get me killed if he wanted, and what would my tale be worth then? 'It's only everything. My whole life,' I said.

'But if the mill's not yours, and never has been, how can it be your whole life?'

He had a point – there was some truth in this. Tom had said the same thing to me once, but I hadn't wanted to hear it. I didn't speak to him for a week.

I began kneading my knuckles, popping and cracking them in the way Gran hated.

I said, 'I suppose it's the not having it that makes it important. It was taken away from me before I was born, but the mill still exists in reality. I see it– saw it, every day. Everything in Fairy Cross centres around the mill, everyone's jobs, everyone's gossip. I have to think about it all the time.'

'But why? Who cares what everyone else is talking about?'

'You wanted the truth, Henry,' I said, 'and the truth isn't straightforward, it's not just about me.'

'And?'

'And what?'

'You haven't answered properly yet.'

'I think I'd rather you told Florian I tried to escape.'

'You really don't,' Henry said.

'Alright. I suppose by *not* having the mill, it's all I can think about. That sounds stupid, I know.'

'Very.'

'Have it your way, Henry. Yes, I'm stupid. But it's still what I think. The mill's at the centre of my thoughts every day and every night. Like being starving hungry, perhaps. All you can think about is food because you haven't got any. It's sort of like…there's a space in my life where the mill should be and…that hole is so huge it casts a shadow over everything else.'

I'd never told a stranger so much about myself before. But maybe Henry wasn't a stranger anymore.

'Like with your parents?'

'How have you gone from the person who asks no

questions, to the one who asks the most difficult questions of all?' I tried to laugh, but I was near tears.

'I just want to know. That you're in earnest. That you won't lie to me, even if you're lying to the others.'

Discomfited by his plain speaking, I said, quietly, 'You want to know who I am, and if you can trust me?'

'I just want to know. That's all,' he said, irritation in his voice again.

I thought about what to tell him. Trust was a thing that formed over years and years of knowing a person, of that I was sure. Like with Tom. Years of sharing confidences, experiences and hardships. A thing you had to earn, and work always to maintain. Fixed to a place, and bound by your family's ties, interwoven. Not something that could spring up in a few days, no matter that it was born of desperation. Confusing big feelings, in a short space of time, for something deep and true.

When I was little, I'd asked Gran lots of questions. She told me stories of my father as a boy – how he used to build dens in the woods and go tramping across the fells, always late home for supper and sometimes not returning until breakfast. But she never worried, she knew he could look after himself and that's why we shouldn't worry about where he was now, he'd be alright.

I believed her then, when I was six, seven and eight. Then I began to doubt. How could you know something with such certainty when you could never prove it?

Growing older, I stopped asking Gran what my father was like, at age ten, twelve, fourteen, and what she knew of my mother, fixed forever at eighteen. I don't know why. I think I was afraid I'd discover I was like them.

In all these years, why had my father never written to Gran, and found out about me? He may well be alright, wherever he was. But he'd never know whether I was alright. And when I wasn't. Was I like him at all?

Or was I like my mother, who died giving birth to me? Perhaps she'd been weak in her heart or in her blood. I only wanted to think of myself as strong.

Through the mill, I sought my father, in a way. My connection with my mother had always been adrift because there was nothing of her in Fairy Cross. The promise of finding my great-uncle in Manchester was becoming strong now I was so close. This great-uncle was my grandfather's youngest brother. My mother's uncle, who'd known her as a girl growing up in Bath.

'Is this a trap?' I said.

'Why would I need to trap you?'

'Can you miss what's already missing?' I said.

'Don't know what that means.'

'I miss the mill even though it's never been mine. Maybe it's everything to me, or maybe it's nothing and I've been aiming in the wrong direction all these years. Maybe I have to let it go.'

'Not before tomorrow,' Henry said. 'You have to do what Florian wants first.'

'Right, yes, of course.' For a while I'd forgotten Henry was here to watch me, not be my friend.

It was getting late now. The innkeep's girl was snuffing out the wall lamps, though no one seemed to be taking the hint; the tavern was busier than ever. I felt all those darting eyes were watching me now.

How would I ever get away tonight? How would I get away tomorrow, with the others watching me too? For the first time I began to consider that I might actually have to go through with Florian's plan. I couldn't go back after I'd done what he asked, back to being an innocent person. If that's what I was now.

Was I weak in my heart and my bloodline? It wasn't

usual for a lakeland girl to fall in with a gang of highway-men, plotting to kidnap a rich young lady. But here I was. There must be a reason for it.

'What trades can a man learn in the lakelands?' Henry said. 'Beside bobbins.'

'What?'

'Trades. In the lakelands.'

'Loads.'

'Like what?'

Wearily, I said, 'There's wood-coppicing, or saw-milling...um, er...mining, for all sorts of stones and metals, but it's dangerous underground. Or there's quicklime-making, but you'll get nasty burns. There's also–'

'And what about the books in your Grandpa's library? Has he something on draughtsmanship?'

'Er, maybe. Never looked.'

'Or anything on steam locomotives or modern navigational instruments...I heard about those in the shipyard.'

'Yes, I think so,' I said, though I knew there wasn't. 'And plenty on ship design and how the, er–' I didn't know anything about this but my mind was racing, wondering why Henry was so keen to know, '–shape of the, um...'

Henry was watching me sternly. 'Don't pretend you know what you're talking about.'

'I don't know anything, I really don't,' I said, despair getting the better of me at last. 'Don't know what I'm doing here, don't know what you want from me, I don't know–'

How I'm going to get away.

I took a deep breath to stop myself from crying, then said, 'I used to think Grandpa William's library contained the whole world. But the world out here... It feels like I'll never get back to Fairy Cross. But where will I go instead? And what does it matter anyway, Florian's just using me to get what he wants, I never believed for a minute that he'd really help me–' I cut myself short.

'You're right not to trust Florian…' Henry said.

I expected him to tell me again I had to go through with tomorrow's plan anyway.

But he continued: 'You have to do what you must, to get what you want. And you do know what you want, don't you? Like I do.'

I began to sweat in my jacket. My mouth felt as if a desert wind had blown in; my tongue stuck to the back of my teeth. I remembered his odd way of talking that night in the tent, the emphasis on Kit and Cavendish being an *alliance, trusting* each other, *bound* together. Who was he really talking about? And what's he saying now? He's not, in his roundabout way – is he? – saying that he wants to come with me to Fairy Cross?

I stood up, clumsily. 'I have to go to the privy.'

My stomach churned, I thought I was going to be sick. I realised I did want him to come with me to Fairy Cross, I didn't want to do it all alone. With Henry's help I could escape Florian and Cavendish, find my great-uncle, confront Robin.

But to tell Henry my plan risked everything.

'The privy,' I said again, like a buffoon, trying to untangle my feet from where they'd hooked around the chair legs. I stumbled beside the table and Henry got up to help me.

'Alright?' he said.

'Yes. Er, just hungry. Makes my head go funny.'

'Better ask in the kitchen if they've got any bread while we wait. Florid will pay. Or…' he said, and paused. His hand was clammy on my mine, and he gripped it so tightly the tips of my fingers began to pulse with trapped blood. He said, 'Maybe that girl from the stables can get us some.'

There was no mistaking it now. He'd heard me ask Theo about St Ann's Square and guessed I had an escape plan. But there was no need to ask her to get us something to eat.

He let go of my arm and sat back down.

'Aren't you, uh, coming with me?' I said. 'Being responsible for everything I do. In case I, you know, accidentally spoon out a man's eye?'

'To wait beside the privy? No, thanks. I trust you. And,' he called after me, 'be sure to ask Theo-not-Dora for what you need.'

38

Something was being thrashed in the stables. A whip cracked, and someone cried out.

I lingered outside, listening for other voices. Heard none. The whip snapped again. I crept in.

It was dark except for an orange glow from the far stall. I sidled along the closed stalls. The straw on the ground rustled beneath my boots and a horse whinnied as I passed its stall. A long face appeared over the stable door: Samson. I padded back to him.

'Sh, sh, shhh, Samson,' I said, stroking his nose. He nuzzled my hand; the warm air from his cavernous nostrils tickled my skin.

'Aie-yah!'

The cry came from the final stall. I sprang away from Samson with the surprise. He thumped the ground with his great hooves. Another horse whinnied and something else shifted in the straw.

'Aie-yah. Aie-yah. Aaaiiiie-yah!'

It sounded like Theo. Angry, but not like she was being beaten herself.

I tiptoed the last ten yards to the final stall. I peeped round the open door.

The stall was empty except Theo herself. In the amber

light she was leaping and lunging with her whip, thrashing a saddle slung over a workbench.

'Oh, thank god,' I said.

She whirled around as I spoke, and raised the handle of the whip above her head. The long tail circled towards me, but I lost sight of the end in the low light. I ducked anyway. The leather tip snarled around the doorpost just above my head.

'Whoa,' I said.

'*You.*' Theo tugged on the whip once, twice, to release it from the post. 'I oughta–'

'Watch what you're doing with that.'

She gathered the tail of the whip, folding it from her left hand to her right, in which she held the handle. She looked like she was getting ready to strike again.

I jumped out of the stall and behind the partition. 'What did that saddle ever do to you?' I said.

'Not half've what you done.'

The whip slapped on the thick hide of the saddle.

I poked my head round the door. 'What *I've* done?'

'Yes, you!' Theo raised the whip once more, then stopped. 'Urraarrggh.' She turned and flung her weapon against the back wall of the stall, where, in the moment of contact, it appeared to me as a snake. She dipped down to her boot and jabbed her hand inside. She stood up and held aloft a short dagger.

'Theo...?' I stepped slowly backwards.

She charged at the saddle and plunged her dagger into the seat; she sawed and chopped frantically through the leather. The stuffing burst out. Then she did it again cross-wise, and left the knife stuck in. She flopped backwards onto a pile of hay. 'Damn you to wherever's worse than hell.'

'Are you done?'

'Never.' She punched her fists deep into the hay, and threw handfuls in the air. 'Pth, pth, pth,' she said, as hay and dust fell upon her face.

'Whose saddle is that?'

'Me father's.'

'I see.'

'No, you don't, you wou'nt be here if you did. But you come here cos you want my help, dontcha? Directions to some secret place or sommat. I got what you want, and you got what I want.'

'What have I got, Theo?'

'Don't call me that. S'a stupid name.' She began to dig the hay out from underneath herself. She sank gradually into the hole until her knees drew up to her chest.

I went to sit beside her on the hay. 'No, it's not. It's a good name, it's your name.'

'He thinks it's stupid,' she said, from deep within the hay.

'Who, your father?'

She tried to nod, then scratched at her neck like dog at a flea.

I said, 'Well, he doesn't get to decide what you call yourself now you're…'

'Twelve.'

'Yep, now you're twelve, or any other age. Theo–'

'You're not gonna tell me how things were when you were twelve?'

I laughed. 'No. I was going to ask what you think I have that you want so badly.'

She scrabbled out of her burrow and rolled onto her front, kicking a bundle of hay onto me. She put her face in her hands.

'I don't have anything, you know, nothing,' I said. 'Only these clothes, they're not even mine,' – the ill-fitting

211

cast-offs of someone in the camp who'd, ahem, died – 'and the things in my knapsack– Oh, no, you don't mean… Henry? He's not mine.'

'Who?' she said, turning face up. Even in the dim light I could see tears had washed stripes down her grubby cheeks.

'Henry.'

'Don't know him.'

'Who I arrived with.'

'That gloomy beggar? Nah. You got my job.'

I looked around the stall. 'Your job?'

'Tomorrow, you dunce. That rich girl–'

'You know about that?'

'Course I do, it was my idea. *He* stole it and cut me out.'

'Who did?'

'Me father.'

Florian? No. Henry said the plan was Kit and–
Cautiously I said, 'Cavendish is your father?'

'When it suits him,' Theo said.

I sank back into the hay to enjoy a small moment of relief, and to think.

'Did you tell your father what I asked you earlier?' I said.

'Course not. But then I found out who you were–'

'And did you tell him then, or anyone?'

'Nope. I gotta keep sommat for meself. That's how I'll get into their gang. They gotta *need* me or I won't be allowed to join.'

Ideas swam into my mind, slippery like eels, but with definite shapes. Theo was angry and upset, maybe she even thought she hated Cavendish. But that didn't mean she'd betray her own father for me. She'd kept my secret so far, however. The kidnap was to take place tomorrow. I didn't need her for long.

I took a deep breath and said, 'Can I trust you, Theo?'

'What sorta idiot question is that? You only met me today.' She giggled.

I laughed nervously with her, to dampen my urge to run, run now, run anywhere, before Henry came looking for me. But the recollection of Pope and Shaw catching me in Avandale made me shudder. This was Cavendish's home city. He knew these streets, and probably the street lurkers on every corner – pickpockets, tricksters and every other type of rogue. He'd be waiting for me in St Ann's Square long before I found my way. If I found my way, before the shysters found me.

Running was a bad idea. Was there another way?

I said, 'Theo, do you want to come with us tomorrow? I need your help. I don't know how I'll be able to lure this rich girl out onto the street for Florian to snatch. I mean, why would she go with me? Perhaps...I don't know...maybe you could create a disturbance in the shop or something.'

'A disturbance?' Theo tried to jump out of the hay, but the loose pile gave her nothing to push against; her hands sank further in. She reached for my leg, and clawed her way up my thigh as she pushed herself up.

'Yes, I don't know what. Knock over a hat display, shout some nonsense words, something to unsettle people. And then I– I could sort of come to the girl's rescue, possibly. I don't know if that would work, but there needs to be a good reason why she'd step out of the shop with me. I can't do it with small talk alone.'

'But he'll never let me,' she said. 'He cut me outta my own idea, he'll never let me come.'

'No, but he doesn't have to. You know where we're going?'

'If it's Holland Arcade, like I told him, then yeah. Is it?'

'I don't know, they won't tell me. But I guess it must be. Can you get yourself there anyway? Set off when we do, but go another way to keep out of sight. Then when you arrive, say you followed. And I'll have already started showing my nerves, saying I can't do it.'

'Then I'll turn up and tell him what's what. I done all the hard work coming up with t'idea, not Annie. S'me who should be part o'r it.'

Theo reached for my hand and pulled me up off the hay. She set her face in a determined expression, but her mouth was quivering ever so slightly. She looked like she might hug me. But she dropped my hand and turned away. She went over to the saddle she'd destroyed and drew the dagger from the stuffing. She slid the dagger into its holder inside her boot.

'I don't go nowhere on the streets without this.'

A horrible feeling came over me. A premonition of tomorrow, but not in picture-form – it was a physical sensation, a reaction to events gone wrong.

What would Theo do with her knife? Because it wasn't a disturbance in the shop I needed her for, but the confusion when she turned up unexpectedly. There'd be an argument between her and Cavendish, and Florian wouldn't be able to keep himself out of it. It was this distraction I hoped would give me the moment to slip away.

And Henry? I couldn't risk telling him anything beforehand. If he truly wanted to escape with me, he'd be watching closely. I'd have to rely upon him seizing his own opportunity.

'I ought to get back inside, Theo. A harmless disturbance in the shop, that's all. It'll be enough, no need for–'

'I know what I'm doing,' she said bossily. 'S'been my

214

idea all along.'

I felt annoyed at her manner. Then I felt guilty. The person to most benefit from this new plan was me. I was using Theo as Florian and Cavendish were using me. As I'd used the Gunpowder contender, Lewis, in Avandale. No matter how many times I told myself I'd done Lewis a favour by taking his place in the Sir Tarquin contest, I still felt deceitful. There seemed to be no way to win, without also compromising myself.

For the first time I began to wonder what this rich girl, the banker's daughter, was really like. It was the first time I allowed myself to think of her as a real person. She was called Isabella Astley. In my mind she was a silly, giggly dimwit, like my cousins, Milly, Sophia and Harriet. Girls who'd grow up to be like my aunts and great-aunts, who sat on their squishy bottoms all day, sniping and snarking at one another over their embroidery because they had nothing better to do.

Only Gran was different. And an outsider because of it. As was I. So, if I was an outsider before I was even born, I'd reasoned, then I might as well do something to deserve it.

When the mill was mine, I intended to put Milly and Sophia and Harriet, and all the useless aunts, to work. See how they liked twelve hours a day on their feet, six days a week, breathing sawdust until they could barely breathe at all, perhaps losing a finger or an eye when the gouging tool hit a knot in the wood and the machine span out of control. It was only what they deserved, living off other people's hard work and suffering, while all they could do was complain about the wet, windy weather of the lakelands that filled the rivers and nourished the trees, and made their easy life possible.

If the rich girl was anything like them, then it wouldn't

do her any harm to be shaken up a bit by someone like Theo. Maybe a quick brush with Florian or Cavendish would open her eyes to the world a little, before she was whisked away by her chaperone–

I caught myself in the midst of this vision. When did I become so nasty and resentful? No one deserved to be frightened just to teach them a lesson, nor held hostage, even for a short time. I should know.

The best thing was for Cavendish to call off the kidnap once Theo arrived, and I'd gone. What they did after that, well, that wasn't my responsibility, was it? When I found my great-uncle I'd tell him about the plot and let him decide what to do.

'See you tomorrow, then,' I said to Theo. But she wasn't listening anymore.

She was examining the ruined saddle, muttering, 'I'll say it got caught on a nail and when I tried to free t'blasted thing it stuck on another. That's it. Or, some oaf from t'tavern stumbled in to saddle up and got wrong one, then dropped it on his spurs and ripped it. Or–'

'Tomorrow, Theo.'

She waved her hand over the back of her head.

I left the stables and crossed the boggy yard to return quickly to Henry in the tavern, to show him his trust in me was well-founded. How would things work out for him tomorrow? If I got an opportunity to run, would he have a chance to follow? Was he really with me?

There were no answers to be found in the dark yard, and I felt even less ready to face Henry. I knew I had to ask him about Morris. I guessed the poor man had been awake when I slipped past him, and for doing his 'job' properly he had to die. Henry needed me if he were to escape Florian too, or so he thought. I saw that now.

I'd have to confront Henry sooner rather than later. But

not tonight. There was too much else to contend with.

I went over to the raised troughs. With my fingernail, I dug away the earth at the base of some sorry-looking leaves and revealed a small pale root. It could have been a misshapen potato or some kind of beet.

When we'd arrived, I believed this attempt to grow something in the city was a sign of optimism. But it could just as easily be a sign that nothing flourished here, that everything was stunted, misshapen, doomed.

I just wanted to go home. My courage in my plan was faltering. Could I save myself, and give Henry a chance too? It seemed a lot to hope for.

39

On the fated morning, Florian, Cavendish and I were hunched at a table in The Amnesty's tavern, eating stale bread and drinking tea that looked as if it had been ladled directly out of the filthy river. I missed my usual fortifying oats, but no one ate porridge in the city.

Candles lit the tavern, though the sun, if had been visible through the heavy fog, had risen hours ago. The brown fog had seeped into the tavern too, giving everything a hazy, dreamy look.

I was wide awake, however, nauseated with fear. I hadn't yet seen Theo, and I was already panicking that she wouldn't turn up at Holland Arcade. Or she would arrive and create such a disturbance we'd all get arrested. Or, she'd already told Cavendish my plan, and once we were in a dark alley he'd shoot me in the eyeball. And all the other three hundred things that could possibly go wrong.

Henry arrived and plonked himself glumly on a chair. He had a black eye.

'What happened?' I said. I'd slept alone, locked in a windowless cupboard room, with a chipped milk jug for my extremely awkward chamber pot. Florian and Cavendish had shared a small room, with Henry in the cheap bunkroom in the attic.

'Snoring, were you?' Florian chortled.

'I don't snore,' Henry said. He patted his shiny swollen eyelid. 'Oo-ph.' He blew out through pursed lips.

I tried to catch his other eye but he was too preoccupied with the bad one. We'd had no time alone since I'd spoken to Theo in the stables. I don't know what I hoped to establish by glancing into a single flecked iris, but even that tiny connection would give me some courage.

'Must have been something you said.' Florian slapped him on the back.

'But I didn't speak to anyone, only the man whose bed I had to share. Asked if he could put his shirt back on because the blanket was too narrow to tuck between us.'

Cavendish coughed and spluttered. A piece of chewed bread landed, splat, on the table between us. He coughed again and laughed. He slammed his palm flat on the table. 'Thou asked him to put his shirt on? Put it back on?'

'Why's that so funny?' Henry said.

'Put his shirt *on*.' Cavendish managed to stop laughing for a moment. 'Th'art supposed to take thy shirt off. And trousers. T'lot. Sleep in thy skin suit.'

'Naked? Next to a stranger?'

'Course. In those rags o' thine he'd have thought thou were from out o' town, from t'country.'

'But I am.'

'And thou've got lice. They're everywhere in folks' clothes and bed linen. In t'bunk rooms th'art supposed to take off thy clothes and wrap 'em up under thy bed, so thou don't pick up lice that's brought in by country folk.'

'He thought I had lice?'

'Well, thou do now.'

'And a black eye to boot.' Florian laughed. 'Not your morning, old chap.'

'Told youse,' Cavendish said triumphantly. 'Thou can

get anything thou want in Angel Meadow, anything at all.'

'Even a punch in the eye before bed?' Henry said.

'Lucky that's all thou got. But t'lice are for free.'

Henry flicked invisible somethings from his coat sleeves and trouser legs. He fidgeted in his chair. He stood up and went to the window. He began examining the stiff elbow creases of his coat, scratched his neck violently, then leapt upon his own foot and wrenched off his boot and sock.

'Give it over, lad, and eat up,' Cavendish said. 'Got thy costume-fitting soon, and then we're off.'

This slum of Angel Meadow was where Cavendish had grown up. Only a hundred years ago the slum had been an actual meadow. Merchants and artisans built grand houses in the fields, planting formal gardens and orchards.

Wealthy people visited the area's pleasure gardens, to dance on lawns lit by thousands of coloured lanterns. They marvelled at wild beasts in cages. They goggled at the gardens' enormous cucumbers, one of which, at over seven feet long, was sent to the Prince Regent so he could behold its glory, and therefore, by association, Manchester's.

The merchants looked out of their long picture windows onto the delightful River Irk. Now that river was a poisonous slick of black water transporting pig offal, dead cats and other rubbish downstream, depositing the filth on the banks, where toshers sifted it.

It was the paupers' burying ground that finally killed this neighbourhood. When the city began burying its poor people next to the church's graveyard – thirty thousand of them, dead from fever, starvation and other miserable fates – the rich merchants and their families didn't want to live here anymore. Now the paupers' boneyard was a dumping ground and the slum's children played football with skulls.

'Ah, there she is.' Cavendish leaned back in his chair. He beckoned to a woman in a black puff-sleeved dress that she wore over a huge crinoline petticoat. She could hardly squeeze between the other tables and chairs. She had to lift the large sack she carried over her head, where it dragged strands of her brown hair out of her bun.

'Who art thou mourning?' Cavendish said, as the woman approached. 'Is it that Irish fella who comes crooning after Saturday pub?'

'Ach, thou devil, thou,' said the woman, slapping him on the shoulders and leaning to kiss him on the cheek. 'He's long gone. Again. Wotcher been up to then? Still wearing thy head on thy neck, I see.'

'Nowhere to put me hat otherwise.'

I couldn't get used to this new, cheerful, Cavendish. It must have been because he was home, back where he belonged, but I thought this even stranger. I didn't feel this cheery at the thought of being back in Fairy Cross. But if it weren't for what the day held, I could have almost enjoyed the banter too. It was how Gran often spoke to me, on the really bad days, when she couldn't be serious at all, when she became more jovial the worse things got, when all you could do was laugh at yourself and what the world had dished up for you – stale bread and tea from the poisonous river – because if you didn't laugh, you'd cry and never stop.

How I missed Gran! What would she say to me now? She'd tell me with the utmost conviction that my plan was the best one possible. And I'd believe her, because her confidence was so persuasive.

'Thought I saw thy ugly mug on a poster, wanted by t'blues, down Goulden Street,' said the woman, dropping her sack at Cavendish's feet. Her face was deeply wrinkled, hair greying at the temples. She said, 'Wanted for thieving deer, trout-poaching and neglecting to visit thy dearest sister t'second thou got into town.'

'Trout-poaching in River Irk, Annie? Might be some eels still, grown fat on grease, big as sea serpents. Thought I heard some kiddie got swallowed whole just last week–'

'Nah,' said Cavendish's sister, Annie, suddenly teary. 'That were plain drowning. Mary's young 'un.'

'Oh, sorry, lass,' Cavendish said. 'That's bad luck for the li'l 'un. Where'd they fish him out? Sorry, mind me. Not 'fish'. He had a good send off?'

Annie wiped her eyes. She pinched her nose and blew into it, rubbed her thumb and two fingers together, then kneaded her hip with the same hand. I noted the slimy smear on her black dress when she removed her hand. She said, 'Ach, well, Mary's other ones may get through winter now there's one less. He were a greedy fat one, Tommy, probably ate t'monster eel himself before toshers dredged him up.' She cackled.

I laughed too. She glared at me, as if I'd just myself held Tommy's head under the water until he drowned.

'Sorry,' I said, 'just, you know, monster eels.' I'd remembered Tom and I catching the eels that had once swum into the millrace, but couldn't now think why I'd found that funny in the context of a drowned toddler. Something bleak was happening to my sense of humour.

'This one?' she said to Cavendish, who nodded. 'Right voice, s'pose. But sure she won't get youse smugged?'

'Arrested,' he said to Florian, with a knowing look. 'Not now she knows thou'll be coming for her. Eh, Lizzie, eh?' He playfully punched my arm. It hurt. 'Annie, how about that basement o' thine?' he said. 'That'd do for a dungeon, good place to chain up a lass, no one'd find her there. Thou like a gruesome tale, dontcha, Lizzie?'

I didn't know whether this was a joke, or a threat. I laughed anyway; he seemed to want me to.

Annie studied me, pursing and twisting her mouth to

suck something from her teeth. Whatever it was, she found it, plucked it out between her torn fingernails, looked at it, then put it back in her mouth.

'Got thy dresses, luv,' she said to Cavendish, eyeing me still.

First from the sack came a smart frock coat, nipped in fashionably at the waist, then woollen charcoal-coloured trousers with a strap at the bottom, to button under the shoe. Everyone in the city, I'd noticed, wore dark clothes, unlike in the country where working people mostly wore white, cream and brown. No one, not even the rich, could escape the grime here.

Florian said, 'Not bad, not bad,' and took them from Annie. He leant back in his chair and draped the coat over his chest, admiring himself.

'Wait till thou see this,' she said, and produced a pink silk waistcoat with a royal blue floral pattern.

'Ooh, la, la, London here I come,' Florian said. 'If I'd known it was this much fun in town I'd have given up highwaying long ago.'

'Don't mind t'stain,' Annie said, passing the waistcoat over the table. 'Just one previous gentleman owner.'

'Stabbed in the back?' Henry said, coming back to our table.

He took the waistcoat from Annie. She shrugged.

Henry showed me the waistcoat. There was a brown mark, about the size of a large poppy, on the back. The cream cloth had been patched then scrubbed until the nap of the cotton furred, but the telltale bloodstain remained.

'Woulda been quick,' Annie said, as if a man dying quickly in the waistcoat made wearing it less ghoulish. 'S'where t'heart is.'

'Won't trouble you, Florid,' Cavendish said.

Sullenly, Florian waved away the waistcoat. 'Don't like

pink. What else have you got?'

Out of the sack came another frock coat, navy, with brass buttons, and looser about the waist. 'For thy lad,' said Annie, handing it to Henry. More items followed.

Henry said, 'Where've these come from? Have they got lice?'

'Been sulphured and camphored and scrubbed like they had blue fever.'

Henry threw the pile of clothes onto the floor.

'Such a bunch o'r ungrateful wretches I ne'er met,' Annie said. 'I shopped for hours at t'secondhand market for youse lot. D'youse think me some kind o' snowdropper, with no care for t'task?'

'Stealing washing from clothes' lines,' Cavendish said. 'That's plenty for our lad, Annie. What about her?'

'This's *the* best.' Annie reached into the sack. She drew out an emerald green silk dress with so many ruches I momentarily mistook it for a stage curtain. But I could see it was meant to be worn over a crinoline with hoops as wide as Annie's.

'Din't even know about thy pretty eyes, lass. Thou'll be matching like a Christmas present.'

I didn't know what she meant by this. She pulled out a tiny corset and I realised these items were meant for me.

'Oh my god,' I said, 'I can't run in those.'

I drew a sharp intake of breath at my slip. But everyone was laughing so much at the thought of me in the dress they didn't hear.

'S'been made for a lady o' twenty years old, this corset,' said Annie, holding it against her own tubby waist when we were upstairs in my cupboard room. 'Th'art fifteen, right? What's matter with thou then? Got stout like a tree trunk in t'country. Should try a bit o' city life, that'll take t'meat off thy bones. Wotcha got that look on thy phizog for? I've not really got a dungeon. Well, maybe…I s'pose…nah…hmm…'

She tossed the corset aside, bundled me roughly into the chemise, petticoat, crinoline and dress, then nearly throttled me tying the ribbons of a bonnet under my chin. She measured a pair of faded satin slippers against my stockinged feet.

'Lord above and li'l baby Cheesus in his crib. Who's feet are those? Th'art a monster eel if e'er I saw one.'

'Eels don't have feet,' was all I could say, but I was relieved to be spared the slippers and corset.

Annie dived under my skirt before I could stop her.

'Hey, what're you doing up in my nethers?' I said, but she only grumbled. I felt her loosen the waist of the petticoat and retie it lower down.

She emerged from under the skirt and tugged the hem of the petticoat down. 'Thou'll prob'bly trip on it and smash that pretty face in t'gutter, but at least them daisy roots'll be hidden. Put 'em on then. Cheesus Christmas, I'd sooner dress up a scullery cat. Done,' she yelled to Cavendish, who was beyond the door of my tiny room.

She wrestled the straw mattress, upon which we stood, up against the door. She dragged the door open and crammed herself through the gap onto the landing. 'Come on,' she said.

'Just a second,' I said, 'I need to, um…'

'Thy drawers are thy own business, but I'm not doing nowt with that milk jug,' Annie said. 'Just get a wriggle on. Ha. Monster eel.' She snorted.

I let the door close under the weight of the mattress. I snatched the cast-off breeches from where they'd wedged between the mattress and wall, and quickly put them on

225

under the crinoline. The flint I'd had in my own breeches was still in the pocket, half-wedged in a small hole at the bottom. I left it there as a reminder of home, along with some crumbled leaves and wizened berries inherited from the previous owner.

I found my shirt and tied it around my waist, also under the crinoline; there was plenty of room. I couldn't run in the dress, and I didn't know how I was going to get it off unaided, but if I got free I didn't want to dash through the streets in my underclothes – I'd end up in the lunatic ward of the workhouse if I were seen by an over-zealous policeman. I pulled on my boots and fumbled to tie them.

I tried to work out how to hide my knapsack under my crinoline, realised I couldn't, so slung it over my shoulder in a jaunty way. It looked ridiculous, but no more than I felt. I opened the door.

'Passable,' said Cavendish. 'But thou can't take that thing.' He seized my knapsack.

I clutched it to my chest.

'Take it off.'

I held it tighter.

He looked at me oddly, and tugged at the strap.

I held on still.

'If thou gotta have t'cursed thing, Henry'll take it. Thou can have it back after.'

40

Holland Arcade was about two miles from the lodging house. Annie had been watching the comings and goings of the arcade for weeks, she said, though I suspected Theo had actually done the work. Annie joined us now.

Mid-morning, the five of us headed out into the damp. Porter and Gaunt, who'd stayed in a different lodging house, as per the plan, would make their own way there.

On the main road at the outer reaches of the slum, the street lamps were still lit; they glowed some ten feet above our heads but illuminated nothing. Down below on the paved sideway we tramped through slippery pools of dirt and dung. The hem of my petticoat, which Annie had tied low to hide my inappropriate footwear, swept through these pools, drinking mud. I was grateful to be wearing my boots.

We crossed the bridge over the stinking river.

Annie said, 'Oops, forgot. Back there's Allen's Court, look. It's been fumigated and whitewashed now, but it were known as Cholera Court seven-year ago, when we had that outbreak o' blue fever. It were like a cesspool down there, with cat-gut factory and tripe-boiling works, and all them privies overflowing with diarrhoea and fever up-chuck.'

Florian groaned. As he had when Annie had described the men who'd abandoned a dead baby girl in the cemetery, disturbed in the act of burying the body because they couldn't afford sixpence for a proper burial, and when Annie told of the policeman swept away in the river while trying to save a boy from drowning, the policeman's half-chewed corpse found downstream by mushroom pickers three weeks later. But Annie took Florian's groans as encouragement.

She continued, 'Caused a riot, that cholera, when a doctor cut off a li'l laddie's head, to keep for examination. After he died. T'poor laddie, that is. Hospital were near demolished by a mob.'

'Cavendish,' Florian said, 'tell your dear sister to save the city tour for our return trip. We don't have time to see where each of your cousins got his teeth knocked out, nor suffer your translations of whatever it is she's chuntering about. I haven't the stomach for more dead babies or headless corpses. Does no one do anything but die gruesomely here?'

'Whadcha mean?'

'She's just excited,' said Cavendish.

'This isn't a outing for tourists, orphans nor ladies of vice.'

'Watch what th'art saying about my sister, man.'

'They sewed that laddie's head back on, eventually,' Annie said, cheerfully. 'A priest found it in t'doctor's lodgings. Wrapped in a hanky.'

'What kind of hanky?' Henry said, trying not to laugh. 'Men's? Ladies'? Cotton, silk, monogrammed?'

'Ooh, d'yer know, I dunno. Let me think. He were a doctor, so some kinda–'

'Henry,' Florian growled. 'What's got into you the last few days?' He glanced at me. 'Bad influences.'

228

'You can't mean me?' I said.

Henry laughed. 'Must be something in the air.'

'That were the cemetery back there,' Annie said, pointing into the fog below the bridge, 'for t'cholera dead. And we'll troop by t'workhouse in a minute. Home sweet home, eh?' She poked Cavendish in the ribs.

I thought of Billy, and hoped he hadn't ended up back in this repugnant place. I wondered whether there was a way to visit him, or if he'd feel worse when I left. Then Annie's comment came back to me. Had she and Cavendish had grown up in this workhouse? I didn't want to ask, and find out the best future Billy could hope for was right before my eyes.

'Better look to t'task ahead, Annie,' Cavendish said, putting his arm around her shoulders. 'This's what we been working towards. We all got a big part to play.'

'Right-choo are,' Annie said, and tooted on the cow horn she'd brought, with which she'd give the signal at Holland Arcade.

Beyond Manchester Cathedral we joined the northern end of Deansgate, the busy thoroughfare – once a Roman road, now a fashionable shopping street at one end, with more slums to the south. The black snow of soot and grime continued to drift down through the fog, leaving a greasy layer on our clothes and skin.

Manchester's black snow. The bobbin mill's creamy wood dust. The contrast, nay, the complete inversion of one to the other, made me gasp out loud. I couldn't comprehend how I'd come from Fairy Cross to this extraordinary city in such a short time. Nor did I understand why I wasn't as afraid I should be, to be here, in this company.

229

'Use this,' Florian said, reaching into his pocket and giving me the silk handkerchief Annie had procured. Almost everyone on the street had covered their noses and mouths with hankies, scarves or shawls to protect them from breathing the polluted air.

'Thanks,' I said, though I knew it was only to keep me from complaining.

He looked at me oddly when I spoke.

'Thanks,' he murmured, as if no one had ever thanked him before.

Florian had now assumed his role, as my doting uncle, in earnest. He gripped my forearm in his gloved hand. When we'd left the slum, he'd tried to link arms so he could hold me close against him. But my crinoline was so wide he'd become irritated at the steel hoops dragging against his legs.

To prevent a tantrum Annie had produced a short plaited leather cord, and deftly tied a loop at end each. She scrunched up the glove on my right hand and slipped the loop around my wrist, then pulled the loop tight.

'Ow,' I said.

'Th'art alright, lass, with them fat wrists o' thine.' Annie drew my glove back over the knotted cord.

She put the other loop gently over Florian's left wrist and gave him a coy smile. He didn't notice. He grasped my forearm and the length of cord was hidden by his arm. He beamed at the simplicity.

'Always wanted a puppy, did thou?' Annie said.

And thus we strolled, as false uncle and captive niece.

On Deansgate, Cavendish and Henry now dropped back a few paces.

Annie leapt to Florian's side and said, 'Mind them omnibuses, you don't wanna slip and end up under t'wheels. Mind you don't get caught up in that cotton workers' march. Shoulda been cancelled cos t'smog, but them bludgeon boys from New Town'll be out anyway, working for them Leaguers and stirring up trouble. And mind them scuttlers, they's happiest in t'smog.'

'I haven't a clue what you're on about,' Florian said, 'but we can look after ourselves.'

'Thou don't know about omnibuses, fella? They're just stagecoaches what stop in t'city.'

'Thank you, Annie.'

Cavendish called her back and she let us walk on. I turned to look at Henry. He was carrying my knapsack with the bag on his hip and hand resting upon it, as I usually did, keeping it safe from pickpockets. I took it as an omen – that he knew what my few remaining belongings meant to me.

Cavendish, Annie and Henry were walking loosely together, allowing other pedestrians to mingle among them. Henry smiled at me. I didn't know how to reconcile his kindness with the boy who'd killed a defenceless man like Morris. But the way I saw myself, the coherent whole of me, was being sorely tested too, stretched and twisted and torn.

Henry winked his good eye at me, though perhaps it was just a blink and meant nothing at all. Then the three of them disappeared into the fog.

I stopped, thinking they'd catch up again. But they didn't. 'Where've they gone?' I said.

'They know what they're doing,' Florian said.

'But I don't.'

'You don't need to. Hold your nerve, Lizzie.' He pulled me along and my feet stuttered beneath the crinoline.

The smog was so dense here you could only see five paces ahead and behind at a time. People seemed to swim out of the chocolatey vapour, sweeping their arms to feel their way, shuffling on the slippery pavement, trying to locate obstacles before they tripped over them.

Milliners' assistants materialised, brandishing hat boxes. Butchers' boys in smocks and aprons sailed into us with trays of meat balanced on their shoulders. Clerks darted to and fro during their dinner breaks.

Somewhere there was a brass band – the solemn tune of a horn seemed sung by the fog itself, some sort of spirit voice from the ether. I wondered what it was telling me. It sounded like a funeral hymn.

'No rich young lady would go shopping in this weather,' I whispered to Florian, hoping to unsettle him.

I thought of Milly, Sophia and Harriet, who bullied me for going out in all weathers, to ruin my complexion and coarsen my hands. I never found anything to envy about their indoors life, however – they were always in a state of near-starvation because their mother believed a full belly encouraged dangerous passions. They didn't get to go shopping either, because the closest shops were in Avandale, to which they weren't allowed in case they saw handsome youths and developed corrupting thoughts.

I said, 'She won't be at the arcade today. This isn't going to work.'

'Shut up, Lizzie, and play your part. How would you know what a rich girl– Urff.' He tipped forwards at the waist.

I stumbled too and stepped on the mud-heavy hem of my petticoat, which ripped with a hiss.

A voice from the fog cried, 'Watch it mister.'

'What the–?'

'I'm here where I always am, it's thou with t'rhinoceros feet. Want thy boots shined?' It was a shoe-black boy, crouched near the kerb with his box and stool.

'No, I bloody don't,' Florian said. He'd already tripped

over one shoe-black lad, and an oyster girl, spilling her shells into the gutter. She'd chased us, wanting the ruined oysters paid for, until Florian kicked her away.

From nowhere Annie appeared, saying, 'I got it, I got it,' and leapt upon me, tearing off the ripped lower portion of my petticoat.

'Get off, woman,' Florian said. 'You're drawing attention, it's not a matinee performance. Go with the others, we don't need you here.'

'Don't need my help, is it?' Annie said. 'Well, I don't need thine.' She disappeared into the fog with the strip of petticoat trailing behind her.

Florian continued striding through the fog, ignoring how crowded the streets were. He was as unfamiliar with city conditions as me. I was heartened to see him struggle.

On the road beside us, horse-drawn omnibuses clattered by. Conductors hollered for passengers.

'Royal Exchange, climb up, climb up, outside seats a-begging.'

'Liverpool Road Station, the train waits for no man.'

The conductors bawled at the drivers of other buses or carriages that came too close, misjudging distances in the poor visibility.

'How will you be able to watch me in the shop from the other side of the street,' I said, 'when you can't see more than five paces?'

'Change of plan,' Florian said, 'I'm coming with you inside. The others'll wait on the other side of the street for us. Porter and Gaunt will be in the alley behind.'

'But will we be able to find them when we're in a hurry? I can't even see them now, the smog is so thick,' I said, growing increasingly worried about how, if I got a chance to run, Henry would know.

'It's the smog that makes everything possible,' he

snapped. 'How else do you think we're going to get away with a girl screaming for her papa? The smog is perfect. Anyone would think you don't want us to succeed. And why would that be, little lost Lizzie? Don't you want my help with your uncle and your precious mill?'

I was glad for the smog then, to account for the extra drops of moisture in my eyes. 'I'm as committed as you are.'

We walked on, dodging people and lampposts, my eyes smarting and nostrils burning from the smog. When we hesitated a few times, sidestepping left, right, left, in a dance with another person we were trying to pass, I heard the scuff of boots halting behind us. I didn't turn to see whether it was Cavendish or Annie or Henry, because I didn't want to find out it wasn't Henry. I'd almost given up on Theo.

'St Ann's, St Ann's Square, St Annie our saviour, Annie our saint,' a conductor blared almost into my ear.

I twitched at the surprise of it and Florian gripped my arm tighter. My own destination just a leap away!

A man swung onto the ladder on the outside of the St Ann's omnibus and climbed to the seats on the roof, tilting his topper hat as he ascended into the brown cloud.

From inside the omnibus, a woman spilled out. She tried to scrape the sodden straw, which carpeted the inside carriage, off her ankle boots with the point of her umbrella. Then she plunged into the sludgy gutter with a cry of frustration.

There must be crossing sweepers at work somewhere, trying to keep the mud and dung away from pedestrians, but how they felt their day's work was ever done I had no idea. The whole city was fighting a losing battle, being engulfed by filth from the ground upwards and from the sky down, by pollution and fog.

The St Ann's omnibus rattled away. I felt crushed like a beetle, between finger and thumb, at the lost opportunity. We were all beetles here, the people in Manchester, squeezed between the sky and the ground that cared nothing for our hopes and our woes.

'Nearly there.' Florian drew me close, clinching my arm tighter with his free hand. My crinoline flounced up to the left side and a passing clerk tutted as it boinged into him.

'Nearly there,' I repeated, as if an echo. How close was 'nearly'?

We walked for perhaps a minute more in this stiff embrace. Then Florian stopped underneath the awning of a shop with murky windows.

'Here,' he said, with a note of relief. 'We're here.'

'Here,' I said, as the echo again, out of time.

41

Florian and I waited for Annie's signal.

On the opposite side of the street, lost in the fog, was Holland Arcade – an ornate, glass-ceilinged structure of mosaic floors, wishing pools under fountains and date-palm trees from Arabia. Part of me wanted to go in, to see the exotic, the marvellous; the things Grandpa had yearned for too.

'We're early,' Florian said, 'but don't lose your cool because you can't stand the delay.'

I still didn't believe a wealthy young lady would venture out in this weather, but neither could I afford to be wrong. My legs began to twitch and shake under my crinoline, but not with the tremble of fright; they were getting ready to run. My belly wanted to empty itself. I clenched my fists to distract myself from the urgent sensation. My shoulders tensed and my arm pulled at Florian's.

'Stop that,' he said. 'I'm risking my reputation on you, don't let me down.'

'I can't do it,' I blurted. 'You should've got that woman, Kit, to do it. Or Theo. She wants to do it, and she's coming anyway.'

'Who's Theo?'

'Cavendish's daughter.'

'Daughter?'

'The stable girl. At The Amnesty.'

'Cavendish has a daughter?'

'Yes. You didn't know? This is her plan, only he wouldn't let her be the one to go into the arcade, but she wants to, she knows what to do. She's going to meet us here–'

'Who else have you told?'

'No one, I didn't tell Theo. I told you, it was her idea.'

'Have you snitched on us?'

'No, no, I haven't. Theo already knew, she tried to beat me with a horsewhip she was so angry. She said she was going to follow us,' – I allowed myself the one small lie – 'I couldn't stop her. There's no police.'

'What about the police? Is this a trap?' Florian shook me by the shoulders. 'This's Cavendish's doing, he's stitched me up, I knew it. You're working for him.'

'No, I swear, it's not a trap, it's just Theo wanting to join–'

'What's Henry's part in this?' Florian said.

'Henry?'

'I knew I shouldn't've let him get cosy with you.'

'No, Henry hasn't done anything. He doesn't know–'

'I'll kill him.'

'No. You're worrying for nothing, there's nothing wrong. I'll go into the arcade when Annie gives the signal, to show you there's no police. I can do it, I can get the girl. There's no police, Henry doesn't know anything. There's nothing to know.'

'We're going back.'

He began to drag me along the street. Then from the fog came the sound of the cow horn, but not the tune Annie had demonstrated in The Amnesty.

'Who's that signal for?' Florian said.

'Don't know, she's probably just got it wrong. Wait, she'll do the real one–'

'You're done, Lizzie. Henry too. You're both done.'

'Help,' I cried. 'Hel–'

Florian clapped his hand over my mouth. I tried to bite it, but his hand forced my cheeks together. I chomped and chewed at the inside of my own mouth. I tasted the iron of my blood. He tightened his grip and caught my nostrils too, and blocked them.

Desperately, I sucked for air.

Florian wrested my arm upwards behind my back. I thrashed against him. Unbearable pressure built up in my head. His hold on my mouth and nose loosened ever so slightly.

I gulped and wheezed. *'Herrh-herrh.'*

He twisted my arm harder. I gulped again like a dying fish, a fish-out-of-water – a country girl in the biggest, wickedest city in the world. I shouldn't be here. Why am I here?

Where do you go in death if you're already in the nine circles of hell, is there somewhere worse than this? Will slum children in a hundred or two hundred years, in the far far future of 2039, play football with my skull? Will it show signs of my death at Florian's hands, like the skeletons of warriors dug up from ancient battlefields?

I dreamed then of myself as an ancient warrior, out of time, out of place, buried a thousand years ago in the Viking lands, now resurrected in this modern-day battleground of Manchester. Here, people fought every day to survive: against the factory owners who paid them less and made them work more, against the machines that took their jobs, against the filth and toxic air and their own failing, malnourished bodies. None of it was a fair fight, hand-to-hand with another warrior renowned for his strength and courage.

As this vision faded, because my air-starved mind was disappearing too, I had one last clear thought: The bobbin mill is a part of all this. I can reclaim the mill from Robin, but I can't separate it from Manchester. Nothing is pure or simple.

…and then…I breathed.

Florian's hand was gone from my face. I breathed again, deeply, twice as alive. My ears began to hear again. There was a choking noise behind me. My tethered arm was being pulled upwards.

I whirled around in the fog.

Florian…with a garrotte around his neck. A pair of rough knuckles drawing the garrotte, a belt, tight. My hand hanging from the leather cord. On the other end Florian's hand, scratching at his own neck to get a fingertip under the belt. His other hand scrabbling at his hip for the pistol. A gravelly voice shouting, 'Yurraaghhh.'

I remembered Annie's warning about scuttlers being happiest in the fog. I'd thought them some kind of sewer crab – giant, mythical, like the monster eels of the River Irk. Then I remembered Cavendish telling us about scuttlers: they were gangs of brutal street fighters and thieves.

Florian thrashed his legs as I'd done only a few seconds before. I didn't think he was death-dreaming of Vikings and travelling through time in his mind. I didn't care if he were.

He cried, 'Liz-*uch*-ee.'

I ripped off my glove and wrenched at the knotted leather cord around my wrist. The slipknot had pulled tight and the plaited leather had locked itself. I tore my fingernails on the cord, then went at the strips of leather with my teeth. My front tooth wobbled, I stopped with the pain, and tried again with my molars. It wasn't working fast enough.

Another ruffian appeared and said, 'Wotcher got, missie? Coin in yer reticule? Jewellery? Hand it over.' He brought a knife to my throat.

I remembered the flint in the pocket of my breeches, found by the river on the night of the fire. A piece of home still with me, stone from the earth, from mountain to city.

To the scuttler, I said, 'Take what you want, but I've got nothing.' I lifted my skirt slowly.

The scuttler said, 'Ooh, what's this...?' and lowered the knife from my neck.

I grappled with the crinoline to reach my pocket. I found the flint, grasped it until it cut into my hand. I wheeled my arm and speared the flint into the man's face. One for the Vikings! He stumbled back clutching his bleeding cheek.

I brought the jagged edge of the flint to the last strands of the leather cord and began to saw frantically. I'd almost cut through when Florian slumped to the ground and the flint was knocked from my hand. I landed on top of Florian. The scuttler shoved me off, to rifle through Florian's pockets. The attacker I'd speared was groaning and cursing somewhere behind me.

With the flint gone, there was nothing for it but to yank my bound arm as hard as I could. My wrist or the leather – skin of another dead beast – something had to give. I stood on the cord and pulled. The bones in my hand began to stretch away from my arm. I paused, summoned my Viking spirit and pulled again.

The leather plait snapped. I flew onto my back, into the mud. I jumped up, hoiked my skirts, ready to run, but the groaning man lunged with his knife.

I leapt back, and hit a wall.

The man came towards me. 'You ragged little– I'm gonna cut you up for t'rats.'

'Lizzie!' Henry appeared from the fog. He skidded into the man. 'What's going–? Oh.' He ducked as the man swiped at him with his knife.

I pushed myself off the wall and yelled, 'Henry, come on.'

Henry punched the knife man in his wounded cheek. The man howled and bent double.

'Florian?' said Henry.

The other attacker stood up from ransacking Florian's pockets and squared up to Henry with a cutlass, a two-foot long blade on a wooden handle. 'Yer man's down, lad. D'you fight any better?'

'Henry, come *on*.' I grabbed his arm. 'Leave him.'

'I can't,' Henry said.

'What do you mean?'

'I just can't.' Henry pulled the pistol from his belt.

The man with the cutlass said, 'Ohhh, s'like that, is it. I got me one o' those too.' He drew Florian's pistol and pointed the long barrel at Henry. 'Best run away wiv yer girl, lad.'

'Henry,' I pleaded, one last time. He didn't move. I ran.

42

I didn't know where I was going. Most immediately, anywhere would do. I pelted along the paved sideway, grateful Annie had ripped away the front of my petticoat so I could run more freely.

'St Ann's, St Ann's, Annie our saint.' The omnibus conductor's patter sang in my head. I was so close to finding my great-uncle I couldn't believe my luck. Quickly, I tore off my bonnet, but couldn't unlace the dress while on the run.

I moved as if in a bubble, within walls of brown vapour. People stepped into my bubble and out again, but not before I'd bumped into and sent them reeling, along with their hat boxes and trays of meat. I lurched and slid across the muddy paving, leaving a trail of angry pedestrians and lamb chops.

Florian was dead, probably. And Henry?

Running made it difficult to be worried about more than one thing at once. I was grateful for this too.

I had to get off the main street but couldn't see the turns before I was halfway past them. I'd missed an alley and a side street already, being on the wrong side of the pavement both times, blocked by a small group of people and then a costermonger's barrow.

Would Cavendish come after me? He'd been nearby, with Henry and Annie. And he couldn't let me run to the police and tell them of the kidnap plot.

My boots slapped in the mud. I swerved a lamppost. My ankle went over on its side. I yelped and hopped with the pain, got caught up in the dress and skidded on my good foot off the kerb. I fell onto my knees in the road. The gutter sludge was shallow and my kneecaps hit the cobbles. I inhaled sharply and tipped forwards onto my hands to recover.

To my right, the sound of clattering horseshoes became louder. I threw myself back. The wheels of a hurtling omnibus rolled where my knuckles had just been. The breeze drew the loose strands of my hair across my face, and the conductor, swinging on the pole at the back, hollered something unpleasant about my moral virtue.

Up on my feet, I floundered into a burly man in an apron. We scuffled under a shop awning, trying to get past one another; he was holding a metal hook above his head.

'Whoa there, lassie,' he said. Behind him, legs of fat-wrapped beef pressed against the inside of the shop window; garlands of sausages hung above and below. 'What's thy hurry? Art thou lost, or been thieving?'

'Get out of my way,' I yelled.

He grabbed the crook of my arm. I tried to shake him off, but his grip was that of a man who pounded raw flesh and sawed bones day after day after day. I whirled around, trying to get loose. He span on the spot with me, face to face. His expression changed from one of alarm to sympathy.

'Why dontcha come in t'shop for a li'l sit down?' he said. 'We got some pork pies fresh from t'oven. Whatever's t'matter we'll get a police fella to sort it out.'

'I don't need a beggaring sit-down, I'm not an invalid or

243

a lunatic,' I screamed, like a lunatic would.

'Now then, missie, I can't let thou scram into t'smog. There's all sorts o' folk who'd do thou harm.'

'That's why I'm running, just let me go. Let me go!'

The butcher pondered my words. His hold on me slackened. I wrenched my arm free and leaned into a run.

My first fast steps took me beyond his shop.

'Come back and I'll help thee,' the butcher cried.

My next, longer strides took me to the edge of the adjacent shop.

'Where did she go, man?' said a familiar voice behind me. 'Where did she go?' It was Cavendish.

I stumbled off the kerb, and realised I'd reached a side street. I swung my body left, nearly fell over my own feet, which hadn't yet received the message, and sprinted down the unknown road.

Busy streets were a blessing. In the smog you couldn't tell one person from another. I'd ended up on another main road, or the same one further along, I don't know. To be sure I'd lost Cavendish, I'd turned in the back streets and kept on turning.

This road teemed with people. Men, women and children spilled off the pavement into the gutter, hollering at carriage- and omnibus-drivers to 'Shift over, the people are a-marching'. I allowed myself to be swept up.

These people were workers from the big factories. Must be the cotton workers' march Annie had warned of. The workers mostly wore loosely-fitting trousers or pinafores, jackets and floppy caps in dark colours. Their clogs, thousands upon thousands of them, squelched through the pavement muck.

Cloth banners and wooden placards with slogans

bobbed overhead. Some of the men used the placard poles to divert carriages from the kerbside, so people could walk in the road and ease the crush on the pavement.

I'd never been in such an exhilarating press before. There was power in the heat and noise of the other bodies, carrying me along, and away.

Shopkeepers, arms folded over prim aprons, scowled as we streamed past. Crossing a side street, we fanned out, then clumsily bunched together outside a general store on the corner. Trestle tables fell over, packets and tins tumbled.

The shopkeeper yelled, 'Get back to work like the rest of us, you lazy whatnots.'

Some people jeered and lobbed the trampled packets, while others apologised and tried to tidy up.

Time passed strangely as I marched. The usual ticking of seconds and minutes was suspended, replaced by the rapid beat of my heart.

My skin began to fizz and tingle, my vital organs seemed to double in size. I'd never been so much of myself and at once so little, subsumed. I had a strange feeling, which at first I couldn't name. Then I identified it. A feeling of belonging. Not in Manchester, city of brick, steel and grime, but in this crowd. Robin always insisted the mill's value was in the land and machinery, the materials and products. I thought it was in the people who made the bobbins. Now I knew I was right. People mattered more than bobbins or cotton cloth. Of course they did. Without people there'd be no need for either.

I marched with the workers because I didn't want to be alone. I knew I'd have to leave the comfort of the crowd eventually to find my great-uncle. Yet I wasn't ready to be separate, to be an individual, shouldering a burden I knew was mine to bear. I was sure I'd be crushed by it.

I'd abandoned Henry, left him to face the scuttlers alone. And I'd left Florian to die. I didn't know what else I could have done, but it most definitely did not feel right. I was so, so ashamed of myself I felt a crawling all over me, as if red ants were trapped under my skin, scurrying back and forth trying to bite their way out through my pores.

Is it possible to live a whole year in a week? I feel as if I have. I'm not who I was when I left Fairy Cross. And I don't know if I'm now who I want to be.

Thinking myself protected, I marched. When I got the gist, I began to sing the slogans on the banners, though people looked at me oddly in my green silk dress. I didn't know then the dangers of crowds.

43

The way became congested when we turned off the main road and into a narrower street. I found myself squashed between a tall man with an uneven gait and a girl in a bobbled brown pinafore and loose jacket.

She wore her woollen cap pushed back on her head. She had the pale, almost grey, skin of a factory worker, but she had a lively step and we couldn't help knocking into one other. She may have been about my age, or much older, it was hard to tell. I glanced at her. She was looking at me.

'Just looking,' she said.

'At what?'

'What's with your dress?' she said.

'Oh, s'what my mistress gave me,' I said, thinking quickly, pretending to be a lady's maid. 'She gives me so many frocks and hats that've gone out of fashion, doing her bit for charity, she says, like I'm a charity case, that I don't have time to sell them. You want it?'

'T'dress off your own back?' said the girl.

'S'all right, I got clothes underneath.' She looked at me even more strangely. I said, 'Proper ones, course. Not just chemise and drawers. You want the dress?'

The lanky man with the wobbly walk missed his footing and teetered into me. I bumped into the girl in turn, and she reached for my arm to steady me.

'Sorry,' I said, and stared too long at her hand.

On her right hand one of her fingers was missing at the second knuckle. I looked up at her face, embarrassed at being caught staring. And there on her forehead, crossing her hairline, was a patch of shiny pink skin. It was about the size of a pocket watch, where her brown hair should have been. I'd heard from Annie how girls' long hair could get caught in fast-moving machines, and the hair, with the skin, ripped from their heads.

'I'm no charity case,' said the girl, pulling her cap down over her forehead. 'Just looking, are you?'

'No, sorry, course not. This isn't charity, just you know, solidarity, all of us standing together,' I said, feeling even more awkward. 'What're you marching for?'

'Striking from t'factories.'

'Cotton?'

She nodded. 'But police stopped us from meeting at Tinker's Gardens.' These were the pleasure gardens of the previous century, of the coloured lanterns and enormous cucumbers, now a meeting place for workers and troublemakers alike.

She continued, 'So we're marching past t'Royal Exchange instead. Tis where them toffs trade cotton, when we're the ones breaking our backs to make it. Then some-one famous is gonna tell us how to get what we want from t'bosses. Maybe. If he turns up. Because he's wanted by t'sheriff, he's some kinda outlaw these days, so...' She shrugged. 'You're really giving away your frock?'

'If you want it.'

'You got sommat proper underneath? You don't wanna be caught in your drawers amid this lot. It's not just cotton workers here.'

'Shirt and breeches underneath,' I said.

The girl raised her eyebrows.

'Promise,' I said. 'You'll have to unlace me though.'

'Not here, I'll lose me pals. Hold up, Josie,' she called ahead.

Several rows in front of us, three girls in caps and pinafores turned. One of them said, 'You gotta keep up, Norah.'

'Don't lose me,' Norah said.

The girls waved as they walked on.

'Or me,' said a small boy, tripping along behind us, holding onto Norah's long skirts. I hadn't even noticed him; he couldn't have been more than six years old.

'Wish I could lose you.' She snatched the brown skirt out of his hand. 'You're not a li'l kiddie, Alfie, and I'm not Ma, so leave off my skirt. You know how to get yourself home so it's better you beggar off now. I don't wanna hear no complaining about your sore feet or itchy bum.'

Alfie scowled and slapped her bottom. She flicked her foot back and caught him in the knee with her clog. She laughed.

He dropped back amongst the people walking behind, clutching his knee, hopping. Then he scurried to join us again.

'Alright then, Alfie,' the girl said. 'Now I know you'll be scrummaging with t'best o' them, when things get nasty. But serious, don't get yourself lost, there's men here who snatch li'l boys and send 'em to be slaves on ships.'

Alfie looked thrilled at the prospect.

'I said, 'slaves', Alfie. No one's gonna make you a pirate,' Norah said.

'Not straight off.'

She groaned and shook her head. She smiled at me and said, 'Once we get to that square, we'll get t'dress off you like world's giantest Christmas pressie. Sure you don't want it?'

'Definitely not,' I said.

'Is she sticking with us, Norah?' said Alfie, trying to squeeze between his sister and my ludicrous crinoline.

'I am if I may,' I said.

Norah gave me a gentle pinch on the arm. She turned her head away but not before I saw her smile again. She adjusted her woollen cap, letting her pink scar show.

'There's gonna be a fight,' Alfie said excitedly. 'There's gonna be a riot. I never seen a riot, but I'm hoping for one.'

'No, you're not, Alfie. A fight between bludgeon boys and some o' them loom-smashers might be entertaining, from afar. But you don't wanna get in a riot. You'll get yourself killed, then Da'll kill me for letting it happen, then Ma'll kill him for killing me, then t'blues will hang Ma for murder, and then everyone'll be dead cos o' you. You'll be happy then, will you?'

'Won't care cos I'll be dead first.'

'You'll be miserable in your grave, I'm telling you. And you won't be going to heaven for making everyone die cos o' your stupid behaviour. She, er–'

'Lizzie.'

'Yeah, Lizzie'll tell you, Alfie.'

'It's true,' I said, with a huge sense of relief.

This crowd was the safest I'd felt since leaving home. I was so glad for Norah and Alfie's company that I put my arm around Alfie's shoulder, without thinking it might be odd to do this to a stranger. For a moment I was able to forget about everything else. I wanted to chit-chat about nothing in particular and not think at all.

I said, 'Rioters don't go to heaven, they go to purgatory where they get tortured for all eternity. It's in an old poem by an Italian man called Dante. There are nine circles of hell, and in the centre is the devil, who's a winged giant

250

trapped in ice. He's got three heads and in each mouth he's eating a traitor.'

'What's a po-ehm?'

'You know,' said Norah, 'like limericks and verse that Mister Fitzgerald tells you. Only not rude.'

Alfie nodded, but he was smirking too. When his sister looked away, he punched the air like a boxer.

'We'll be at St Ann's in a minute,' said Norah, 'then we'll find a good spot for t'dress-fitting.'

'What did you say? St Ann's?' I said, thinking I hadn't heard right.

'Yes, St Ann's Square, t'one with a big red church. Tis where we're all gathering.'

The smog was a little thinner in St Ann's Square, which was a long narrow plaza lined with elegant four-storey buildings, mostly the premises of banks and cotton merchants.

St Ann's church stood at the southern end. The church was constructed from red sandstone, which was quarried from the same type of sandy soil around Manchester in which the famous cucumbers thrived.

The church tower was said to be the centre of the city, and from where surveyors measured city distances. I had a feeling there was a distance I needed to know, but it couldn't be measured in miles. Yet it was a distance between two points: me, as I was at home, and me here, now.

Soon, the strike leaders would congregate in front of the church and address the eager crowd. No one could be as eager as me, gathering any information I could about how to organise a strike. Would my great-uncle, when I found him, support me in this? I didn't know, but I'd have to do it

251

anyway. How about Tom? I was more nervous about his reaction.

Norah, Alfie and I huddled together, squashed near her friends, waiting for the announcement. Most of all I wanted to learn how I could arrange the mill's production without one person having to be in charge.

'Lizzie, you want some scran?' Alfie said, holding up a crust of bread.

It was the same kind of stodgy loaf I'd eaten for breakfast, but this piece was smeared with dripping. My stomach rumbled at the sight of it. 'No, that's yours, Alfie, I couldn't. But thank you.'

'I en't licked it.'

'That's not what I mean. I can't take your food, you need it. I'll get some dinner later, when I–' When I find my great-uncle, I thought. But that felt too big an event to be happening soon. Yet how I wanted the relief, and the rest. To sleep like King Arthur and his knights in the mountain for a thousand years. The peaceful, dreamless sleep of a man with a true and undisputed purpose.

When Arthur awakes it'll be to fight a worthy battle and restore the rightful order of things. He doesn't have to worry about what's right and what's wrong, just do the duty that's already been spoken in prophecy. But that's a fairytale world. What's 'right' in this world? And who decides?

Alfie said, 'Suit yourself,' and opened his mouth wide to receive the chunk of bread.

'Oi,' said Norah, grabbing his arm, 'I told you to share it. Guests first.'

'She don't want it.'

'She's just being nice.

'That's her fault.' He bobbed to the hand Norah was holding and licked the bread. Norah cuffed him on the ear.

His cap fell off and Norah let go of him. Then he shoved the whole piece of bread into his mouth and showed us the achievement, though he couldn't close his mouth around it. He dived between people's legs to find his cap.

Norah said, 'I'd say he's sorry but he'll only do it again.' She put her hand in her satchel and brought out her own chunk of bread. 'Here.'

'No, really, thank you, I can't.'

'Go on, I can see you want it.' She paused. 'You're no lady's maid, are you?'

'No. Sorry I said that, just didn't want you to think I was a rich girl, in this dress.'

'S'll right. Din't think so anyway, your face is browned like a nut. Work outdoors in t'fields or sommat? Is that why t'shirt and breeches under your dress?'

'Sort of.'

I wanted to tell her everything. But unburdening myself of my troubles and secrets would mean burdening her. I knew I should have done something about Cavendish and Annie and the plot to kidnap the banker's daughter. But if I went to the police, I'd have to explain how I came to be involved or they wouldn't believe me. And they'd arrest me too, for being part of the scheme. I hated myself for being such a coward.

Norah offered the bread again and I took it gratefully. I ate it with my back turned to her as she began unlacing my dress.

'Who knotted you into this?' she said, after some minutes of tugging. ''Tis like they've trussed you as a ham for t'pot.'

I laughed at the thought of myself as a ham for the cook-pot – and how big that pot would have to be – which made me think of food again, and of Alfie licking his bread. I realised we hadn't seen him for ten minutes or so.

'Where's Alfie?' I said.

'He'll be back, know's where we are.'

'But I think we've moved,' I said. 'I can't see much for the smog, but when you started on my lacing we were by that passage between those buildings there.' I pointed. 'Now we've moved forward, and we're also more in the middle. The crowd's taking us towards the church.'

'Oh, pilchards. I knew I shoulda sent the li'l git home.' Norah bent down to look amongst the forest of legs. 'How's he gonna find us? He's three foot nothing, without two wits to call his own. My Da really is gonna kill me.'

'You stay here,' I said. 'I'll go look back where we were. And try not to let the crowd move you anymore. I know where you are, I'll find you.'

44

How far could one mischievous boy roam through such a dense crowd?

With urgency but not panic, not yet, I squeezed through the people behind Norah and me. When we'd entered the square, from a side street halfway along the length, the northern end had been mostly empty. But now, as far as I could see in the thinning fog, the square had filled up completely.

I made my way back to where we'd been when Alfie went looking for his cap. No luck. I went to the edge of the crowd, and to the head of the passage I'd pointed out to Norah.

Earlier we'd seen two scruffy boys here, trying to entice people into playing the thimble-rig game. You had to find a dried pea hidden under one of three thimbles, which the dealer moved around so quickly you couldn't follow. The game was rigged and you could never win. Alfie had wanted to play but Norah dragged him on. I was sure this was where he'd be.

But the thimble-rig boys had gone, and there was no sign of Alfie. I stood with my back to the buildings to keep out of the way. It was nothing but people, people, everywhere. And one small boy to find among them.

I scouted around. It wouldn't be long before Norah moved enough that I lost her too. I needed a better vantage point if I had any hope of finding Alfie soon.

Amongst the rubbish on the pavement I found some squashed oranges. Nearby, I found the toppled orange crates. I piled three on top of one another and climbed up.

Above the level of people's heads, the smog was moving strangely. The wind had picked up since the morning. As I watched, the breeze lifted and carried pillows of vapour, revealing then concealing the crowd. There was no chance of spying Alfie himself, he was too small and the square packed. But I scanned the tops of people's heads, for any sign that he was causing a bother, like Frankie Flash had, barging through the festival crowd in Avandale. I hoped Alfie was causing a bother so I could see it and find him. I didn't want to lose anyone else today.

There were pockets of minor disturbances here and there, as someone tripped over, or a small group foolishly sat down and others bumped into them. But my gaze kept returning to one area in particular, on the limit of what I could see, and more often hidden by the fog than visible. Something about the to-ing and fro-ing of the men's heads didn't look like the usual friendly jostling.

The brown vapour of the smog descended and I lost sight of the trouble. I hopped off my orange crate tower, shooed a dozing dog out of a fourth, stacked the new crate, then climbed up for when the clouds lifted again.

I waited. Sounds were travelling strangely in the square, both muffled by the fog and bounced around by the tall buildings. But I was sure I could hear shouting from the same direction as the disturbance.

Still the fog remained. I heard the clopping of hooves close by, but thought nothing of it until I heard orders being given.

A procession of five horsemen approached. I jumped down off my crates and dragged the pile out of the way. The men were wearing uniforms: the blue jackets and white trousers of yeomen, local mounted soldiers. They had rifles slung across their chests and sabres hanging from their belts.

Slowly, the yeomen passed. I got onto the crates again. The fog had lifted. The disturbance was still going on. It was now a fist-fight.

The yeomen had seen the fight too. The third man in line said, 'Sir!' and pointed. The leader said over his shoulder, 'No, leave it, not yet.' They walked on towards the end of the square.

Behind me I heard the clop of more hooves coming from the side street. I turned. More yeomen on horseback. They turned left and went the opposite way to the others.

Yeomen circling the square. Circling, I wondered. As in, surrounding? Why are they doing that? To protect people? Yet they're doing nothing about the fight...

I looked towards the fight again. More people had joined in: the cluster of heads and shoulders moving violently had grown from a few feet to an area of about fifteen in diameter. And still the yeomen did nothing. The last of the new group disappeared into the fog.

Then I remembered Gran's story of Peterloo, the march-turned-massacre of twenty years ago, when a man called Henry Hunt held a mass meeting, for voting reform, in the fields of St Peter's on the outskirts of Manchester. Soldiers had charged into the crowd to stop Hunt addressing his followers. People had panicked, soldiers too, who'd slashed at the crowd with their sabres. Gran said twenty people had died, but she told it with such melodrama I thought it was one of her tales to put me off wanting to visit the city. Until I found out Mr Ivison had been there. And it was all true.

Would Alfie have gone towards the fight? I hoped he wasn't that stupid. Even if he were, I wasn't.

I plunged back into the crowd to find Norah. I didn't know what the yeomen were up to with their cool parade. But I knew we had to leave the square.

45

Immediately, I regretted entering the crowd so far away from where I'd left Norah. I kept getting tangled up in people's linked arms, and there was still a long way to go.

'Sorry, sorry, I have to get through,' I said, trying to prise apart two women.

One of them glanced over her shoulder and said, 'We're all more squashed than we wanna be.' She had a cloud of mousy hair and a deep crease between her eyebrows. She drew her friend closer with her arm. 'Thou don't get no priority cos th'art in a fancy dress.'

'I've lost a little boy,' I said, 'and a girl.'

'Tha and me both.'

'Let her be,' said the other woman, who had a slight stoop. 'She's not talking about typhoid.' To me she said, 'Thy brother and sister? They'll find their way home, I s'pect.' She tried to unhook her arm from her friend's.

The other woman wouldn't let go at first. Reluctantly, she then dropped her arm.

'Thank you,' I said, and pushed through.

Beyond them was a wall of five people, each clutching part of their long banner.

The first woman jabbed me in the back. 'Get on thy way then, girl.'

But the banner was a cordon. I tried to go under, but one of the men caught me by the dress-laces Norah had half undone.

'Would youse look at this?' said the man holding my lacing. 'We're here striking, losing a day's pay, and prob'ly t'week if boss has anything to do with it, and here's a lass taking advantage to rob us blind.'

'I'm not a pickpocket,' I said. 'I've lost my friends.'

'Well, I'm not so stupid to think th'art working alone.'

'That's not what I mean. Please let me go.'

'Wotcha got in thy pockets then? Empty 'em out and we'll see.'

'I haven't got any pockets.'

'Don't be funny with me, lass.'

Desperate to find Norah, I punched the man in the gut. He let go of my lacing.

I dived under the banner, headfirst into a woman's bottom. It was the worst getaway ever. I rebounded into the same man. He grabbed me around the waist, trapping my arms by my sides, and lifted me off the ground.

I kicked furiously and yelled into the air. 'Alfie! Norah! The yeomen are here. Get out of the square.'

The man said, 'Hollering won't do no good, we're gonna get thy filthy mates too.'

One of his companions caught my left ankle. I put my right foot on his chest and pushed him away.

The first man said, 'Right we're not joking anymore. If there's yeomen about we're taking thou straight to 'em.'

'Let me go!' I shouted.

Again, another man tried to seize my legs but I hoofed and booted and kept him away.

The man holding me leaned backwards to counter my weight. My heel found one of the metal hoops in my crinoline. It wasn't much to grip, but my heel in the hoop created tension in the crinoline – it was almost a sort of ladder. I dug my other heel into the man's thigh, and climbed up and up.

The crinoline began to pull down, then stuck on the waistband of my breeches, which were tied tight above my hip bones. I scrabbled, climbing upwards within my own clothing. The half undone laces of my bodice began to strain and loosen. The man helped, inadvertently, his grip pulling down on my dress as I pushed upwards.

A head higher than the crowd, I had a mad thought that I was about to be released from the emerald chrysalis of the dress into the sky as a giant, demented butterfly. I flung my head side to side and twisted my shoulders, thinking I could wriggle free if only I kept on long enough. The waist-cord of my crinoline snapped.

I thought I spotted Norah and her friends, a group of four girls in woollen caps, but then I couldn't find them again. I thought I saw the fight that had first alarmed me. But it was too close, perhaps it was another. Or perhaps I'd got it all wrong and it had never been a fight, just the sort of disturbance I was now creating.

Maybe I really had got it all wrong, assuming the worst when spying the yeomen. What if I just let it all be? Stopped interfering, trying to make everything right, when nothing was actually out of order. In his own time, Alfie would find Norah, who was still safe with her friends, and after the speeches everyone in the crowd would go home safely.

I'd been worrying about nothing. I suppose I'd end up in the police station for being a pickpocket regardless, or in some other place where no one would come for me because they wouldn't know I was there.

And then the shooting began. The man dropped me. I landed in a heap. He hunched over me as he ducked.

Not everyone took cover on the ground. Some people ran from the sound of the shots, battering into one another. The man's body, in an arch over me, pressed down as someone fell over him. The falling man rolled and landed on his front; his head wrenched sideways. Our eyes met for a second. I saw his terror. He tried to get up but another man knocked him down.

People screamed and shouted, but nothing was as loud as the blood pumping in my ears.

The man protecting me became a burden. I could only breathe short breaths in this constricted position, and the sweltering animal heat of his body was frightening. The people around me were animals too, beasts fearing for their lives, stampeding.

Where I'd fallen, my knees were bent underneath me. I put my hands to the ground and tried to push myself up, but the man was too heavy. And unconscious. His head lolled over my shoulder. His eyes were open but glazed.

More people tumbled over him. A boot stamped on my hand and crushed my little finger.

I managed to shift position under the dead weight of the man. He was my turtle shell, my armour. I shrank beneath him, and curled over my knees. I felt the blows his body took as they resounded through my own. I wondered how long I could stand the suffocating heat. I felt as if I were in the wooden helmet of the Sir Tarquin contest again, and marvelled at how a hundred years seemed to have passed yet I was still only fifteen years old.

Is this the age at which I'll be preserved forever, like my mother, dead at eighteen? I'd thought her short life tragic and pitiful, but never thought I'd better it in the waste. Will my great-uncle, in his business premises somewhere on this square, ever know how close I was to finding him?

Only Henry, Florian and Cavendish can trace me back

to where I've come from in Avandale – does this mean they're now as close as kin?

And what's happened to these conspirators? Are they free – alive and well – kidnapping a girl for her father's knowledge, while I cower here using another human being as my shield?

I couldn't get Norah and Alfie out of my mind. I'd never find them now. I thought I'd found something with them, here, in this crowd – myself as a part of something bigger. But what was that big thing now? A massacre in the centre of a city that cared so little for the people that made it great.

I'm not going to die here!

I wriggled under the lifeless man. The bodice of my dress loosened. I wriggled again, and trapped one arm as the dress slid down over my shoulder. I put my hands on the ground, tried to heave myself free. Fabric ripped somewhere, but one side of me was still caught. I squirmed to reach my stuck shoulder, and tore at the sleeve.

The whole side panel of the dress came away in my hand. I slithered out from under the man. He slumped to the ground on the shed skin of my dress.

Springing to my feet I laughed, near choked, then sobbed at the sight of myself, the ragged moth that had emerged. In a dead outlaw's breeches, my own clumpy boots, and two flimsy chemises, probably stolen from a washing line by Annie. I wrested off the last of my petticoats, untied the sleeves of my shirt, which had ended up around my ankles, and threw the shirt on.

'Gotchoo,' said a boy. He snatched my hand and held it so tightly I thought his fingers would slice like wires through my skin.

'Oh my god, Alfie,' I said. 'I was looking for you.'

'I was following, but you din't ever see me.' He grinned,

showing the gummy gap where his front teeth should have been, but his eyes were wide, darting side to side. He wouldn't let go of my hand. 'I lost you, then everyone went mad and started running and yelling. Why's everyone going mad like that?'

'Alfie, we can't stay here. Have you seen Norah?'

He shook his head, his face fixed in a terrified grin.

'We've got to go anyway.'

The crowd around us had thinned, and people were running and limping towards the church end.

'Alfie, we'll go this way, to the other end, away from everyone else. It'll be too packed by the church, could be more dangerous.'

He didn't say anything, but ran with me, clutching my hand. We'd not gone more than ten paces before I saw the reason for the crowd's charge towards the church.

Ahead, the square was unexpectedly empty, and walled in by smog. From within the smog came the sound of horses snorting and neighing.

Alfie and I slowed to a cautious walk. A few strides closer and we saw the line of horses' heads, then the white trousers of the yeomen riders, and their sabres, stretching as far as we could see, in both directions, into the fog.

'Stop,' I said to Alfie.

He tripped. I hoisted him up by the arm. He skimmed the ground and span on his toes.

'What're they doing?' he said, getting his footing.

The yeomen cavalry advanced no further. I wasn't sure if they'd seen us. They weren't moving but they were doing something. They must have come from the other side of the square, spurring people towards the middle.

One of the soldiers bellowed an order. The horses emerged fully from the mist. They walked slowly towards us.

To our right, one horse broke from the line. It startled the others beside it, and a skittish group of four swelled from the ranks. Off to the left, two other horses were swinging their heads wildly. The riders couldn't hold them still. One of the horses pivoted on its front legs and rear-kicked the one beside it. The yeomen riders shouted at each other but they couldn't control their beasts. There was nothing to do but run.

46

Alfie and I ran as best we could. Hurdling shattered crates and placards. Stumbling through the debris of abandoned parcels, clothes and banners. We tried to weave between people who were erratically weaving too – tripping over each other, shoving others aside.

Something snapped under my boot. Only the dry twigs of a basket.

Alfie veered into me. We parted again around the island of a woman, who was bent double in a tattered skirt, clutching her ribs. She reached out to me, but my instinct was to run not stop. I couldn't help her, and help myself and Alfie.

The clamour of shouting, clogs on the cobbles and what sounded like the banging of pots grew louder. We'd taken a diagonal course towards the edge of the square so I'd expected to steer close to, but not into, the masses. At this end there was still enough room for Alfie and I to manoeuvre, if we were quick. But I could no longer see the row of buildings I was aiming for. I paused, and held onto Alfie.

'We've lost our bearings in the smog,' I said.

'Are all them people coming towards us?'

'Or we're going towards them.'

'Which way do we go?' Alfie said.

I didn't know. And I didn't want to say.

'Which *way*, Norah?'

'Alfie, I'm not–'

He looked up at me. He didn't like what he saw. He tugged his hand from mine and ran back the way we'd come. His skinny bowed legs rocked him side to side like an old man with arthritic knees.

I shouted after him, but if he heard, he wasn't stopping.

Then my shoulder was bumped from behind. I pitched forwards and said, 'Hey!' forgetting for a moment that this was how the world was now.

A man, his torn shirt billowing, ran beyond me. Another man flew past on my other side. Two women were dragging a limp girl between them. I began to run, and just in time, because from the smog came the multitudes.

I drew level with the women, who were slowing, struggling to carry the girl. Two more strides and I was past them. I heard screams and a scuffle. Didn't dare look back.

Something had happened at the church end. But these people didn't know about the disorderly cavalry ahead.

The last thing I wanted to do was run with the masses, but to stay put or go cross-wise would get me trampled. And poor Alfie, hampered by his short stiff legs: if the cavalry didn't knock him down, the charging people would do it.

Hemmed in by the crowd, I couldn't weave around obstacles, nor leap over things I couldn't see until I was upon them. People fell as they ran, but no one stopped, unless they fell too. Something snapped under my boot, again, but it wasn't a basket because it cried out.

I ran on, in the grip of instinct and fear, as a bison in the midst of its herd across the great plains of America, hunted by men shooting arrows, and later, on horseback with guns. Don't fall, don't fall, I told myself over and over. Don't fall. Keep running.

Then I stopped running. I had to. I slammed into the people in front of me, a barrier of four or five packed rows facing the cavalry line. Others slammed into me from behind. I was trapped.

The horses were in a frenzy – rearing, snorting, stamping. Hooves flying, as if galloping through air. Heads wrenching against the reins. They were desperate to do what their nature demanded: they wanted to run.

Soldiers fought to restrain their horses under the barrage of flying objects – cobbles prised up from the ground, placards, poles, the stripped carcass of a roast chicken. And in the no-mans-land between, a small boy scurrying back and forth, throwing whatever he could find, oblivious to the danger from both sides. Alfie.

I pushed my way through the confusion, swapping places with people muscling backwards to seek cover. I scanned the cavalry line, which was just about holding, for any gap to escape through. I saw one such gap, off to my right, away from Alfie, but it closed as suddenly as it had opened.

Alfie bent down, wrestling with his shoe. The horse nearest him reared. Its front hooves struck the cobbles inches from his head. Alfie stumbled back and plopped onto his bony bottom. He stared up into the sky for a second. The horse tried to buck its rider.

Then, to my disbelief, Alfie jumped up and held his arms out to the frantic animal, as if it were Pegasus, the flying horse of myth and legend, and had just that second landed on earth to offer him salvation.

I couldn't hold my nerve to wait to see what would

happen next. I dashed into the no-mans-land and scooped Alfie under my arm.

'Rrrr-aarghhh!' he cried and fought me too.

And then everything happened at once.

The horses broke their line. The soldiers, panicking as their mounts charged into the people, drew their sabres. Screams and blood, that's all I remember, that and the breach in the cavalry line dead ahead of Alfie and me. The horses parted as they charged, only by a few feet, but to me it felt as huge as a rift between mountains.

I threw Alfie onto my shoulder and sprang forwards. I took us through that great rift to the near-empty square beyond the yeomen and horses, I don't know how. I just reached the other side and collapsed to my knees, dropped Alfie, and heaved a huge sob. Then Alfie pulled me up and we carried on running.

47

In the old boneyard of the Angel Meadow slum, the dead are always rising up through the earth. But the dead don't walk, or dance eerie jigs for the joy of non-being, or haunt anyone. Only their bones come to the surface, when slum dwellers dig up wheelbarrows of earth to sell for compost and cart away fallen headstones to rebuild their homes.

The city's always changing – being built up, being knocked down. Old making way for new, over and over. Manchester was a Roman settlement once. The Romans thought they'd rule forever. But their empire weakened and died. The cotton barons of Manchester believe cotton is king – how long do they have until a new king is born?

Whatever I thought I'd been part of, amongst the cotton workers on strike, was gone.

Alfie and I hid in an alley until dark. I didn't know where to start looking for Norah. I knew I should have taken Alfie home, but I couldn't face explaining to his parents what had happened. They'd hear soon enough, and perhaps by then I'd have better news. We sat in a gutter behind the square, and listened until it seemed the chaos had died down.

Alfie had slept, on and off, in the hours that we waited. But I didn't. I kept thinking about Norah and, for some

270

idiotic reason, my green dress, which must be lying somewhere in the square. I'd hated wearing that dress, and the purpose of it, yet I had a strange urge to find it. I wanted some relic, some sick souvenir of today, otherwise I might forget what had happened, quickly, deliberately, because it was just too awful to remember.

Beside me, Alfie woke. He blinked several times, then frowned.

'We're still here,' I said, cradling my throbbing little finger, which had swelled to the size of a sausage. 'Not been swept into the sewers just yet.'

When he was fully awake I led us out of the alley and back to the square. The street lamps were alight, except those that had been smashed. Small fires burned. Whoever was clearing up or searching had brought lamps too. The baubles of fuzzy orange light bobbed in the dark. I was so tired I fell under the spell of the lights – I stood fixed to the spot, dreaming and aching, erasing the day from my mind.

Until I remembered: those bobbing lights are probably carried by policemen, who are hurrying to where something's been found. And those lights, as they cluster prettily in a new constellation, then descend, are where the policemen are crouching to examine a body.

Alfie and I found a horse. Or rather, tripped over one of its splayed legs, snapped at the shin. Alfie touched his finger to the shard of bone that had broken through the horse's skin. He brought his sticky bloody finger level with his eyes. I hoped to god he wasn't going to lick it.

An inch away from his face, he traced his finger from eyes to nose to chin. He looked as if he were going to mark himself with the blood, but perhaps that's just what I would have done. Then he wiped his finger on his breeches.

'Poor old horse,' he said. 'Not his fault.' He stood up.

271

'Where's Norah? I thought you was her before, but she'd tell me off for poking a dead horse. When will we find her?'

I hesitated, then cuffed him gently round the head. 'That's for poking a dead horse.'

'Bet he was a nice horse.'

'Even though he could've been the one that nearly trampled you to death?'

'E'en though.'

I led Alfie around the edge of the square so we didn't have to see what the bobbing lights had found. I checked the numbers of the buildings as we walked. At number thirty-one, I stopped. Ahead, two doors along, a man in a tricorne hat was leaning with his leg crooked against the wall.

'Alfie,' I whispered, 'sit here for a minute.' I pushed him a bit roughly onto the stone steps to the door beside us, but he neither complained nor resisted.

I walked slowly towards the man outside the building in which I hoped to find my great-uncle. The man pushed himself away from the wall and took a few steps to me. I knew who it was before he spoke.

'There's no one here, I already knocked. It's just an office.'

I'd thought him dead. In a way, I'd hoped he was. Not truly, not for him. But for me. I wanted to close a door on everything that had happened since leaving Fairy Cross.

'Did you hear, Lizzie? It's just an office, some sort of legal firm, your great-uncle doesn't live in this building,' Henry said.

To close the door, firmly, and forever. To forget, and start afresh. I'd taken a wrong turn and now I needed to go back. But I knew I couldn't. Henry, and everything that had happened, was a part of me now.

'Aren't you going to say something? Aren't you surprised to see me?' Henry's voice was raised. A mixture of excitement and almost anger.

'How did you find me?' I said calmly. 'You can't have followed. No one could, not through all that…'

He bent to the ground and picked something up. 'I've been keeping it safe for you.' He handed me my knapsack, and fiddled with his hat, Florian's battered tricorne, pulling the front corner down to hide his black eye.

I took the bag. 'You've been through my things. You read my letter.'

'How else would I have found you?'

How had he found me the first time, when he and Florian had 'saved' me from Robin in Avandale? As a consequence of my own actions. Fighting in the Sir Tarquin contest, believing myself some noble warrior, some righteous saviour. Attracting the wrong sort of attention. Everything had been so uncertain then, but now, looking back, it seemed inevitable that things had turned out as they had. What else did I think would happen, when I joined with a couple of rogues who held Robin and his men at pistol-point?

'Who's that?' Henry pointed to Alfie, who'd turned himself upside-down on the damp steps two doors along and was sliding down on his belly.

'That's Alfie. I–' I was going to say, I saved him from being trampled by the cavalry. But to explain that would mean admitting I hadn't saved, or even found, Norah.

I said, 'He's lost, I'm looking after him.' What I meant was, I'm lost, I don't know what to do, I'm holding onto Alfie because then I've got a clear purpose: to get him home safely. I said, 'Even if it's only an office, I'm going to wait till morning, till my great-uncle or someone who knows him turns up.'

273

'Alright.' Henry sat down on the steps.

I began to walk towards where Alfie was running up and jumping off the steps, then changed my mind, wanting to say something to Henry but not knowing what.

Alfie landed a final time and trotted over. 'Who're you?' he said to Henry. 'Is Norah here?'

'Who's Norah?' said Henry.

'My sister, course. We was all together before, having a picnic–'

'Alfie, we weren't having a picnic,' I said.

'I was. When I went off. Got a bit o' cheese from a woman, nearly got a sausage.'

'You were having a picnic?' Henry said. 'While I was…while I was– I thought you were in trouble.'

'We weren't having a bloody picnic, we were caught up in *that*.' I turned towards the square.

'I killed a man for you.'

I didn't turn back.

'Which man?' Alfie said, and skipped further into the square as if to find the corpse.

I watched him watching the investigations. There were fewer searchlights now and they moved around less. Soon, all activity would die down for the night. In a few days, the square would have been cleared of debris, the prised-up cobbles replaced and to all appearances it would be as if nothing had ever happened. But it wouldn't be like that between Henry and me. We'd been part of a plot to kidnap a girl. And he'd killed a man for me.

'Morris,' I said, facing Henry.

'Oh, and him.'

'Then who else?' I said, aghast at Henry's casual manner. 'One of the scuttlers?'

He said nothing.

Afraid of what his silence meant, I filled it. 'Those

scuttlers attacked us, and who knows what else they've done. They deserved it.'

'Not the scuttlers. They ran when Cavendish appeared.'

'And Florian was...?'

'Florian was–' Henry put his hand over his eyes.

'You couldn't come with me because you thought he was alive?'

'No. I mean yes. I don't know. I did want him to be alive. I don't know why...it's been so long since I left home I– I felt like I owed him after all.'

'Who then?'

'Cavendish.'

'But he ran after me. You were following? Why didn't you shout?'

'It wasn't like that, he came back when he lost you. There were loads of people around us by then. We had to leave...Florian there...because–'

'There'd be too many questions?'

Henry nodded. 'And then Theo told Cavendish where you'd gone. She turned up when we were waiting outside Holland Arcade. That was your doing, wasn't it? She went through your things before I thought of it. You asked about St Ann's Square, remember?'

'I wish I didn't.'

'Cavendish was coming after you, said he couldn't have you running around free to tell someone about the plot. Told us to meet him back at The Amnesty and that he'd, er, get you.'

'*Get* me, how?'

'You know how.'

I knew. From the forest camp, I knew.

Henry said, 'But when he'd gone, and Annie and Theo went to the Arcade and told me to tell Porter and Gaunt what was happening, I went after Cavendish. Thought I

275

could get to you before he did, that we'd find your great-uncle and never have to see Cavendish again.'

'But you couldn't come here,' I said, pointing to the closed door at the top of the steps, 'because of the crowds and then the...'

'Yeah. So I went around and around the back streets for hours, as much as I could, thinking you'd have to do the same. I wasn't looking for Cavendish...but I found him.' He paused. 'He never saw me. But I couldn't let him go, could I?'

I didn't know what to say. I'd forgotten my great-uncle's address had been in my knapsack all along. Why hadn't I destroyed the letter? I could have done so easily, and many times over. It wasn't as if the letter were a comforting missive from my loving family. Just some sick souvenir, with which to berate myself further when I felt worthless. And with it I'd brought both Henry and Cavendish to my great-uncle's, and now only Henry remained.

'I'll have to go with you to Fairy Cross now, won't I, now I'm a fugitive from the law?' Henry laughed.

'Weren't you always?' I said, numbly, without thinking how it sounded. 'A fugitive from the law, I mean. Isn't everyone in the forest camp an outlaw of some kind or another?'

Henry looked up at me. He saw that I was crying. 'Yes,' he said, woodenly, 'yes, I suppose you're right. Nothing's changed. I'm still what I was before. Not worthy. Of you.'

'That's not what I mean.'

'Whether you do or not, you owe me.' He stood up on the steps, a head higher than me.

'I'm grateful for what you did for me, I am, b–' But what? But you killed two men...? But I didn't ask you to...? But what do we do now?

Then I remembered what he'd said about Annie and Theo.

'Why did Annie and Theo go to the Arcade, Henry?' I said. 'Why did you need to tell Porter and Gaunt what was happening? What was happening exactly, after Cavendish came for me?'

48

Suddenly, Henry put his hand to his hip, to the pistol. Then, as if reassured it was still there, he let his hand drop. I span around to see what he'd seen.

'Nothing,' he said.

'In the square?' I said. Then, wondering whether he was trying to distract me: 'Or nothing happened when Cavendish came after me?'

He looked everywhere but me. He shrugged.

'Henry, *what*?' I said, trying not to raise my voice in case we woke someone in the building above.

'Dunno.'

'You do know, tell me. Why did Annie and Theo go to the Arcade? What were you supposed to tell Porter and Gaunt?'

'Not my business anymore.'

'How can you say that? Henry, we have to stop it.'

'Stop what,' he said, listlessly. It wasn't a question.

'The kidnap. Annie and Theo are going through with it anyway, aren't they? Tell me.'

'What, I'm supposed to kill a man to save you, *and* stop a girl being kidnapped?'

'I don't need saving,' I said. Then wondered whether perhaps I did. But what sort of salvation was there for me?

'No? How far would you have got without me?' Henry said, tapping his pistol again. 'Well, we can't stop it anyway, it'll have happened by now. Yesterday afternoon, in fact, after you *ran*.'

'Then we have to undo it.'

'Undo it? You can't undo a kidnap, it's not a mistake you made in your bloody embroidery, Lizzie.'

'Then we have to get the girl back. Get her home.'

'Good luck with that.'

'Where will they take her? The Amnesty? They won't have known about Cavendish at the time, so they'd be expecting to rendezvous with him there. They may still be waiting at The Amnesty.'

'They're not going to take a kidnapped girl to a lodging house.'

'What about the forest camp? Porter and Gaunt had the cart. Or Annie's house? Cavendish joked about her basement, said she could use it as a dungeon. Maybe that's where they've gone. Do you know where she lives?'

'Why would I know where Annie lives? I met her when you did. Let's just wait for your great-uncle–'

'And tell him, then tell the police.'

'No! You can't tell him anything, and you can't tell the police. Or they'll know what we've done, what I've done. Who are you trying to help here, Lizzie? It doesn't seem to be me.' He came down a step, and I had to back away to make room.

'I won't tell him everything,' I said.

'You will, you'll have to. Or how'll you get to the part where we know a kidnap's just taken place and who's done it, how they drink their tea, and where they may be hiding out?'

'But we can't do nothing.'

'Yeah, we can. You were tricked into it, and I– I was too.

279

It wasn't our fault. It would've happened with us or without us. And has, in fact, happened without us. How're we to blame?'

'Henry, you know that's not right, this's our mess, where's your,' – I struggled to think of any word but 'honour', no matter how pompous it sounded – 'honour?'

'Honour? I'm just trying to survive, Lizzie. You've never made a mistake?'

'Loads.'

'And I'm one of them.'

'I can only make up for my own.'

Henry leaned into my face. The front corner of his hat snagged my hair. He said, 'You want me to turn myself into the police.'

'I don't want you to do anything,' I said, pushing him away. 'You have to do what you think is right.'

'What's right for you? Or what's right for me?'

'I don't know. Just what's right. I don't know what that is, but I know it's not twiddling our thumbs here while a girl's been kidnapped. I know why you did what you did for me, twice, and I'm grateful, but it's still wrong.'

'Wrong? Alright, have it your way. But the first time...you knew what I'd done to Morris. And you said nothing. When we talked on the way to Manchester...you want to talk about choices now? Your choices. Don't tell me you didn't have a choice, Lizzie, you've always got a choice.'

'Henry...' I said.

'No, don't bother. I know what you see when you look at me. You think you're different, better. You've found your great-uncle, you've got your grandmother who loves you. That mill you think is yours. You think you're owed but you– You're right, I'd never fit in there, in Fairy Cross, I'd never belong.'

'I didn't say that.'

'You don't have to. But more importantly, *you'd* no longer fit in. With me there, you'd never be able to forget what I've done, what you've been part of. What *you* knew and didn't stop. Well...' He held out his hand for me to shake.

I hesitated. Shaking his hand will mean goodbye. Is this what I want? To say goodbye, and to forget. Because if he's right...

If we tell the truth, to Gran, to Tom, to anyone, then the truth will be present forever, a cloud hovering inches above my head, my own personal fog. But if we lie to everyone about what's happened, about what we were part of, we'll have to lie forever. Either way I'll never be able to forget and I'll never be free.

I was about to take his hand when he dropped it. Quickly, I thrust out mine. He ignored the gesture. Instead he reached inside his jacket, the navy one with the brass buttons, his costume for the kidnap.

'Take this.' He proffered the same emerald and gold necklace Florian had shown me in Kit's tent. 'You may need it.'

I dropped my hand. 'What for?'

'To sell?' He looked up at the dark windows of my great-uncle's business premises. 'Or wear?'

'It's Florian's.'

'Not originally.'

'I don't want a dead man's chain,' I said. 'You went through his pockets while he was– while he was dying?'

'The scuttler dropped it when he ran.'

'Still not right.'

'I'll take it,' said Alfie, appearing from behind me.

With a sickening jolt, I wondered how long he'd been listening, and what he'd heard that he might repeat.

He said, 'To look after. For you, Lizzie.'

'No, Alfie, don't do that.'

'I don't wanna keep it, just to see it. I'll look after it, I will.'

'Alfie, no.'

'You en't my sister, I can take it if I want.'

Henry gave Alfie the necklace. 'Take care of it, and be sure you don't forget.'

'Forget what?' Alfie said.

'Lizzie'll tell you.'

'Just to take care of the necklace, Alfie, just to look after it,' I said, before he could ask.

I knew what Henry meant: this necklace was a chain binding us. He wasn't going to let me forget anything, nor forget him, even if he were gone from my life.

Henry began to walk away, adjusting his hat, then he turned back and said, 'Don't suppose it matters anymore, but Florian told me about the previous chief. Do you want to know?'

'No.'

'How have you gone from the person who asks so many questions, to someone who doesn't want to know the most important thing of all?' Henry laughed. 'You don't want to know what Florian told me when I asked?'

'No, I don't.'

'That old fellow,' Henry continued. 'The one you said you cut down and buried, remember?'

'I remember.'

'That was him, the old chief. He'd retired, supposedly, but was assembling a gang for another job. It was never mutiny, Florian taking over. Somebody snitched. The old guy got lynched, and Florian invented the mutiny story to strengthen his position as the new chief. He'd left the family trade when his father did, fourteen, fifteen, years ago, something like that, when he was about my age, but he came back for the new job too–'

'Left the *family* trade?'

'Ah, you're interested now.'

'You don't mean–?'

'The old highwayman was Florian's father? Yep. He said that was the making of him, his father's lynching. Couldn't go back after that.' Henry held out his hand to me again. 'You see, you belonged with us all along.'

I couldn't take his hand, mine was shaking so violently. 'No.'

'You buried Florian's father. He was grateful. Wish I'd been able to bury mine. Well,' – he took hold of the tricorne and doffed it with a flourish – 'see you around, Lizzie.'

'Where will you go?' I said. 'To The Amnesty? Or the forest camp, back to Florian's men? Oh, are they your men now?'

'Not your business anymore.' Henry put his hands in his pockets, and walked across the square towards the last bobbing lights.

49

'You can't sleep here,' a man said.

I blinked up at the new morning. It looked just like the previous one: smoggy, brown. But the face was unfamiliar. The man had a neatly-clipped mahogany beard, which was most of my view against the pillar of his topper hat. He rapped my shin with the end of his ivory-tipped cane.

'Move along, you'll get no alms here.'

I uncurled my stiff body from the alcove of the doorway. Alfie groaned but didn't wake. He was upside-down again, his head and shoulders lolling over the top step, his legs tangled in mine.

'I'm waiting for my great-uncle,' I said.

'He'll get no alms either. Take yourselves off to the soup kitchen.'

'Dr Emerson Beaulieu.' I stood up on the top step and looked down upon the man. He was short, tubby, smartly-dressed. 'Are you…him?'

'Certainly not,' the man said.

I glanced at the engraved brass plate beside the door pull and checked the names again.

'This is his place of business,' I said. 'Are you, then, Mr Dorville?'

By the manner in which the man fussed with his cravat

I assumed he was.

He said, 'In the first instance, and of superior priority, who are you?'

'I'm Lizzie. Greenwood. Elizabeth, that is. Dr Emerson Beaulieu's great-niece,' I burbled, thick with sleep. 'He won't know me by sight, I've never met him. Though I suppose he's met me. I've got a letter here, from my aunt in Bath, who's his niece. My mother's sister.' I rifled in my knapsack for the letter, but it wasn't there. 'Oh, somebody's taken it. But my aunt, Miss Vita Moncrieff Beaulieu, instructed me to find my great-uncle here.'

'I see. Very well. Indeed,' Mr Dorville said. 'If, in the unlikely event, this is true, verifiable and forthwith verified, which kind of juridical service would you have my business partner or myself render unto you and yours?'

'Pardon?'

'What do you want?'

I stared at Mr Dorville wondering whether the odd man really believed I wanted the services of a man-at-law. Then wondered whether perhaps I did.

'I have a legal conundrum,' I said, which I supposed could describe Robin's possession of the mill, 'that warrants some disentanglement.'

'Very good, very good. And the particular nature of this conundrum requires which level of attention, arbitration or pursuance?'

'Ah...um... Can't I just come in and wait for my great-uncle? When do you expect him?'

'We said our adieus yesterday eve, so I expect him two months hence.'

'Two months?'

'You can't wait here,' Mr Dorville said quickly, as if I'd been showing signs of setting up home in his doorway.

'Two months...'

'Unless, of course, he has not yet departed.'

'Well, has he gone or hasn't he?'

'I am not in possession of such knowledge. He said he intended to set off early this morning, but he also said he may drop by for additional papers. But that was before this dreadful strike business. You weren't part of that, were you?' he said, taking further note of my ill-fitting, ripped and dirty clothing.

'I don't work in a factory,' I said.

'Glad to hear it. You could, perhaps, wait in the back stairwell.'

'For two months?' I said, hopelessly confused.

'No, no. For an hour or so. To see if he does indeed intend to call in.'

I slumped down on the doorstep.

'I really must insist you remove your personage, and the boy's, from the doorway. I have urgent business and a highly-esteemed guest due. I may perhaps pen a letter to your great-uncle, on your behalf?'

'I know how to write.'

'Then get off my doorstep!' Mr Dorville screamed, flapping his arms in frustration.

Alfie woke with a start.

'Goodness,' said a white-haired gentleman, at that moment pausing on the pavement. 'My dear man, whatever is the matter?'

'Emerson, there you are! This determined beggar insists she is your long-lost niece. But whoever she is, it is my utmost wish that she no longer be visibly present on the doorstep. The Countess Ossalinsky is in a frightful state, and will be along in,' – he checked his gold pocket watch – 'oh dear, oh dearie me, very soon indeed. Emerson, you must resolve this untidy matter immediately.'

'I'm not an untidy matter,' I said to the white-haired

gentleman. I couldn't yet think of him as a relative, it was too much to comprehend. 'Actually, I suppose I am.'

'I'm an untidy matter too,' Alfie said.

'Yes, I rather see so.' The gentleman strode up the steps towards Alfie and me.

His snowy moustache advanced before him – the long, twisted tips of it investigating us, be we friend or food. He was tall and lean, dressed in dark trousers and a well-fitting frock coat, with a scarlet waistcoat beneath.

The vibrant waistcoat made me think of Florian, and the pink one he wouldn't wear. I held back sudden tears. It was me who'd caused Florian's father to be lynched, when I'd boasted to my cousins about what I'd witnessed at the old gent's cottage – the strange visitors at curious times of night, the packets and loads delivered and smuggled away. If I'd made Florian, and he made Henry, then who'd made me?

'Lizzie?' said Dr Emerson Beaulieu, halting two steps down. He squinted at me with eyes as blue as glacier water, and just as forgiving. 'Or is it Elizabeth? You nearly missed me. I gather you've come rather a long way.'

'Yes. I–' I faltered as I scanned his face for the re-assurance I sorely needed.

Deep creases, white against the tan of his weathered skin, radiated around those icy blue eyes, as if from straining too long into the blazing sun. I felt he'd seen the distant horizon of the end of my life, through every scene beyond this moment on the steps and back again. And oh! how those eyes told me I should never *never* ask.

What should I tell him, about my long, long way here?

I couldn't think of anything to say but: 'Did Gran write, sir?'

'She did.'

'What did she write?'

287

'Rather a lot. You can read it yourself.'

'No, thank you. I don't want to see myself described on the page, as I was when she wrote it.'

'Very wise,' he said, and when I flinched he added, 'There are a number of things about myself which I don't enjoy being reminded of. Your grandmother, thorough as ever, was kind enough to include some of them in her letter.'

I smiled to think of Gran writing such rebukes. I wondered if she'd used some of the words she'd learnt in Paris.

'She gives me to understand you require my help,' he said.

I thought again of Gran, of how I longed to see her soon. And of Tom, who may never forgive me for bringing about his humiliating demotion. How I hurt most the ones I love. Because of who I am and what I do.

And then I thought of Robin. I could never not. He was always there, connected to home and to everything I knew and loved.

His last words to me in Avandale rang in my head, now transformed into the chorus of a mocking song: 'Will you fall further? Time will tell. Will you fall, will you fall, will you fall further?'

Look at me now. Robin was right. And if he's right, he wins.

What help can this great-uncle possibly give that doesn't involve me being arrested for plotting to kidnap a girl, and being an accessory to two murders? Because I can't tell him anything about my journey and not tell him all. I have to be honest.

50

Time will tell, Robin had said. But what will it tell?

'You have only to ask for my help,' said this new uncle, Dr Emerson Beaulieu, whom I'd longed and dreaded to meet.

Something must be done about the kidnapped girl. But how can he help with that?

And how can I truly say to Tom and Gran, and everyone else, that right now I am better than Robin, that I am a better person to run the mill?

Until something is done about Isabella Astley, I can't. I don't know whether I can climb back up to wherever I should be, but I'm sure as nine hells not going to fall further. I'm not going to prove Robin right.

'I can't go back to Fairy Cross. At least, not yet,' I said, with a sudden shift in perspective. For a moment I saw through my father's eyes. Had he always meant to return, to make everything right, whatever he'd actually done? Then found himself changed by his misdeeds and adventures. He could only go onwards, with all the world before him.

'Very well. Then may I venture a proposal?' said the new uncle. 'I've been rather looking forward to meeting you. I hoped we could– that I may be able to–' He paused, then said hurriedly, 'But of course, I don't expect you to feel the same way.'

'I don't have a gran,' Alfie said, standing up from the doorway with, I noticed in dismay, the emerald necklace strung over his hand. He said, 'Who wrote for me?'

'And who may you be, my good sir? I was given to expect just the one adventurer.'

'Alfie,' said Alfie, puffing up his scrawny chest. 'Short for...Alfred? Lizzie en't my sister though. That's Norah. Is she inside?'

'Not another one,' Mr Dorville cried. 'Please, Emerson, indoors or off the step before all the waifs of Manchester descend upon us. The Countess will arrive any minute, and already the distinguished lady will have to proceed through this dreadful scene.' He swept his arm towards the debris-strewn square. 'She's in a frightful state about her associate and will require all our resources.'

'And what's that you have there, Master Alfred?' the new uncle said, ignoring Mr Dorville's plea.

'It's Lizzie's,' said Alfie, holding the necklace aloft. 'I'm looking after it for her.'

'I see.'

'It's not mine,' I said. 'Someone gave it to him.'

'An unusual gift for a young boy.'

'Why,' said Mr Dorville, coming up the steps. 'I believe I have seen a very similar choker around the Countess's neck.'

'A dead man's chain,' said Alfie.

'Pardon me?' Mr Dorville said.

'That's what it is. A dead man's chain. I dunno what that is, but Lizzie don't want it. She said so t'man who give it her.'

'My, this is a strange affair. Emerson, I implore you to–Oh! Oh my. The Countess, the Countess. She is here!' Mr

Dorville leapt down the steps and scuttled along the pavement towards a lady on horseback. He stepped into her path and waved his arms furiously. She began to dismount; he tried to stop her.

'It's a very distinctive gift, this necklet,' the new uncle said, glancing at Mr Dorville's frantic efforts. 'Quite incongruous with, and please excuse my frankness, Lizzie, your rather jumbled appearance.'

'S'not her fault,' Alfie said. 'Men on horses tried to trample us to death and we din't have a picnic and Lizzie saved me.'

The new uncle stared at me as if I'd just removed a mask. 'You weren't caught up in the riot?'

'We were.'

'However so?'

'Well...' I said, wondering where I'd start, if I were to spill all, wondering where the start was, how far back I needed to go. Back to The Amnesty? To the outlaws' forest camp? The Sir Tarquin contest in Avandale? Back to the fire at the mill, or Mr Kirke's accident?

Or even further back, to events outside my lifespan, to when my father gave up the mill, or when Florian's father had fatefully set up home on the east-west road. Maybe even to before Gran arrived in Fairy Cross, when Grandpa's wanderlust had set everything in motion.

There was no beginning, not really. At least not one I could pinpoint. Everyone, and everything, was moving forward all of the time. Bowling and lurching into one another, clashing and tangling over who wants what, then ripping apart, and stumbling on. Doing it all over again.

I said, 'Well, it's done now and we survived. But Alfie needs to find his sister.'

'I can help with that.'

'Thank you. And I need to– I need to–'

291

'Go on, Lizzie, I can help if you ask.'

'No, I don't think you can,' I said, at a loss as to what to say and what to do.

Should I search first at The Amnesty? Try to find someone who'll tell me where Annie lives. But what if Cavendish's body has been found and the police have traced him back there? And what of the investigation into Florian's death? Someone might recognise me, even without the emerald dress. And what of Henry? Has he gone for good? Or…will I run into him again in rather less friendly circumstances?

But I didn't have a chance to speak further.

'I appreciate your extensive warning, Mr Dorville, thank you,' said the lady, who'd now dismounted and was striding towards us on the steps. 'However, there is no breed of untidiness or inconvenience with which I am unacquainted.'

The lady was slender, wearing a full-skirted black mourning dress, though without the usual volume of petticoats to obstruct her determined pace. The chiffon veil of her riding hat covered her face. With her riding crop, she appeared to stab the smog upon each step.

'I am, I assure you,' she said, striking the bottom stair with her boot, 'quite unshakeable.'

My great-uncle hastened aside to let her pass.

Two steps below Alfie and me, she halted. 'Good God.'

With her crop, she hooked the emerald necklace from Alfie's hand and said, 'That's mine.' She placed the necklace into her gloved hand and stared at it for several awkward moments. Then she said, 'The, ah, bearer of this…where is he?'

Alfie said, 'He's dea–' and I clapped my hand over his mouth.

The lady came a step closer.

I looked past her, at my great-uncle. He seemed composed, showing no signs of interest in the lady, which was odd, given that she was evidently of some means and purpose. And on his doorstep.

Instead he was trying to calm the flustered Mr Dorville, saying, 'Dorville, she's my great-niece. Her appearance is by-the-by, she's had a rather troubled journey and we're not to judge her on this alone.'

Do either of them know who this lady is?

She lifted her veil. Quietly she said, 'If you know, Lizzie, tell me. Please.'

'That's my uncle,' I said, 'the white-haired one. My great-uncle, that is, not the one I was running from.' I paused. Then, taking a small chance, I said, 'Have you as much to hide as I do?'

'Rather more, I expect,' the lady said, sadly. It was Kit, the woman from the outlaws' forest camp.

This was my chance. With Kit's help I could track down Annie and Theo. If not them, then at least Kit would know where to find Porter and Gaunt. It was a start. But why would she help, when she was at the heart of the plot?

I have to try anyway. I can escape Robin, but I can't escape myself.

I took a deep breath and whispered, 'Cavendish is dead. Henry killed him because he was coming for me, here. And Florian is dead too, because we were attacked while waiting near Holland Arcade. And I ran, to save myself, leaving Florian to die, and only Henry to fight.'

'Oh,' she said, looking up to the sky. 'I see.' Then she looked at me and frowned. 'You're taking a big risk telling me the truth.'

'I know.'

She waited a moment, for me to fill the silence. I didn't.

She said, 'Why did you tell me first about Cavendish, when I asked you about the bearer of the necklace?'

'Because you and Cavendish were an alliance before you joined Florian, I thought you'd want to know about him most.'

'Well, yes. And yes, we were an alliance, of sorts. We have a common cause. Had, I should say. But our methods, hmm, they've always differed somewhat.'

'Because you're a Countess?'

'Huh, yes. And, no,' she said, looking more amused than sad. 'And, not really.'

'You're not really a Countess?'

'That's a longer story. Are you testing me, Lizzie?'

She glanced down to where Mr Dorville was hanging his head and shaking it, jabbing the tip of his cane into his own foot, while my great-uncle was trying to console him.

My great-uncle didn't seem to have noticed Kit glance at them, but he took Mr Dorville's arm and led him several yards away. Strange timing, I thought.

'Testing you?' I said to Kit. 'Of course I am.'

'Have I passed?' she said, with smile creases beginning at the corners of her mouth.

'Don't know yet.'

'What do you want from me, Lizzie?'

'The kidnap went ahead anyway.'

'Ah. Oh dear, I'd hoped to be in time to stop it. Why did you leave The Amnesty so early?' Kit said. 'Never mind. Was it Annie in the end?'

'And Theo. So Henry told me. What will Porter and Gaunt do when they find out Florian and Cavendish are gone?'

'We'd better see.'

'Really? But it's the main part of your plan to ambush the bank's coaches...'

'Should never've been. Ah, Mr Dorville!' she exclaimed as my great-uncle and Mr Dorville approached the steps. She grasped Mr Dorville's hand and spoke words I couldn't hear; he gave me a suspicious look.

Then I felt a tug on my jacket. It was Alfie.

'Were you listening, Alfie?' I said.

'Not really. Heard everything, course.' He grinned his gummy smile. 'You saved me, now I gotta help you, Lizzie.'

'Oh, god.'

'Breakfast for the five of us, Mr Dorville?' Kit said loudly, and before he had a chance to reply: 'Splendid. Make it snappy, we each have our urgent tasks.' She dropped his hand and turned to me.

I let her join me on the top step. Her fine clothes smelt ever so slightly of the forest.

She said, 'Did you want this back?' She dangled the emerald necklace on her finger. 'I suppose it was someone's family heirloom once.'

'No, I'm not ready for that, not yet.'

Kit looked at me quizzically. 'Your inheritance? Your family's mill?'

I nodded.

'Then we'd better hurry up and find this girl, so you can get back to your mill,' she said, appearing to understand me perfectly.

'I'm ready.' And I was.

One day soon I'd return to Fairy Cross, but not to the deer den, forest bed of birch and moss. I was made of other things now. Things I wouldn't choose, with more no doubt to come. My conscience was far from clear. Probably it never would be. But I had to go on anyway, onwards into the world. Whatever lay ahead for me.

"I've finished! What now?"

If you loved *Emerald Noose*, I'd really appreciate a review.
I hope you enjoyed reading it as much as I loved
writing it. Thank you!

To find out about the sequel to *Emerald Noose*,
for occasional news and events, and more about my
writing process, sign up to my Blog at
www.georgiebelmont.com/blog.
See you there!

If you have any other feedback or questions, please get in touch
through my website, www.georgiebelmont.com/contact.

www.georgiebelmont.com